{sierra's story}

degrees of betrayal

sierra's story
{DANDI DALEY MACKALL}

ryun's story
{JEFF NESBIT}

kenzie's story
{MELODY CARLSON}

{sierra's story}

degrees of betrayal

DANDI DALEY MACKALL

Tyndale House Publishers, Inc.
Wheaton, Illinois

Go to Degreesofbetrayal.com or areUthirsty.com for more info.

Edited by Ramona Cramer Tucker

Designed by Julie Chen

Scripture quotations are taken from the *Holy Bible,* King James Version.

Library of Congress Cataloging-in-Publication Data

Mackall, Dandi Daley.
Sierra's story / Dandi Daley Mackall.
p. cm. — (Degrees of betrayal)
Summary: Scarred and in pain after a car accident, a high school senior turns away from God, especially after remembering how her boyfriend and best friend were involved in the crash, and plans her revenge while the elderly woman sharing her hospital room urges her to forgive and forget.
ISBN 0-8423-8726-9 (sc)
[1. Traffic accidents—Fiction. 2. Revenge—Fiction. 3. Amnesia—Fiction. 4. Interpersonal relations—Fiction. 5. Conduct of life—Fiction.] I. Title. II. Series.
PZ7.M1905Si 2004
[Fic]—dc22 2004001498

Printed in the United States of America

08 07 06 05 04
7 6 5 4 3 2 1

To Maureen,
the most loyal sister in the world

I have to give thanks and credit to the women
who bailed me out of the corner I painted myself
into when I made my main character a shoe freak.
Since I have about three pairs of shoes—
all of them black—and, as a friend of mine explained,
"Dandi, you don't shop for shoes. You restock,"
I desperately needed help.

Thanks to my nieces, Becca Pento and Kelly Brigmon,
who have spent sizable portions of their lives
researching shoe styles.
Thanks to Andrea Martin, whose love
for shoes is boundless.
Thanks to Caitie Kindig's immense shoe closet.
And thanks to Kelsey Knowlton,who not only
supplied me with brand names, but many shoe stories,
which I have stolen for this book.

My arm is ice. I can't lift it. It feels like it's buried under an avalanche of heavy white snow. I could be buried alive.

Maybe this is one of those dreams—those trapped dreams—where you have to get away, but you can't move no matter how hard you try. And you can't scream.

Clank!

I'm awake again, I think. Something woke me, I think. *I think. Therefore I am.* Right? But *where* am I?

The *clank* happens again. Metal on metal? Voices too. But they're on the ceiling, bouncing around, refusing to be trapped into separate sounds. Tangled and interwoven words.

And the smell. Like a too-clean bathroom.

I would be scared, terrified, if I could line up my thoughts in a straight row. But I can't.

I can't open my eyes. Or maybe they *are* open, and I still can't see. Is this what it's like to be blind? Am I blind?

"There's a disturbance on 8th and Maple. Suspected 10-15. Vehicles respond. We have a 10-23 at Highview Heights. Copy."

The words are words now. But together they don't make sense. And the voice is scratchy and filled with smoky air. A police scanner? Somehow I know this. Am I in a police car? But nothing is moving. No high-speed chase. No turns or speed bumps.

"You turn that thing off. You hear me? Don't make me tell you again. I don't care if you're the Highview police captain. You turn that thing off in this room. My girl here doesn't need to be hearing that scratchy thing."

This voice is familiar, but I don't have a face to go with it. Just the soothing sound of the words rolling. Female. African-American. Middle-aged. Is it racist to think this? Is it age prejudice? Gender prejudice?

"It's regulation. I have to keep it on." The voice is young, male. I picture a rock singer, tall, clean-cut, out of place in his own band. Laughed at behind his back. "She can't hear it anyway."

She can't hear it. Does he mean *me?* Am *I* the *she* who can't hear?

I want to scream at him. *I can too hear it, you pitiful excuse for a rock star!* But nothing comes out.

"She can hear us." The soothing lady's voice

again. In my mind she becomes Lady Smooth, a woman as at home in mules as she is in Skechers.

"That's not what the doc said," mutters Officer Geek.

Lady Smooth whispers in my ear, "I know you hear me, sugar. You'll come back when you're ready."

I feel something at my shoulders. A blanket being pulled up? I *felt* that. I *feel!*

I can't tell if seconds have passed. Or hours. Or days. Or eternity.

Maybe I'm dead.

I've always believed in heaven and kind of in hell. But this isn't like either one of them.

I remember a sleepover. Sixth grade? My friends piled onto my bed. Our fingernails wet with pink pearl polish. Cotton between our toes. And somebody started talking about what it would be like to be dead. Before I could get them to talk about something else, like Jason Weaver or the new boy who just moved from Texas and had the cutest accent, they took turns imagining what it was like to be dead. Most of them believed in heaven, like me. But Molly Jacobs, who moved away the next summer, insisted death was darkness and being cut off from life. A degree of life.

I can't move. It's total darkness wherever I am now. Grave dark. I'm cut off from life. Is that *dead?*

But I smell scrambled eggs. I can't be dead.

"There you go, sweetie. That better?"

That voice again. Lady Smooth. I fight to stay

above the darkness so I can hear her voice. It's the only thing in my world that doesn't hurt. She's doing something around my head. A pillow? I'm in a bed. With a pillow and a blanket.

"Honey, I'm sorry these officers keep disturbing you. I can't keep them out. Believe me, I tried."

Officers? Is this the army? Am I in a war?

But I remember the police scanner. They're police officers, not soldiers.

And I should know where I am. Pillows. Blankets. I do know, but the answer keeps melting out of my head.

"This is Sergeant McCarthy," says Lady Smooth. "And this youngster is Officer Williams. They keep coming back, so I thought it was about time you got introduced proper."

"Are you sure she can hear us?" One of them—I'm thinking the geek rock star Williams—whispers this. Why is he whispering? Is it a test?

A deeper male voice says, "Uh, ma'am . . ." Then he clears his throat and tries again. "I'm McCarthy. I'm . . . we're sorry. . . ."

He's sorry? Sorry about what? I try to pull in my thoughts, but it's like trying to get pieces of bread back together after I've tossed them into Eden's Pond for the ducks.

Eden's Pond. I remember ducks.

"We just need to ask you some questions," says deep-voiced McCarthy.

"Like she's going to answer? This is crazy, Mac." It's the rock geek. Williams.

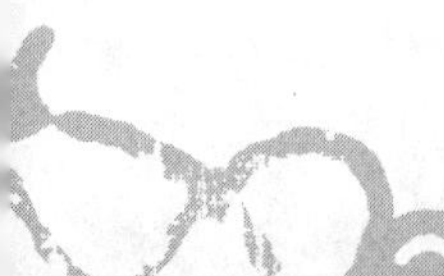

A sigh comes from my friend Lady Smooth. She doesn't like Williams any more than I do. "Sierra . . ."

Sierra. I'm Sierra. I remember that. Sierra Reynolds. Sierra Emily Reynolds. A senior at Highview High.

". . . they're wanting to know about the accident."

Accident. There's been an accident. A 911 accident? An airplane crash?

I can't remember. I can't remember an accident.

But inside my cold dark skeleton, there's no doubt. There *has* been an accident. A terrible, terrible accident. I was in it.

Maybe I still am.

It's quiet again. The only sound is friendly laughter far, far away.

I am in a hospital. A hospital bed. I'm not sure how I know this. Everything is still black. I still can't move. But the knowledge is here, inside my black cave.

The cold dripping into my arm isn't snow. It's an IV. I've seen them on *ER* reruns. I've seen them when we visited Grandpa Reynolds in the hospital. He had tubes everywhere they could think of.

Do I? Do I have tubes like Grandpa Reynolds?

Memories are rolling through my mind so fast they're bumping into each other. Grandpa Reynolds. He moved east because he had only one son, my dad. Grandpa hated chewing gum and loud music, and I don't think I ever knew what he liked. He spent the last three weeks of his life on a life-support machine in Highview County General. I remember the "quality of life" arguments my parents had when Grandpa was on oxygen, the clear bag expanding and collapsing according to the commands of metal dials on metal machines.

"We should tell them to turn off the machines," Dad insisted. "What kind of quality of life is this?"

"You can't do that," Mom whispered. "You can't betray your own father like that!"

Gotta wonder if Mom and Dad have had that particular discussion about me. I haven't moved since I've been here, however long that is. I can't even open my eyes because they're heavier than lead. Eye leads. A joke—*leads.* How can I have a sense of humor here?

The blanket lifts, and I feel a rush of cold air.

"Vitals still stable, Nurse?" It's a doctor. I've heard his voice before. I've heard lots of doctors, male and female, come and go, this one more than the others.

"Ninety over 70. Pulse rate, 65."

The cold stethoscope shocks my chest. Inside, my skeleton jumps so high, it smashes on the ceiling. But I don't move.

He squeezes just below my knee, then moves my leg. It hurts. "That hip will take some time. But the leg looks good."

Should I be flattered? My mother has great legs. Mine are okay. They're not my best feature. But thank heavens I got Mom's feet. Size 5 1/2. Nothing weird about the toes. A foot made for sandals, Steve Maddens.

I concentrate, trying to call up an image of myself. I see my feet first. Toenails painted, a tiny flower on each big toenail. Perfect with cork-heeled Bebes.

What else? Average height. Five-five. I'm *cute.* I guess that's what everybody says: *Sierra, you are so cute.* I don't get over 122 pounds, or Mom starts leaving dieting pamphlets in my bedroom.

Cute. I'd rather be gorgeous. Or beautiful. Or striking. Like McKenzie Parker, my best friend. She's tall and tan, with streaky blonde hair that turns heads in the mall.

When I think of Kenzie, something inside twinges, like a physical pain. That's odd. She's been my best friend since summer. I got to know her on yearbook staff our junior year, when she was still pretty mousy. But over the summer, she changed her hair, her style, everything. We went shoe shopping a couple of times and hit it off. We've been best friends our senior year.

So why don't I want to think about her anymore? Did something happen to her? Did she get hurt too?

In the blackness behind my eyes, my own image finally comes into focus. I have shiny auburn hair, deep red really, with natural blonde highlights. I can't remember when it hasn't come at least to my shoulders. My hair is my best feature, and I know it.

And my eyes. Green and deep set. People say they're Irish eyes. Ryun, my boyfriend, says they're the biggest eyes he's ever seen.

Ryun. When I think about Ryun, I can hardly breathe. Longing? Fear? Where *is* Ryun? Why isn't he here?

Above me, Doctor and Lady Smooth are talking about cutting back drips, consulting specialists. They argue about something, but I can't keep the thoughts together, so I let myself sink into the mattress and fall all the way through.

I smell Old Spice. Someone's leaning on my bed. The Old Spice has to be my sister's. Jacqueline's in eighth grade, and Mom won't let her wear perfume to school. So she wears men's cologne. That's Jacqueline. I picture her in flip-flops—never mind it's no longer the season for them. Not the cool flip-flops with designs on the inside of the sole. Not like my turquoise pair with bright edges and straps and the palm tree design. Just plain yellow thongs. And overalls with a T-shirt—the slogan, thankfully, illegible because of the overall buckles. Her friends all wear skater clothes.

Jacqueline would have her wild red hair stuffed under a hat. Maybe the broad-brimmed Panama or the one that looks like she's going fishing and it should have hooks and worms on it. My sister loves hats.

"Hey, Sis!" she shouts. "Can you hear me? Wake up! I miss you, Sierra. I'm not kidding. You need to meet your roommate. You have the coolest roommate. Her name's Missouri. Isn't that amazing?" She pronounces it *Missou-ruh,* not *Missour-ree.*

I think I'm not hearing her right. I have a roommate? A roommate who is a state?

"You should have seen Dad when he walked in," Jacqueline continues. "After you got out of intensive care and into this rehab unit, Dad demanded a private room, which they didn't have. And anyway, he's the one who wrote this discovery grant. Remember? For University Hospital and rehabilitation? Putting old people with young people—*The Nurturing Program.* So Dad couldn't just say, 'This is ridiculous,' which you could tell he wanted to say. It was great though. You should have been there. Oh. Okay. You *were* there. Anyway . . ."

Jacqueline takes her weight off the bed. Her weight isn't much. She's skinny as a Granny boot. "I don't know what to do for her. Except talk. Do you think she can hear me?" she asks.

"I think she can. Sometimes," Lady Smooth answers.

"I hope so." My sister lowers her voice. "Why is her face like that?"

My face? Like what? Why is my face like what?

"It hardly looks like Sierra," Jacqueline says.

Why doesn't it look like me? What happened to my face?

"Your sister's face is just swollen, honey. She'll be all right. That scar on her forehead will fade too. You'll see."

Jacqueline asks more questions, but I can't hear them. All I hear is *scar. Scar on her forehead.* Blood is pounding in my head. If I'm disfigured, I don't want to live.

How could this happen to me? God, if you're out there, why did you let this happen to me? What did I do to deserve it?

I don't want to wake up, not ever.

"Hospitals are bad for you."

Jacqueline's talking. Still? Again? I can't fix time. There's no time where I am, and there's nothing but time.

"Hospital mistakes kill 50,000 people a year, you know. One in 20 patients gets the wrong medicine. And don't get me started on infections! You should consider a new profession."

The familiarity of my sister's tirade pulls at me, tugging me closer to the surface. Jacqueline believes everything is bad for us. And she's never shy about giving out her facts and stats.

"You're not married to a doctor, are you?" Jacqueline will ask anyone anything.

I feel sorry for Lady Smooth.

"I married a carpenter who became a teacher."

Lady Smooth sounds close. I think she's changing my IV bag. I imagine her . . . short, plump, gray at the temples, standing on the tips of her square-toed, white nurse's shoes as she lifts the bag off the hook.

"That's good." Jacqueline doesn't miss a beat. "Doctors have high suicide rates. My dad's a shrink. Talk about high suicide rates."

I hear heavy footsteps outside my room.

"Here they come," Jacqueline whispers.

"*Again,*" Lady Smooth adds softly. "I think they actually believe your sister's faking it." Her footsteps move away. "Evening, officers."

"Any change?" Sergeant McCarthy asks. I know his voice now. Deep—and kind, I think. I wonder how many times they've come here. And why.

"Jack Reynolds."

I picture my sister sticking out her hand, taking charge. My mother hates it that Jacqueline calls herself "Jack."

"Sierra is my sister," she continues. "She's not really up for visitors at the moment. I'd like to know why you've been giving her the third degree."

"Easy, sister." This from the rock star geek Williams. I already know he's no match for my sister. I almost feel sorry for him.

"Who are you?" Jacqueline demands.

"Williams. Officer Will—"

"Puerto Rican?" she asks, direct as ever.

"Yeah. Fourth generation."

I wonder how Jacqueline knows this. There's no accent.

"We should go dancing sometime. I love Latin jazz. Or salsa!"

"Wh–"

"I'll show you."

I can only imagine what Jacqueline is doing to embarrass Officer Geek Williams. Lady Smooth laughs, a wonderful hearty sound. If I could lift my hands, I'd applaud.

Expensive, leather-heeled shoes pound in the hall outside my room. Fast clicks of high heels trail behind. I know my parents' shoes. I know their entrance. It's like they've been here before, but I can't remember.

I can feel my dad in the room now. Everything changes, even the air. Even though I still can't open my eyes or speak, I know my dad will make all this go away. He can make the police run back to the station. He can do anything.

"I told you I wanted to be notified at once if the police entered this room again." Dad's voice is controlled. He's had lots of practice controlling things. He has his own psychiatric practice. No new patients. That's how popular he is. People wait for years to get in to see my dad.

"They just arrived, Dr. Reynolds." Lady Smooth isn't ruffled. "How are you, Mrs. Reynolds?"

I imagine my mother smiling, then feeling guilty for smiling. So she bites her lip and assumes the martyr stance. She makes a great martyr. Her eyes will be tear-filled, with just the right degree of concern, of regret, of *We gave the girl everything, did our best–and it's come to this?* in her face. People think my mom looks like Mary Tyler Moore. Not the spunky, all-American version with the grumpy newsroom boss. The *real* Mary Tyler Moore, the one who looks about two hours away from a nervous breakdown.

"Jacqueline, how did you get here?" Mom asks.

"Bike. Officer Williams' police motorcycle, actually." Vintage Jacqueline.

"Jacqueline!" Dad scolds. But it's hard to tell if he's scolding her for riding the motorcycle or for lying and saying she rode the motorcycle.

"It's okay," my sister assures our parents. "We wore our helmets."

"No, we didn't. I mean—" Poor Officer Williams.

"Jacqueline," Mom pleads, "I want you to tell me what's going on."

It's almost funny. Mom's worry isn't an act now. It's not the motorcycle. I know that edge in her voice. She had it the first time she met Ryun, when he came into the house to pick me up for our first date. Ryun is Komerican, Korean-American. Normally my mother would have a problem with this. But that was just until she met Ryun and saw how he dresses, how he acts—always a gentleman. He even talks to my mother on the phone if I'm not home.

But this is different. Her daughter with a Puerto Rican? A policeman? I could tell my mother was just about ready to have both Jacqueline and Officer Williams arrested.

"Okay." Jacqueline sounds like she's giving in. I know better. Mom never does. "Williams and I are engaged," she says. "I want to have his baby."

At least two people choke on that one. Mom and, I think, Officer Williams. Maybe McCarthy too. I picture steam coming out of Dad's ears.

I'm laughing so hard inside that it seems impossible they can't hear me.

"That's not funny," Mom says. She stops. I imagine her glancing at Dad to make sure. It's the Dad-glance she gives when she tells a joke, but it's Dad's joke really. And she has to get his nod, his permission, before she can deliver the punch line.

"That will be enough, Jacqueline," Dad says sternly. "Which one of you is in charge? If either of you comes into this room again without our lawyer present, I'm calling your captain."

Our lawyer? We need a lawyer? I *need a lawyer?*

"Officer Williams and I were the ones called to Route 58. We're just doing our job, Mr. Reynolds," McCarthy says calmly.

Their job? What job are they doing in my hospital room? Why is Dad so mad at them? It's scaring me to think about this.

Then I get it. An accident. A car accident. Did I cause it? Was I driving? I remember . . . sliding into Dad's '57 Chevy. He collects classic cars, and the Chevy is his prize. I remember moving the seat forward. The keys felt icy cold in my palm.

Then the blackness settles over my mind like a heavy curtain falling, and I can't see what happens next.

Their job? Is their job to get me to confess? To arrest me for the accident?

Is that it? Is that why they're hovering over my

hospital bed as if I'm going to escape? They're idiots. I can't even escape to the bathroom. I can't cry.

It wouldn't be the first time I've combined beer and high speeds on Route 58. I *am* a senior. I don't drink much because I don't like the taste. But I'll have a beer with my friends. Is that it?

And was I alone?

I'm trying so hard to remember that my head is splitting into pieces. I see white specks in the black, like tiny bone fragments. Who was with me? Not Ryun. *Please, God, not Ryun.*

But I can see myself behind the giant wheel of the old Chevy. I'm driving—to a football game. The last one of the season. I pick up Kenzie. And I know I'm driving to Ryun's.

Somebody tell me! Where are they? Are they okay? If I hurt them, I don't want to live. Is that why the police are here? I hurt McKenzie and Ryun? Did I kill them? Did I?

The room feels empty now. I want to scream for the police to come back so I can confess. *Yes! I did it! I don't remember, but I must have done this.* They won't believe me if I tell them I can't remember anything.

Not that I care if they believe me or not. It doesn't matter.

If I can ever talk again, I'll cry out so loud the whole state will hear me: "Yes! I did it. Bring on the judge. Bring on the gas pellets or the lethal needle. Take your pick. I don't care. Just let it be over."

Life, I mean. It might as well be.

I think it's the middle of the night. It's quiet, except for a *plip, plip* that seems to come from the ceiling and a *beep, beep* from some machine I'm hooked up to. From farther away come the sounds of friendly laughter, the squish of rubber soles on the hall floor. It's what I've come to think of as night music. It's the only peace I have now.

I'm empty without Ryun, without McKenzie. Every minute I'm awake I hate myself and wish I were dead. Every minute except these interludes of night music that play on as if none of the rest of this is happening to me.

But even the music of the hospital hurts. I miss music. I miss everything. I miss Ryun most of all. I remember the first time I really noticed Ryun Lee. I'd seen him around before, at school, playing soccer. It was second semester, junior year, a warm spring day, when some of us girls were hanging out in the bleachers watching the soccer game. Ryun caught my eye and made this little signal, promising that the next goal he made would be for me. He made the goal, of course. So afterward I told him that a bunch of us on yearbook staff would be looking through photos and could use a guy's perspective.

And Ryun had showed up the next day. We had the radio tuned to WYII. They were doing the Top 40 countdown. Ryun said he'd always wanted to work on the yearbook. He started fingering through party pictures until he came to a group shot of my friends and me, back when I dated Michael. "That's a good picture of you, Sierra," he commented. "Nice dress. But the shoes are amazing."

I couldn't believe he'd noticed my shoes—Stuart Weitzmans, deep maroon, straps to the ankles. No guy had ever noticed my shoes. I think I knew then that we were destined to be together.

I can remember that moment as if it just happened. Funny. I don't remember days, not really. Or years. I remember moments. But I think it's always like that, not just here in the cave. I see snapshots or movies of the past.

I don't remember how I got here, in this hospital bed—it just feels like I've been here forever. But I remember everything else.

Like the first day of my senior year. Since I was old enough to understand the difference between elementary and high school, I'd dreamed about my senior year. With all my heart, I believed that my senior year in high school would be the best year of my life, the time I'd think about for the rest of my life.

I'd started planning for this day the end of my junior year. Highview High has a tradition of first-day themes based around togas. Past High High—short for Highview High—senior classes had gone classic, with everybody ordering Greek and Roman togas. Boring. Or Mardi Gras togas, with sequins and beads. Skanky. One year some uninspired juniors chose farmer togas and had to wear them under overalls. Jacqueline would have loved it.

Our class, at my suggestion, decided on prison togas. It was the best ever. Lots of kids went with prison orange—big mistake. Since Kenzie and I had been hanging out so much lately, we coordinated our togas. Hers was black with white stripes, and mine was mirror image, white with black stripes. We wore each other's pillbox hat. I knew she looked better in her outfit than I did, but it was okay. I was glad to see her come out of her shell. That girl really had transformed herself over the summer. Seriously, there were kids who didn't recognize Kenzie when she walked in the first day of class, all trim and tan, with streaky blonde hair, instead of mousy brown.

I'm trying to hang on to every one of my memories because I don't think I'll be making any new ones.

I remember something else, something closer. McKenzie's boyfriend, Taylor Hatfield, broke up with her before the last game of the year, the final football game of our senior year. I wanted to punch his lights out. The loser didn't know a good thing when he saw one.

I'd talked Kenzie into going to the game with me. With Ryun and me. So I picked them up. Why did I do that? I remember. Dad made a big deal about letting me drive his prize '57 Chevy for our last high school game. He was so cool about it. He won't even let Mom touch that car.

And so I was driving. . . .

My head throbs, as if the memories have razor-sharp edges and pulling at them slices through my brain. So I let them go.

"How is she?"

The voice startles me. It's deep. Yet I'm picturing a guy my age.

It's funny how voices spark memories, and I don't really get the connection. I remember a kid, Andrew, I think. African-American. Got into all kinds of trouble when we were in second grade. We had a class pet, Grady, a black-and-white hamster, with a serious overbite. I got it into my head that Grady was unhappy and wanted to roam the woods with other hamsters. Never mind that there were no woods, no other hamsters. So one day I snatched Grady from his cage and set him free on the playground.

The teacher, Mrs. Swindler, was convinced this kid Andrew did it. I was such a good kid. Couldn't have been me. I was terrified when she demanded to know who turned Grady loose. All I could think about was how disappointed Daddy would be, how I'd let him down and he'd never forget it. But Andrew was sitting next to me. He raised his hand and said he did it and he was sorry.

I couldn't believe it. I remember thinking that maybe Andrew really did do it. Then the hamster wandered back into the cage, and *I* set him free.

So at recess I asked Andrew if he'd really let the hamster go. He laughed and said, "*You* ought to know, Sierra." I asked him why he'd said he did it then. He shrugged and said, "I figured if I got in trouble one more time, it wouldn't make any difference." Then he ran off to shoot hoops.

I have no idea why I'm thinking about this. The boy in my hospital room is talking to Lady Smooth, and I try to listen in because I think they're talking about me.

"Do they know what happened?" he asks.

"They think they do. If those other two hadn't pulled her out of the car, she would have burned to death."

"They were all over the front page again today. I saw that girl, McKenzie, in school. She just had a few bruises. Pretty amazing."

I'm lapping up their words. McKenzie. Kenzie is all right. I think I'm crying, and I wonder if they can see it, if I'm getting any of these tears outside my shell.

I want him to talk about Ryun. Two kids pulled me out of the car. Two—Kenzie and Ryun. Then

Ryun has to be okay, doesn't he? If he could pull me out? Unless he got hurt pulling me out. . . .

My throat is on fire, and I'm so thirsty. On fire. I can almost feel the flames. . . .

■ ■ ■

"You don't look so bad, in case you're wondering." It's Kenzie. I've been hearing her voice, but I thought I was dreaming. Now I'm sure she's really here, sitting on the foot of my bed.

"You're not missing much at school," she continues. "Everybody asks about you."

I want to break through the cave and talk with my friend. I want to hang on to her so she won't leave. So *I* won't go back.

"This feels silly," Kenzie says to someone else in the room. "Are you sure I should keep talking?"

"I'm sure." Good ol' Lady Smooth. "I have a feeling Sierra can hear you. You just keep talking."

Kenzie sighs. "Well, they said your ribs are just bruised. Your hip isn't broken, but it's bad. Dislocated, your dad said."

My hip? She's wrong. I would know if I'd dislocated my hip.

"Anyway, Ryun's doing better."

Ryun. I try to grab hold of the word as the letters float past me. *Ryun.* If he's doing better, then he wasn't killed. He's alive. But the other words push through and hover around me. *Doing better.* What does that mean? Better than what?

I scream in my head, "Kenzie, tell me about

Ryun! What happened to him? What did I do?"
If I've hurt him, if he's *damaged,* I won't be able to live with that. I will never, ever forgive myself for that.

Kenzie is rattling on about the kids at Little Lambs, a day-care center her church sponsors. She's teaching them to draw and play the guitar. She spends a lot of time there after school.

Kenzie! Tell me about Ryun! I scream so loud, it's a miracle (a reverse, perverse miracle) that she can't hear me.

Time passes, but I have no idea how much time. There are visits from Jacqueline, never with my parents. I think she had two friends with her once. They cried, then had a giggling fit, like they were eight, instead of in eighth grade. Lady Smooth had to shush them. The boy whose voice made me think of Grady and Andrew in second grade and the hamster escape has been here a lot.

Dad has come, at least once by himself. Surely more. And I know I've heard Lady Smooth talking with my mother several times.

There's a presence most of the time when I come up from the darkness. That's how I think of it, like coming up for air. At first I thought it was "a God presence" or even an angel. But by now I know it's not. I think it's the woman Jacqueline called my roommate. The one who is a state. Sometimes I hear her humming. She always hums hymns. "Amazing Grace." "Go Tell It On the Mountain." Other songs our elementary music teacher called "Negro spirituals." Maybe that's why I thought of an angel.

We don't sing these songs in our church. I go to Baker Avenue Church, the oldest, most historic church in Highview. I remember every Vacation Bible School I attended there, every Sunday school class. My friends and I would try to wear the same color and always sit together. We played games and talked about school and the poor. I used to want to sing in the choir. But there are 100 singers, and you have to be pretty good to get in.

Since freshman year, a lot of kids have dropped out. They don't come to church, except maybe on Easter. Even Jacqueline has to be dragged to church with us. But I've never even thought about quitting. I've never had problems with God or church or anything.

Until now. Because it doesn't seem fair that I'm trapped in darkness. I don't deserve this. I'm not sure what I did that put me into this frozen state. But it couldn't have been bad enough to deserve this.

I used to pray every night, naming all of the people in my life and thanking God for everything. I had the list memorized. When Grandma died, it took me two weeks to stop giving thanks for her and take her off the list.

But I don't feel so thankful right now. And I don't think I could talk to God if I wanted to. He's not down here. Or if he is, I sure haven't seen him.

■ ■ ■

I've discovered that I can choose to listen to the "aboveground world" or shut it out. I've been shutting it out more and more lately. I'm not sure why. I shut out the hymn-humming whenever I can. I think I'm mad at God. I don't like his songs.

Suddenly, like a flash of a favorite TV show while you're channel surfing, I hear a channel, a conversation worth tuning in. And I know the two most important people in my life are here in the room with me–Ryun and Kenzie.

"She doesn't even know we're here, Ryun. We shouldn't do this to ourselves, especially you. You've got enough to worry about."

"I know."

I can't stand this. What is Ryun worrying about? How much did I hurt him?

"She's not going to wake up. That's what everybody's saying. You know that." Kenzie is whispering.

It makes me laugh inside. If I can't hear her, why is she whispering?

"Even if she does wake up," Kenzie continues, "she's going to be a vegetable for the rest of her life."

A vegetable? What a strange idea. It can't be me they're talking about, can it? Then I want to ask Kenzie which vegetable they think I'll be if I wake up. Calmly I consider my options. Not a tomato. Too cliché. And maybe it's a fruit anyway, like a cantaloupe or a watermelon. I should have paid more attention in Mr. Russell's science class.

But anyway, they can't be talking about me. Not about Sierra Reynolds.

I think I've passed out or fallen into the black pit again, when I hear footsteps fading away. I want to yell for Ryun to come back, to please come back.

Then he does. For a second, I think maybe he heard me. Maybe the words, the sounds finally made it out of my head.

Ryun comes to the bed. He leans down, his head next to mine. I can feel him. Breathe him. His breath is on my ear.

I want him to hold me. I know I could feel it if he holds me. I try to swim to the top.

He stammers, "I-I'm sorry, Sierra."

I want to tell him it's not his fault I screwed up. I have never seen *him* drunk. Ryun is an athlete. He always says alcohol and athletics don't mix.

I hear him move away. But it sounds funny, like he's dragging one leg. And I wonder how bad he's hurt. How bad *I* hurt him.

There is something chasing me. *A lion or a bear. But it's human. I run as fast as I can. I stumble, cursing my clumsiness. Then I'm running again. I glance over my shoulder. The thing is closing in on me. I'm trying to speed up, but my legs wind down, as if they're on a coil that's coming unsprung. I'm in slow motion. My arms drop to my sides. I can't lift them. I'm not moving. And all the while, the thing, whatever it is, gets closer and closer.*

It leaps onto me, making me free-fall into blackness.

Then we're in a car. The car is speeding. Faster and faster. Out of control. It hits something and flies into the air. I feel the crash and hear the boom. *We roll over and over. Something's hissing. People are yelling. It's getting hotter. I can't move, and it's so hot that I have to scream. And I scream and scream.*

■ ■ ■

"O Lordy! Lordy, Lordy! Nurse!" The voice is high, squeaky.

It's the hymn-hummer. My roommate. But she's not humming. She's shouting.

Blurred light bashes my eyes. It's like swimming in chlorine. I try to close my eyes, but it's so hard.

There's cottony light at the end of a long dark tunnel. I don't know if I'm awake or asleep. I could sink back deeper into the tunnel. How easy it would be to slide backward, where nothing can touch me. But it's been so long since I've seen anything but blackness. I want to look. I want to see.

"Come on, child. It's time to come out now," the hummer coaxes.

My eyelids are still heavy, but I can lift them. When I do, it's like looking through slat blinds. A face, or a slice of one, comes into focus, although it might be in my head. I don't know. The face is leathery, black, with thousands of lines running through it. A shock of white hair sticks out all around it. The hymn-hummer, if that's who it is, must be 100 years old. With tiny, deep brown eyes that strike me as the color of heaven, even though I know heaven must be blue.

"That's it. Keep coming. I'm Missou-ruh. I've been praying for you, child. We all have. Where is that nurse?"

I wonder if she's real. Because she doesn't look real. And I'm thinking that maybe I've really died this time. Maybe "Missou-ruh" is part of wherever I've gone to. Her eyes could be angel eyes. But the rest of her? Angels couldn't look like this.

She says Lordy a few more times—it sounds like a prayer. Then she reaches across me and pulls a cord. A buzzer sounds.

Footsteps snap in the hall and run into my room.

"Look at this! She's back to life. Glory be. And God be praised!" sings the hummer.

"Well, welcome back, Sierra." It's Lady Smooth. The voice is real. *I'm* real.

I want to see her, Lady Smooth. When I try to open my eyes wider, I see my own eyelids, dark and sagging, with a tinge of pink. I try to speak, but my lips are too thick and my tongue is lost. My throat is a circle of sandpaper, rubbing against itself.

Then my eyes clear, and I see the old black woman, smiling, inches from my face. She looks like a ghost, her nightgown draped over a skeleton. Her bony fingers rest on my arm, as if she's ready to pull me back up if I start slipping away. I see the tube in my arm, the tape inside my elbow.

"I'm Nurse Miller. Do you know where you are, Sierra?" Lady Smooth asks.

I know I can't answer, but I think I nod.

"You're in University Hospital in Highview. You're going to be okay. The doctor will be here any minute. I called your family."

Everything's white. Except the hymn-hummer. I'm so thirsty.

"Can I get her some water?" the hummer asks, as if she's heard my thoughts. Maybe she *is* an angel.

"Just ice chips, Missouri. Can you get her some from over there?"

The old woman shuffles away, and I see Lady Smooth clearly for the first time. But it can't be *my* Lady Smooth. This woman is tall and slender, not round and soft as jelly. Her black hair is swept up in a comb. She's younger than my mother. And pretty. Maybe beautiful. And elegant.

The hummer is here again. She has a spoon that she puts to my lips. I feel the cold of the ice. My lips move to grab it until the tiny piece of precious ice enters. It fills my mouth and finds my tongue. Nothing has ever tasted so good.

"This is Missouri," Lady Smooth says. "She's getting over a broken hip herself. She's been helping me keep an eye on you. Missouri is 101 years old, the most fit centenarian I've had the pleasure of knowing."

"Likely the *only* one you've had the pleasure of knowing," replies the hummer, Missouri.

For a second I wonder if the state *is* named after her.

I don't want to, but I have to close my eyes. They are too heavy to stay open. It's impossible. Still, even with my eyes shut, the darkness isn't total.

I feel like I'm floating on the surface of life.

"Are you sure she's still . . . awake? What if she's unconscious again?"

It's Mom's voice, and I am awake now. I should swim up and talk to her. But I don't. I'm not sure why it doesn't seem worth the effort. I have a great family, a terrific family. And she's part of that.

But a part of me clings to the belowground world, the safety and ease of it.

I open my eyes. The light is too bright, so I shut my eyes to half-mast. I can see Mom. Mrs. Richard Reynolds, of Dr. and Mrs. Richard Reynolds. She's wearing a white silk blouse and expensive black pants, with the black Cole Haans that are a little preppy for her. Her hair is perfect—shiny brown, layered, with wisps over her forehead.

"She's opening her eyes!" Mom exclaims. "Hi,

Sierra. We're here, honey! We're so glad you're conscious again. Everything's going to be fine."

"Has she said anything?" Dad asks.

I want to see him, but he's standing too far away. He peeks around Mom, then looks away. And I remember what Kenzie said about my face. What Jacqueline said.

Can't my dad stand to look at me?

"You were right, Missouri! She's back." Jacqueline plunges on my bed in front of Mom.

The jarring hurts my ribs and just about everywhere else. I open my mouth to tell my sister to get off, but my throat hurts too much. The sandpaper closes in on itself.

"Cool! Welcome back. And thanks a lot, Sis," Jacqueline says. "Thanks to you, I owe Missouri one Sunday morning."

Mom frowns over at Lady Smooth, my nurse. "What?"

Nurse Miller laughs.

"We had a bet," Jacqueline explains, straightening her black derby. She calls it a bowler. "I lost, so I have to go to church with Missouri one Sunday."

"She's right," Missouri replies. "If I lost, I was going to have to wade in the hospital fountain on Sunday."

I can tell Mom doesn't like this. But she's too polite to say so.

"What does the doctor say?" Dad asks, pacing. "Why isn't he here?"

"Dr. Snyder came as soon as I called him. He checked her out. Your daughter's vital signs are strong." Nurse Miller comes over and wraps the blood-pressure cuff around my arm, as if she needs to prove her statement.

"Tell Dr. Snyder to call me when he gets back to the hospital," Dad commands. "I'll leave my office number. I want a firsthand report."

All of this feels like a dream, as much as when I was in the black cave, hearing their voices. I can barely stay awake.

"You're 18! You had a birthday, *and* you missed Thanksgiving!" Jacqueline shouts, as if I'm deaf now.

"What?" I think I say it out loud. But the voice isn't mine. It's an old man's voice. *I'm 18?*

"She can talk!" Jacqueline cries. She turns back to me. "We saved your presents. And it's no big deal that you missed Thanksgiving. Nobody was too thankful at home anyway. We didn't even have turkey."

I can't take this in. I try to remember, to fix a time, a day, a month. But they're swirling past each other in my head, and my head hurts. Is it possible to turn 18 and not know it? Eighteenth birthdays are landmarks, like 16 and 21. And how could I miss Thanksgiving? We always have a traditional meal, with the best china. Then the next day I go shoe shopping with my friends.

Mother reaches for me, and I think she's going to put her palm on my forehead. Instead she touches my hair, not my head. She doesn't look me in the eyes either. "Did they have to do this?" She stares at my hair.

"What's that?" Nurse Miller asks, hanging a plastic bag of clear fluid onto a hooked pole.

"Cut her hair. Like this?"

Cut *her* hair? *My* hair? Why would they cut my hair? Ryun loves my hair long.

"They had to do it," the nurse explains. "For the stitches on her neck. See?" She touches the back of my neck. "They took out quite a few pieces of glass."

This is too much for me. I think I'm going to be sick. Am I a freak? Is that why they can't look at me?

"Don't worry about it, Sierra," Nurse Miller says. "Everything's going to heal good as new. You won't even see that scar. Or the one on your hip, unless you're doing something you shouldn't."

She laughs. Mom doesn't.

And I know I can't take anything else. I want to go back. Back to the cave and the darkness. Because the aboveground world has changed too much. I'm not sure I can live there now.

I close my eyes and let the darkness take me.

When I open my eyes again, it's morning. Light streams in through a window I haven't noticed before. It seems noisy for a hospital. Dishes *clang* and *clunk*. Somebody drops something, then laughs. A voice shouts down the hall for someone named Jason. I smell cooked cereal and bleach.

"Morning, child. God's smiling down on you this fine morning."

I look across the room and see the old black woman sitting up in bed, eating.

"Name's Missouri, in case you can't remember. Your family was mighty glad to see you last night. We all were."

The visit comes back to me, but in pictures that are cloudy. I know Jacqueline was on my bed. And Mom and Dad were in the room.

My throat feels a little better, and I want to see if I can talk now. "How long have I been here?"

"Well, you have a fine voice after all," she says. "I'm not right sure. A couple of weeks or so."

A couple of weeks? I don't know what I expected.

Nurse Miller comes in. She's as pretty as I remembered.

"My boyfriend? Was he hurt? Ryun Lee. Is he in the hospital? I need to see him—" I try to get up, but my body is solid steel.

"You take it easy," Nurse Miller says, her voice smooth as ever. "Your boyfriend is just fine. Yes. The paramedics brought him in with you. He stayed right down the hall a few days before they released him."

"They released him? He's all right?"

"He'll be just fine. Don't you worry about him."

I take it all in, as if it's a flood of ice chips, bringing me back to life. He's okay. Ryun is fine. I'm so grateful that tears make my eyes blurry. "Thank you, Lady Smooth," I say, the words sounding choked.

She cocks her head at me. "Excuse me?"

I manage a grin, I think. "Lady Smooth? That's how I thought of you, when I was under. When I . . . couldn't move or open my eyes, I kept hearing your voice. I called you Lady Smooth."

Her gaze is so intense it feels like she can see through me. "You heard me, didn't you?" She turned to the old woman. "You hear that, Missouri? I *knew* it! She could hear me all that time. Wait till I tell those doctors! Ha!"

She smiles at me again. “Lady Smooth, huh? Drew, my son, will love that one. His mama is Lady Smooth!”

The rest of the day I keep dropping off to sleep. Each time I wake up, new doctors and wannabes are huddled by my bed. I have become hospital show-and-tell. Dr. Snyder, my main doctor, acts as proud as if he’d given birth to me. They talk in low voices that send me back to sleep.

I think it’s after lunch when I wake up suddenly and see Jacqueline. She’s talking to Missouri. My sister grins at me, then gets up and comes over.

“You’re sure a good time, Sis,” she says, plopping on my bed.

This time I almost tell her to get off. But I don’t. I’m glad she’s here.

She turns and seems to be straining to hear something in the hall. “Here they come,” she announces. The way she says it I know she means our parents.

Dad rushes in first, with Mom trailing after him. They take off snowflake-covered coats and pile them over the only chair in the room. Then they both say hello.

Dad glances at his watch. He frowns into each corner of the room and at all four walls. “Sierra, did that nurse tell you the police were coming here again?”

“The police?” I remember police. I remember police scanners. But it’s more like I dreamed them.

Mom comes to the bed and pats my knee. “Don’t

worry about it, honey. We're here now. Are you feeling okay? I mean, better?" She's not looking at my face.

Dad glares at my sister. "You should tell us when you're coming over here. The school called, asking where you were. Your mother was worried."

"Being worried isn't necessarily a bad thing," Jacqueline says. "*Not* worrying can be bad for you. People without many wrinkles run a bigger risk of basal cell carcinoma."

"Ooo-eee," Missouri squeals. "I may live another hundred years!"

Jacqueline laughs. The sound is a cross between a siren and a truck downshifting.

Dad comes over to my bed, and Mom steps back. "Sierra, our lawyer said you shouldn't answer any questions. So let me do all the talking."

"I don't remember anything, Dad. I really don't."

"Good. But you shouldn't even say that. Let me handle this. If we need Frank, my lawyer, we'll get him over here. Understand?" Dad doesn't wait for me to say that I understand. "All right then."

I know he's trying to protect me. I hear the cops' footsteps a second before everyone else turns toward the door.

"Be calm," Dad commands us. "Everybody shut up and let me do the talking."

"That will be novel," Jacqueline mutters.

"Jacqueline, keep still," Mom seconds. Her voice is tight. I'm afraid she'll have a Mary-Tyler-Moore breakdown.

Two policemen walk in and take off their hats.

I feel as if I know these men. The bigger, older policeman is pretty much like I'd imagined him. He's almost a stereotype of the Irish cop, with kind green eyes. I'm sure he's McCarthy.

"I'm Sergeant McCarthy," he says to the room. "Thank you for meeting with us." He steps around my dad to get to my bed. "Sierra, you're looking a lot better. It's good to see you awake." He's smiling at me, not looking away.

I'm grateful.

"Officer Williams and I have been by to visit you a few times." He nods toward the other policeman.

Williams is physically different than I imagined—skinnier, darker, and he's wearing glasses. But he still qualifies for a geek rock star.

"I know you were here," I say to McCarthy.

"You do?" McCarthy's smile shows straight white teeth.

"Sometimes I could hear you talking."

"That right?" McCarthy seems impressed.

"Hey, Williams!" Jacqueline coos to the geek rock star. She doesn't follow Dad's orders well.

Williams tries to ignore her, but it's like pretending a tornado hasn't landed in Kansas.

McCarthy twists his cap in his hands and leans in closer. "Officer Williams and I have a few things we'd like to clear up about the accident."

"I don't—," I start.

"Sierra!" Dad shouts. He wedges himself between McCarthy and me. "Officer, we have been instructed by our lawyer not to answer any questions about

Sierra's accident and not to allow her to talk with police without her lawyer present."

McCarthy looks surprised. "I'm not sure I understand, Mr. Reynolds."

"*Dr.* Reynolds," Dad corrects. "What part of *not talking to the police* don't you understand?"

"Richard," Mom pleads.

"Go, Mom!" Jacqueline cheers.

It's a rare assertive moment from my mother, and Dad squelches it with one glance.

"Are you intending to charge my daughter?" Dad demands.

"Charge her? With what?" McCarthy asks. I want to know how he can remain so calm when my dad is on the verge of exploding.

"Don't play games with me!" Dad shouts.

I don't want games. I can feel the cool of the cave calling me back belowground, away from this.

I don't want this. I don't want anything, except to get all of it over with. They *should* charge me. For what I did to Ryun, whatever it is. I couldn't feel this guilty without *being* guilty.

"I did it," I say. "Okay? I'm guilty. I don't care what you do to me. What could you do to me that I haven't already done to myself?"

Dad turns to me, horrified. "Shut up, Sierra!"

I try to remember. I don't think he's ever said that to me before. Not to me. To Mom, yes. To Jacqueline, yes. Not to me.

"My daughter doesn't know what she's saying. They have her on morphine drip. She's not responsible for what she says." Dad's sputtering, he's so mad.

"Mr.–Dr. Reynolds, I don't know what you think happened," McCarthy begins.

"I told you not to play games with us. You and your boss are looking for an example. I know how this works. Sacrifice one teen for a don't-drink-and-drive campaign, and the coming election is–"

McCarthy interrupts. "She wasn't drinking."

We're quiet. Jacqueline eyes Williams, as if they really are together.

Williams nods.

"She wasn't drinking?" Mom repeats.

"Blood tox was zero," McCarthy answers. "Not even a sip of beer. First thing we check."

My dad looks suspicious, like he thinks it's a trap. "Why didn't you tell us this days ago?"

"I didn't realize you thought she *was* drinking." McCarthy smiles down at me. "Your friends confirmed that you hadn't had anything to drink."

I picture Kenzie and Ryun talking to the police, standing up for me, telling them I would never drink and drive. Maybe they lied for me. Maybe they claimed I would never take so much as a sip of beer. I am so grateful to my friend and my boyfriend.

"You can't remember anything? About the accident or that night?" McCarthy strains to hear my answer.

I shake my head and feel a knife stab at the base of my neck.

I have the flash of memory again, the one where I'm driving Dad's car and picking up Kenzie for the game. "I remember picking up McKenzie," I tell him. "I was driving the '57 Chevy." I try to keep the memory going, but it's stuck. Then it breaks up and fades out, like the time the computer virus ate my hard drive.

"Well," McCarthy says, "you weren't drinking. And from what we've been able to tell by the skid marks on the highway, you were driving the speed limit."

"So why do you keep coming back here?" Dad's voice hasn't lost its edge.

“We still have reports to file,” McCarthy answers, as if Dad had just asked him how his day was going. “That car of yours burned up any evidence we might have gathered at the scene. We were just hoping your daughter could fill in a couple of the blanks so we could close this case.”

McCarthy stares down at me. “Your friends saved your life, young lady. I don’t know if you know that or not. If they hadn’t pulled you out of that car when they did, we wouldn’t be having this conversation.”

“I can’t remember,” I say, wanting to so much that the stab of pain in my head digs in deeper.

“Well, they did,” he assures me.

I’m crying now. I can’t seem to stop.

Nurse Miller comes in. “Aren’t you fellas about done?” She breezes bedside and wraps the blood-pressure cuff around my arm.

“I think we’re finished.” McCarthy smiles at me, then nods at Mom and Dad. “Thanks again for your time.”

Jacqueline springs off the foot of my bed. “That went well. I’m out of here.”

“Jacqueline,” Dad calls, “you can ride home with us. It’s too cold to bike. We’ll put your bicycle in my trunk.”

“Thanks, but no thanks. I’m good.” Jacqueline walks over to Officer Williams and kisses him on the cheek. His whole face turns bright red. “I’ll see *you* at midnight.” Her voice has a syrupy ring to it. “The ladder under my window.”

“Jacqueline!” Mom’s expression is all that my sister could have hoped for.

"Until then—ciao! And, Sierra, hang tight. Don't let the bedbugs bite." She stops at Missouri's bed and whispers something before making her final exit.

Silence falls over the hospital room. This is a familiar phenomenon I used to call the minus-Jacqueline effect. I remember hundreds of her exits, when she seemed to take my parents' breath out of the room with her. Nothing left but the hint of Old Spice. They'd need a minute to recover and refill the oxygen content of the Jacqueline-less room.

"Well." Sergeant McCarthy is the first to break our awkward silence. "I guess we'll be going back to the station." He places a business card on my night table. "Sierra, if you remember anything more, give us a call."

After they all leave, Missouri and I fill in Nurse Miller on everything the police said.

"You should be so relieved, Sierra!" says my Lady Smooth, when I finish the part about how I wasn't drinking and driving or even speeding.

I should be. I know she's right. But it doesn't change anything. It was still my fault that I drove off the road. I'm not walking away from this, whether I was drinking or not.

Nurse Miller is talking, but I'm not taking it in. Another day has gone by. I've missed another day of my senior year. Ryun didn't come by. Neither did Kenzie. I feel like it's my fault they didn't visit me. Everything is my fault.

"And tomorrow we start physical therapy," Nurse Miller continues. "Good timing, with Christmas just around the corner. Your recovery is nothing short of miraculous, Sierra."

"Mmm-hmm," Missouri agrees. "Thank the good Lord. Miraculous. That's his style."

I think that the good Lord's style could use some serious work. I refuse to stay in this hospital until Christmas. Christmas is my favorite time in the whole year. I love every single family tradition. I still won't let Dad give in to the fake tree epidemic in America. I make us go to the same tree farm every year and chop down our tree, even though Jacqueline holds me personally responsible for the greenhouse effect.

I cannot be here in this hospital. Not on Christmas.

"Mmm-hmm, that's his style," Missouri repeats.

"Some style," I snap. "Whatever happened to the lame leaping off their beds and the sick getting healed in a flash? That's a style I could get behind."

"Sometimes that's his style, and sometimes it's not." Missouri has an answer for everything. I don't think I could rile her if I tried.

"Back to bed with you, Missouri," Nurse Miller says. She escorts Missouri to her bed.

I close my eyes and let myself remember other Christmases. I remember my 16th Christmas, when I got my secondhand blue Toyota. I loved that car, even though it was pronounced dead before my 17th Christmas.

On Christmas Eve Dad plays "White Christmas" on the piano. Then we go to this multifaith service. On Christmas morning I call all my friends to see what they got.

This would have been a special Christmas for Ryun and me. I have a mental list of the traditions I wanted us to start this year, traditions we could pass on to our children and grandchildren.

After a while, I fall asleep, dreaming about Ryun and me celebrating Christmas around a huge Scotch pine in the living room of our own home.

■ ■ ■

I'm sitting up in my hospital bed, about to take my first sip from a cup of real 7UP, when I hear voices. I know instantly that it's Kenzie and Ryun.

My breath stops until they appear in the doorway. I wish I had my camera. I'd have them hold that pose so I could take a hundred pictures of them. I already have hundreds of pictures of both of them, but this would be one I'd hang on my bedroom wall.

Kenzie's mouth is open, and Ryun keeps running his hand through his hair. I'm so happy to see my friends that tears blur their images.

"Hi." My voice comes out as a croak.

"I can't believe it!" Kenzie says. "I saw Jacqueline in the school parking lot, and she said you were conscious, but . . ."

I smile at her quickly, but I can't take my eyes off Ryun. He's even more handsome than I remembered. He's over six feet tall, with perfect black hair and deep brown eyes.

I've had other boyfriends. I guess I've always had a boyfriend, even in kindergarten. But I've never had a boyfriend like Ryun. He's the one. I know he's the one. If I could get out of this bed, I would throw myself into his arms.

Kenzie elbows him.

"Man," Ryun stammers. "I-I don't know what to say."

I lift the arm that's not attached to the IV. "Come over here."

Ryun glances at Kenzie before walking to my bed. He limps closer. That's when I see the brace on his leg, a huge black brace from the middle of his shin, up his calf.

"Ryun! Your leg! I thought you were okay. The nurse said you were fine. What is it? What's wrong with your leg?"

"It's not that bad," he answers. "The brace just stabilizes my leg until they can do surgery on it."

"Surgery?" They should have told me. I should have known. It's so unfair. And it's my fault.

"It's not a big deal. I'll be ready for spring soccer."

"Are you sure? Does it hurt?"

"Nah. Don't worry about it."

I can't take my eyes off the brace. Ryun's whole life is soccer. If he's injured for life, I won't be able to handle it. "Ryun, I am so sorry. I–"

"Forget it. I told you. I'll be good as new." He turns to Kenzie again.

I want him to look at *me*. I want to see his eyes, those deep eyes that shone, even in the darkness of the cave. "Ryun?" *Please look up.*

He doesn't look up. "Yeah?"

Then I remember. My face. My hair. How could

I have forgotten a thing like that? I must be brain damaged. Ryun has never even seen me without makeup. How could I let him see me now? I still haven't looked in a mirror, but I know there's something terribly wrong with my face. Something bad enough to make people look away. I feel panic set in, like tiny lightning bolts.

What was I thinking? Ryun shouldn't be here. I want to throw the covers over my head.

"I won't always look like this," I say. "The nurse said I'll heal and look exactly like myself again. The doctor says none of the injuries are permanent. My hair will grow back. You believe me, don't you?" I know he doesn't. Why should he? *I* don't believe me.

"I'm just . . . I'm just glad you're better. Really glad." Ryun's gaze bounces around the room.

"Me too," Kenzie chimes in. She sounds nervous. "Everybody asks about you at school. You wouldn't believe some of the rumors."

I follow Ryun's gaze to Missouri's side of the room. Missouri is pretending to be asleep, but I know better.

The rational part of me kicks in, the part that can't stand awkward situations, that feels responsible for every conversation. I don't know how I do it, but I open my mouth and let words—normal regular words—come out. I ask them about classes, about other kids, about plans for Christmas vacation.

Ryun keeps peeking back at Kenzie, like he wants her to tell him what to say.

I hate this. I don't know what to say to my own

friends. What's the matter with me? I've never felt awkward around Ryun or Kenzie. I can't stand it. I want them to go. But the thought of not having them here makes me want to burst into tears.

I fight the impulse to bawl like a baby. For Ryun. For me. I remember the one and only time I cried with Ryun. He did not like it.

"I'm so sorry, you guys," I say, choking on the words. Sputtering.

"What?" Ryun frowns at me, like he didn't understand.

"I'd do anything to get that night back," I say. "The police said I wasn't drinking."

"The police?" Ryun wheels around to Kenzie, then frowns down at me. "When did you talk to the police?"

"Today. I guess they've been coming here since . . . since the accident. But they said I wasn't drinking. And they claim I wasn't even driving too fast. They can tell by the skid marks on the highway. But I can't imagine *not* driving that car too fast. Or maybe I just wasn't paying attention. Is that it? Is that what happened? I wasn't paying attention?"

Kenzie comes closer and stands beside Ryun. "Don't you know?"

I shake my head. "I can't remember."

Ryun does it again—looks at Kenzie. "What are you saying?"

"I can't remember the accident."

"Are you serious?" Kenzie asks, her eyes wide, sparking. "You don't remember the accident?"

"I can't remember anything about that night.

Except picking you up in front of your house. I remember driving, heading over to pick up Ryun. We talked about Taylor. Then a Beatles song came on—"Let It Be"—and we sang with it, loud, as loud as we could. And that's it. I can't remember anything after that."

"Nothing? Not the game or . . . or anything?" Ryun asks. He's so intense. I've never seen him this wound.

"I don't remember anything, except picking Kenzie up. Not even picking you up. Not the game. Nothing after the game. We didn't go some place and have a beer or anything, did we? I mean, the police said I hadn't been drinking. Were they right? I wasn't drinking?"

"You weren't drinking," Ryun assures me.

"This is unreal." Kenzie keeps shaking her head, like she can hardly believe it.

All of a sudden I remember what else the police said. "There was a fire, right? The car burned?"

"You remember *that?*" Kenzie asks.

"No. The police told me. They said you and Ryun pulled me out of the car. If you hadn't—" I look at both of them, so overwhelmed with emotion I can hardly get the words out. "You saved my life. I can never thank you—"

"Time's up!" Nurse Miller breezes into the room. She's carrying a metal tray with a syringe on it. "Sorry, kids. Visiting hours were over half an hour ago. You can come back tomorrow though."

Ryun and Kenzie spring into action and move to the door.

"Well, great seeing you, awake and all," Kenzie says.

"Yeah," Ryun agrees. "Take care. Night."

I hold off until Nurse Miller is finished with me, and I hear Missouri's even breaths, her tiny wheezing snore. Then I curl up in my bed and picture Ryun and Kenzie in my mind. And I cry as if I'm never going to see either of them again.

I don't know how much time has passed since Kenzie and Ryun left my hospital room—a minute, an hour, a day. But I hear voices in the hall again. I want it to be Ryun, coming back to tell me he loves me, that he doesn't care what my face looks like.

But it's a girl, a woman. She bustles into the room. "You must be Sierra." She drops a duffel bag beside the bed and flings back my blanket. She's wearing generic white tennis shoes.

"Yeah?"

"I'm Bev, your physical therapist. Party's over."

She's probably a size 3, in khakis and a polo shirt, minus the little Polo pony on the pocket. She pushes me onto my side like I'm a sack of rotten potatoes.

I cry out. The pain is enough to make me see white spots when I close my eyes. "That really hurts," I say as politely as I can. Maybe other patients are too wimpy to tell her this.

"We have to stretch the tissue around that hip and start rebuilding the muscles. Right here." She touches the point of my right hip.

Switchblades eject all along my right leg. I make a wailing sound I've never made before.

"If you let your muscles atrophy," she warns, "you'll have a limp the rest of your life. Got it? It's my job to make sure that doesn't happen." She lifts my right leg.

"Ow! Stop!" I scream. I'm not proud of how I'm acting. But this hurts more than anything has ever hurt before.

"I know," Bev confesses. So she's not ignorant, just brutal. "It's going to be uncomfortable for a while."

Uncomfortable? Bev, Queen of Understatement.

She raises my right leg again, as if it's a barbell. Then she pushes the whole leg forward.

I grip the sheet in both fists and bite my lip so I won't yell obscenities and curses down upon her head.

She keeps it up. Bev has missed her calling. She should have been an interrogator for the Nazis. I think about telling her this, but my teeth are clenched.

I don't help her as she moves my leg in ways a leg should never move. Up and down, side to side. Over and over. I hate her.

When she finally stops, I'm a wet dishrag. I can't even roll to my back from my side.

"Not bad for the first date," she says, picking up her duffel bag. She's halfway to the door—I haven't moved—when she calls back, "Whenever you feel like it, stretch your toes toward the foot of your bed and count to 10. Then release and relax slowly."

"I'll get right on that," I mutter. It's sarcasm, and I almost never indulged in sarcasm in my "other" life. Maybe something did happen to my brain.

■ ■ ■

I wait for two hours the next morning, thinking maybe Ryun will stop over before school. Or surely after school. Kenzie could have come during lunch hour, if she borrowed her mom's van, because seniors get free lunch. But nobody shows, except Jacqueline. She stops by after school and fills me in on all the eighth-grade gossip. I try to listen, but it's so boring that I doze off.

When I wake up, Jacqueline has pulled the only chair in the room over to Missouri's bed. I hear her telling Missouri the same gossip about Tom Somebody getting caught smoking in the john and Jo Beth cheating on her algebra exam. She talks so fast my teeth vibrate.

"She didn't!" Missouri exclaims, as if in her 101 years she's never heard of anyone cheating. She reacts to every piece of gossip the same way.

"Did you see Ryun today?" I call over.

"Nope."

"Did you see Kenzie?" Jacqueline is in middle school, but it's next door to the high school. They use our pool.

"I saw her across the parking lot once." Jacqueline turns around now. "Didn't they come by today? Either of them?"

"They probably have a lot of homework," I say quickly. "Ryun's still making up for what he missed when he was in the hospital."

She looks angry. I don't want Jacqueline to be mad at Ryun. "Well, if you see them, you should thank them. They saved my life."

She stares at me a second too long, then says, "Sure, Sierra."

My friends would be here if they could. I know that. They would do anything for me. They *did*. They pulled me out of the car. They saved my life.

I think of Ryun again, the way he had to drag his leg. What if I've ruined his soccer career? Ryun is High High's star striker, but he's too good for our high school team. He spends more time with his city league, an adult league, where he's still the star player. Colleges have been recruiting Ryun since our sophomore year.

Thinking of Ryun's injury makes me physically ill. I close my eyes and let sleep silence my mind.

■ ■ ■

I wake to the *click, click* of high heels. Stilettos, my mother's. My side of the room is dark, but Missouri is sitting up in her bed, eating from a tray. Somehow the sight of her eases me more than anything else.

Mom makes her entrance and turns on my light.

"Hello, Mrs. Reynolds," Missouri calls.

"Hello," Mom says back. I'm thinking she doesn't remember Missouri's name, and that embarrasses me.

I want to make up for Mom not registering Missouri's name. "Morning, Missouri," I call.

"You haven't been sleeping *that* long, sugar," Missouri answers. She dabs her wrinkled chin with her napkin. "It's just suppertime."

"You look better, Sierra," Mom says. She drags the chair closer to the bed.

I don't know how she would know if I look better. Her gaze doesn't move above my waist. She's staring at my knee under the covers. Maybe my knee looks better. "Where's Daddy?"

"He's gone to Boston for a conference." She says it like it's an apology. "I think he told you."

If he did, I don't remember. "How long will he be gone?" It's stupid to feel so disappointed. Dad's gone lots of weekends. Is it a weekend?

"Two nights." Mom changes the subject. "One of your teachers called today. Ms. Wilcox."

She's an art teacher. I don't have her this year, but she's the advisor for the yearbook. I wonder how they're getting everything done without me. I'm the main photographer. One more person I'm letting down.

"What did she say?" I ask, feeling guilt like an anvil on my chest. My recklessness is messing up our whole school's book of memories.

"Nothing really. Just that they're all thinking of you."

"Anybody else call?" I'm thinking Ryun, of course. And maybe Kenzie. But I know they're really busy.

"Let's see . . ." Mom's pinkie touches her tongue, then smoothes each of her eyebrows. "Someone from the newspaper called yesterday. I let your father talk to her. You're quite a celebrity, you know. And not just in Highview. Your friends are famous too."

"Ryun and Kenzie?"

"People are calling them heroes. I phoned Mrs. Parker to thank her personally for what her daughter did. That woman sounds like quite a character. Have you met her?"

I shake my head. Kenzie has never invited me to her house. I'm sure her mom must have been at some of our school things, but Kenzie's never introduced her to me.

"She brushed off my thanks," Mom continues. "She was polite enough. But she spent most of the time talking about winter squash. I thought she sounded a bit . . . odd."

I laugh. "Kenzie calls her 'earth mother.'"

"I called Ryun's mother too. I don't think she understood a word I said, though. You'd think she'd learn English, wouldn't you? I can't imagine."

"Jacqueline was here," I say, when we're quiet too long. I'm trying to do my part in this dialogue. Mom and I aren't alone together very often. I can't remember the last time we talked one-on-one like this. We're not very good at it.

"Don't get me started on that girl!" Mother the Martyr pleads. "*Her* teacher called too. Seems our Jacqueline has been leading a protest against the use of Number Two lead pencils on standardized tests. She claims they contribute to the rising problem of lead poisoning."

I laugh out loud.

Mom doesn't. "Honestly, I don't know what to do with that girl." I feel the martyr growing in her. "I've tried everything, Sierra. She won't go shopping with me. She won't wear anything except those overalls. It's like she doesn't take me seriously."

I know if I don't stop her, she'll keep going on and on about my sister. I want to get the conversation back to my friends. "Mom, tell me what the newspapers say about Kenzie and Ryun. What exactly do they know about the accident?"

Mom takes in a deep breath. I can tell she'd rather complain about Jacqueline. But she gives in. "From what we can tell, the car rolled over and over. The Parker girl got loose right away. But Ryun was hurt. I guess he somehow managed to crawl out the window on his own. Then they both went back for you. You were unconscious. They probably thought you were . . . that you hadn't . . ."

"Go on. Please." I'm hearing the report and picturing it, as if it's a movie. I want to remember, but there's nothing in my brain to go with this.

"Well, the reports change with every article. You know how the newspapers are. Anyway, the kids worked together. You were trapped. The dashboard had folded almost into the seat of the car. The windshield was shattered. The car was upside down. Somehow they managed to pull you loose and drag you away from the car, seconds before it exploded in flames." Mom's choked up. I think it's real.

"God be praised," Missouri mutters.

Mom glances over at the woman, then back to me. "Can't you remember, honey?"

I try to remember. All that comes are the pictures I've imagined as she was telling me how they pulled me out of the car.

"Well, don't worry about it," Mom says. "It's probably a good thing you can't remember. It would give you nightmares."

"I *want* to remember it," I say.

Mom stands up and brushes the wrinkles out of her gray wool skirt. "Dr. Snyder said you'd get your memory back soon enough. Don't force it. Just be glad you're safe."

After she leaves, I think about how ironic it is that I can't remember the night of the accident. I'm the one everyone comes to when they want to know anything about our past—the name of the sub in third grade, the kid in kindergarten who cried every day, the girl who went to Highview Elementary only the first half of our fourth-grade year, then moved out West. I remember everything. I never forget. I could describe that kindergarten kid down to the blue Keds on his feet.

And now I can't remember wrecking Dad's Chevy? Or being pulled from an exploding car? It doesn't make sense.

Then I remember something. It's just a flash. I'm at a game, the football game. It's night, and the team's already on the field. I'm standing behind Ryun, who's cheering. I think . . . I'm heading for the restroom. Kenzie's not there. Or I think, yes, she's already in the john.

And that's it. It's gone, faded like a bad smoke ring. I can't get it back. But it was real. I'm sure it was real.

"I remembered something," I mutter, not sure how I feel about it.

"What's that?" Missouri hollers over.

"I remembered something," I repeat. I turn on my side so I can see her better. "Missouri, I remembered something that happened before the accident."

"Well, that's fine then, isn't it?" She pushes her tray aside. "What did you remember?"

Then I realize what a stupid fragment of memory it was. "It wasn't anything important. I was at the game, the one we went to before the accident." I give a half-laugh. "I was on my way to the bathroom, I think. And that was it. Pretty dumb, huh? Why would I remember that?"

"I think it's wonderful," Missouri says.

"Don't tell anybody, okay?" I'm not quite sure why I ask her this. It's kind of embarrassing that my first memory would be a trip to the john. But I don't think that's why I don't want her to tell anybody. Not yet. I think I'm afraid of being show-and-tell again. Or maybe I don't want more pressure than I'm already putting on myself to remember.

"Okay," Missouri finally answers. She doesn't ask me why. And I believe her when she says she won't tell anyone.

I lean back down and close my eyes. An image of Ryun pops into my head. He is so handsome and sure of himself. I know at least a dozen girls who are probably waiting to swoop in on him while I'm here.

I don't know how long Ryun will wait for me. I know I would wait for him forever. He could lose both arms and both legs, and I'd never leave him. But guys are different. And I don't want him to stay with me out of pity.

I have to get better. I have to get out of this hospital and back to my life. Every day I spend in this bed is one day of my senior year I will never get back.

And Ryun is waiting.

Slowly I stretch the toes on my right foot. The pain shoots all the way up to my hip. I point my toes as if I'm trying to touch the foot of the bed. It's all I can do not to cry out. But I hold my foot this way for the count of 10. Then I relax and let my toes come back.

And I do it again. And again. And again.

■ ■ ■

For the next two days I stretch my toes, raise my leg, and perform various kinds of self-torture after Bev the Nazi Physical Therapist shows me how. She's so pleased with my unexpected progress that she rewards me by letting me sit on the edge of my bed, an activity that gives *excruciating* a whole new depth of meaning.

Ryun and Kenzie stop by right after one of Bev's sessions. I'm so wracked with pain that I know I'm lousy company. But it's wonderful to see them, and I have to fight off tears when they leave.

Nurse Miller gets me into a chair the next day. I beg her to let me stay in it because I'm so bored with the hospital bed that a chair feels like a vacation. She drags the chair closer to Missouri's bed and turns on the TV. It's a game show.

As soon as the nurse is gone, Missouri turns the TV sound all the way down. "Any more memories?" she whispers.

"I'm not sure." I know it sounds dumb, but it's the truth. Yesterday I pictured a couple of things that might have been memories of that night. But it's hard to tell if they're real or imagined.

Missouri's sitting up, studying my face. Waiting.

"Okay. Like yesterday morning, right when I woke up, I had this—" I'm searching for the right word—"this flash. Like when somebody snaps your picture with a flashbulb? And you get the scene lit up, but then you're blind from the light and can't see anything. It's like that."

"What did you see?" she asks.

"Ryun. My boyfriend. And me. So how could it be real if I saw myself, right? Only I think I was driving, and maybe I just saw my arms and hands on the steering wheel." A wave of fear passes through me. I wonder if I was afraid in the car. Maybe I saw the accident coming.

"Ryun was . . . yelling," I continue, tugging at the memory or whatever it was. "He looked so angry." I turn to Missouri. I don't want her to get the wrong idea. I try to laugh. "Which proves I imagined it, because Ryun never yells at me. We get along great."

"Hmm." That's all she says. After a minute she asks, "What do you remember most from your life?"

I laugh. It's a funny question. "Everything. Seriously, I remember so many details. I have scrapbooks of souvenirs from class parties, birthdays, overnights, dates, everything. You wouldn't believe how many scrapbooks I have, Missouri." I can picture all of them, so full of corsages and napkins and pictures that they don't close.

"So tell me, child."

"Tell you what?"

"Anything. Everything." She smiles at me. I wonder if the tiny teeth are still hers. Something about her eyes, the sparkle deep in them, makes me believe she was beautiful once.

"You don't know what you're asking," I joke. "I could tell you what shoes I wore to the eighth-grade Christmas dance."

"Shoes? How about your dress, child?"

I lean back in the chair and picture myself getting ready for that dance. I went with Brian Chillsworth. "Mom took my friend Elizabeth and me to the mall to shop for my dress. Elizabeth was going with two of our other girlfriends. But I had an actual date. So my dress was a bigger deal."

"Mmm-hmm."

"It only took trying on 50 dresses, but we did it. We found the perfect dress, a teal chiffon, with spaghetti straps."

"Ooo-eee, sounds just right," Missouri agrees.

"Only I was such a novice at the whole special-occasion buying thing that I didn't realize that the real search had just begun. I had to match my shoes to this teal dress. We shopped for four days, hitting nearly every shoe shop in the state. No luck. I refused to ruin that dress with anything less than an exact match."

"What did you do?" Missouri makes it sound like I'm telling a murder mystery, and she's dying to see how it all comes out. If she were 85 years younger, I'd insist that she be in my group at school.

"Are you sure you want to hear this stuff, Missouri? I know I'm a shoe freak. I don't usually bore other people with it, though."

"You keep going now!" she demands.

"Well, we ended up getting the shoes at a bridal shop and dyeing them teal!"

"Did you now?" she asks. "That was right smart. Is it always that hard?"

"Sometimes," I admit. "But now I usually start with the shoes." I could have listed off every dance after that, along with the exact make, model, and color of shoe—Steve Maddens for Spring Fling; Nine West, lime green strappy for my first prom; chunky heel Cole Haans for my first date with Michael; Bebes for Ryun and Arden B. and Rampage. "Last month, for Ryun, I got these great heels, a tiny strap over my big toe and a string-thin strap over the top of my foot. In red."

I grin at Missouri. "I'm sorry. I must be boring you to death." I should have used a different word. You just don't say *death* to a 101-year-old woman in a hospital bed.

"Bored?" Missouri laughs. I picture that laugh in every decade, all the way back to World War I. "I know a bit about shoes too," she says. She nods to the nightstand. There's nothing there but her water glass and the biggest Bible I've ever seen. It's faded black, with a bumpy cover and tattered edges. "Read Ephesians 6:15."

I pick up the Bible, afraid it will disintegrate in my fingers. The cover feels crumbled from use, and several pages are loose. "What verse?" I ask, stalling for time. I know she said Ephesians, but I don't know where it is. It sounds Old Testament-ish.

"Ephesians 6:15," Missouri answers. "There's a directory up front there to help. I know this old Bible is pretty worn."

I'm grateful. She must realize that I can't find the verse, but she's trying not to make me feel stupid. I use the table of contents and eventually make my way to Ephesians. Every page I turn past has lines underlined and notes scrawled in the margins.

"Got it," I say. I start with the verse before 15, so it's a whole sentence. "'Stand therefore, having your loins girt about with truth, and having on the breastplate of righteousness; and your feet shod with the preparation of the gospel of peace.'" I laugh. "A shoe verse!"

"I thought you'd like that one. One more: Romans 10:15."

I'm faster this time, going straight to the table of contents and getting the page number. "'How beautiful are the feet of them that preach the gospel of peace, and bring glad tidings of good things!'"

We both laugh.

"Beautiful feet, huh?" I say. "Very important to a shoe snob. I am so lucky. Size 5 1/2. If I had Jacqueline's 8 1/2s, I'd shoot myself in the foot."

Missouri laughs hard, then slips into a coughing fit that goes on so long I want to call Nurse Miller. I pour her a glass of water.

"I'm fine," she says, when the fit passes. "Thank you, Jesus." She says it as natural as if Jesus had just handed her the glass of water.

I have a feeling she wouldn't let me touch her Bible if she knew the thoughts going through my head. If I ever believe in God again, I'm going to be so angry with him that I'd probably be better off not believing.

"Missouri! Don't tell me I've been replaced."

I recognize the voice before I turn toward the door. I heard it when I was unconscious. The kid who made me think of Andrew and the hamster. He's tall, over six feet, African-American, baggy jeans, nice shirt, great Nikes, and a backward Yankees cap. He looks familiar, but I'm not sure.

I whisper to Missouri, "I heard this guy's voice when I was unconscious, didn't I?"

"Yeah?" the kid says, obviously overhearing. "You could hear me then? Cool."

"Drew and I have been friends a long time," Missouri explains. "He comes and reads to me from time to time."

"Sorry I haven't been around for a while," Drew says. He walks to the other side of Missouri's bed, leans down, and kisses her forehead. "Mom's got me filling out grant applications for colleges." He grins over at me, not looking away. "Good to see you sitting up, almost like a real person."

"Almost?"

Nurse Miller sweeps into the room. "Drew! Well, if it isn't himself!" She walks over and gives him a hug. She keeps one arm around him when she turns to me. "Sierra, have you met my boy?" She whips off his baseball cap. "Andrew Miller. Sierra Reynolds."

"I know," Andrew—or Drew—says. "We're in the same English class."

I'm pretty sure I don't register my surprise at hearing this. But I am surprised.

Nurse Miller grins. "But did you know that Sierra thinks of me as Lady Smooth?"

Drew frowns. "She must be sicker than you thought."

She whacks him with his own baseball cap.

I don't know why it's so hard for me to piece things together. "You're Nurse Miller's son?"

"Guilty," he replies.

She whacks him again with the hat.

I sit with my friends in English class, so I don't always pay attention to other students. But picturing the classroom, I can see a long-legged kid a couple of rows behind me. He asks questions and has intelligent comments when we read stories. It's Drew. I can see that now.

"Didn't you kids know each other before we moved away?" Nurse Miller asks, turning her attention to Missouri. She straightens the stethoscope hanging around her neck. Then she puts the little metal disc to Missouri's chest and listens.

"We knew each other," Drew answers, staring at me, like he's waiting for something. "Second grade. Swindler's class."

"No way!" I protest. I study his face, searching for little Andrew in this giant Drew's face. "You're not *that* Andrew, not the hamster Andrew!"

I can't believe it. How could I have recognized Andrew's voice, a voice that had changed almost as much as the physical person?

"Poor Grady," Drew says, shaking his head, a smile teasing at the corners of his mouth.

"Something tells me we're missing part of this story," Missouri says.

Nurse Miller jots down something on Missouri's chart. "Maybe *you're* missing something. I'm not. I remember that hamster. My boy here tried to set that creature loose. He got himself in a whole mess of trouble. Not the first time–or the last."

"He didn't do it!" I burst into laughter. "*I* did!"

"But he said *he* did it!" She taps her son on the head.

"Hey!" Drew protests. "I got cuffed for setting

that hamster free, and now I get cuffed for *not* doing it?"

Missouri giggles. "'And the truth shall make you free,'" she offers. "John 8:32."

"Thanks a lot, Missouri," Drew replies.

"I was so terrible to let you take the blame!" I'm as embarrassed as if it had just happened. "I can't believe I did that."

"The incident was hardly noticed in my checkered past," Drew says.

"Well, I'll leave you two to reminisce," Nurse Miller says. She takes hold of the privacy curtain and starts to pull it around Missouri's bed. "It's bath time. Out with you. Drew, you help Sierra back to her bed. She's been sitting up long enough."

"Later, Missouri," Drew calls. "I'll be by for you on Sunday."

"Lord willing," she answers.

I try to get up on my own. I'm still wearing a hospital gown, so I wrap the blanket on my lap around my shoulders. I know I've lost weight, but my body feels too heavy to be lifted out of this chair.

Drew takes my arm. I have to take a deep breath before trying that first step. I know how much it's going to hurt. Bev says I'm not supposed to hunch over, but it hurts to stand up straight. I feel as old as Missouri.

A wave of dizziness sweeps through me. "Wait a second, please." We stand there until the clouds fade out of my head. When my vision clears, I see the ugly, fuzzy blue slippers on my feet.

"Drew, if you tell another living soul about these slippers, I'll tell the whole world you turned Grady loose."

"All right. But I think those slippers are pretty cool." He raises his voice. "Mom, you suppose you could steal me a pair of these fuzzy slippers?"

"What am I going to do with that boy, Missouri?" she complains.

I make it to the bed and push the button to raise the head so I'm half-sitting. Drew pulls up the chair.

"When did you guys move back to Highview?" I ask, hoping he doesn't realize that I didn't even know he *had* moved back.

"This year. Mom finished her nursing degree and got a job here. Dad didn't mind the change. He's teaching at the middle school. I think he has your sister in class."

"Jacqueline? I hope, for his sake, he doesn't use Number Two leads."

Drew laughs. "I heard about that. I think Dad gets a kick out of Jack."

"Jack?" Nurse Miller calls out. "Sierra, your Jacqueline is Ty's Jack?" She breaks into a laugh I haven't heard from her before, long and hearty. "I should have known!"

I can only imagine the stories her husband must bring home about my sister.

"So what's happening in lit?" I ask, trying to find a sitting position that doesn't hurt my hip.

"We've been reading short stories. Faulkner, Updike, Hemingway."

"I'm going to be so far behind, I'll never catch

up." I'm glad that I got most of my required classes out of the way. I wanted to have a light senior year. My lit class is the hardest class in my schedule.

"I can bring you your lit book, if you want," Drew offers.

"Really?" I could start catching up. I have the time, if I can just stay awake more in the day. "Thanks." I give him my locker number and combination.

We talk about school until his mom gets off duty. They leave together. I think I'm asleep before they reach the hall.

■ ■ ■

The next day I sit in the chair twice, for an hour at a time. Drew brings my English book, but I don't feel like reading stories.

I watch three game shows with Missouri. She knows the answers to almost every question. I guess after 101 years, you know things.

My mind wanders. I can almost feel my brain trying to grab at lost memories that slip through the grooves of my cortex. I do remember the three of us–Ryun, Kenzie, and me–laughing on the way to the game. I remember sitting in the stands, with Ryun on one side and Kenzie on the other.

Missouri turns off the TV, and I look away fast. I can see my fuzzy reflection in the television, and I don't want to. There's no mirror in our hospital room, and I haven't asked for one. No one's offered. I figure there's a mirror in the bathroom, but I haven't visited there yet, thanks to the lovely tube, a catheter, which has been irritating me more every day. I haven't complained about it though. I'm in no hurry to go into that bathroom, to see the mirror.

I fall asleep in the chair, my head tilted back like an old man's.

"Hey, sleepyhead!" Nurse Miller is taking the blanket off my knees. She's wearing a light blue smock and white pants, with white tennis shoes. "Dr. Snyder's on his way. You're getting rid of that catheter."

"I am?" I'm glad, until I remember. The bathroom. The mirror.

She helps me to the bed. I close my eyes when the doctor comes.

"This will just take a minute," Dr. Snyder lies.

It feels like he yanks my insides out. I don't let myself scream, not outside of my head.

He listens to my heart and reads my chart. "You're doing fine, Sierra. We'll have you out of here in no time if you keep this up."

"Thank you," I say to the man who has just torn my organs from my body.

When he's gone, Nurse Miller pulls back the sheet and takes my hand, which hasn't been connected to an IV for 24 hours. "It's time, Sierra."

I pretend I don't know what she's talking about. "Time for lunch? Already? I'm pretty sleepy." I pull back my hand. "I think I'll take a little nap."

"It's time." She puts her arm under my back—she's so strong—and lifts me to sit on the side of the bed. "We're taking a journey to the bathroom. It's going to be okay. You already look better than when you came in here. Don't get me wrong. Your face is still swollen."

I've known this all along. I've touched my chipmunk cheeks. I can see blurred skin at the bottoms of my eyes.

I don't want to do this.

"That's it. Lean on me." Nurse Miller puts her arm around my waist and almost carries me along.

When we get to Missouri's bed, I catch her shutting her eyes, pretending to be asleep. "I'm onto you, Missouri," I call.

"I'm just praying for you, child," she calls back.

I wonder how bad my face could be, that she feels she has to pray for me. She must have seen a lot of ugly faces in 101 years.

We move past the foot of Missouri's bed, into the tiny bathroom. I know the mirror is above the sink, to my right, so I stare straight ahead of me. The walls are white. Even the shower curtain is white.

The all-night light is on already, but Nurse Miller must be one of those pull-the-Band-Aid-off-fast people—get it over with—because she turns on the light above the mirror.

I take a deep breath and turn.

The *thing* staring back at me, puzzled,
is a monster.

I am not crying. Or screaming. Because the face in the mirror cannot possibly be me, Sierra Reynolds.

"Now, remember everything Dr. Snyder told you, Sierra," says Lady Smooth. "You are not going to look like this. The swelling's already starting to go down, especially around your chin. See?"

The monster face isn't swollen, as in round cheeks or round face, like when I had my wisdom teeth removed. It's lumpy, uneven, as if the skin has boiled into a big bubble and stayed there. Deformed. There is no nose on this face because the cheeks have swallowed up what used to be a nose.

I lean forward and brush back my hair to see the Frankenstein scar on my forehead.

"That scar will all but disappear, Sierra," Nurse

Miller explains. "The stitches will dissolve. No one will even see it under your bangs."

Bangs. She's right. I have bangs. My hair looks like one big set of bangs. I touch my hair, but it's not mine. This hair is chopped off and greasy. It hangs in clumps.

These eyes aren't green. They're red. Even the whites of the eyes have turned bloodred.

My stomach surges to my throat, trying to escape this horrific body. I grab onto the sink and let it come. My body shakes as I vomit, retching and retching long after anything's left to come out.

■ ■ ■

I don't look at the mirror again. Not for the next few days. Ryun calls once, and I tell him not to come by. I can't believe that he saw me like this. No wonder he doesn't visit more often.

I don't believe Nurse Miller. I don't believe Dr. Snyder, who says the same things—how I'll be as good as new before I know it.

Dad stays away two extra days in the city. He stops by the hospital, though, on his way from the airport. I understand now why he stays away, why he can't stand to look at me.

I'm going through the motions of the hospital. Each hour is the same as the last. I'm no longer watching the pretty TV faces of the game-show contestants. I let the physical therapist do whatever she wants to with my legs, but I don't help her. I drink what they bring me and eat when they make me. There is no taste. Not in anything.

Jacqueline has come by every day after school. She ends up visiting Missouri because I can't carry on a conversation. All I want to do is sleep.

Mother comes every day too. She acts as if nothing's wrong. She chatters about Monday club and bridge and lunch with her committees. But she still doesn't look at me.

Me either. I go to the bathroom in the dark and never, ever look up when I wash my hands. I will live the rest of my life this way.

■ ■ ■

It's maybe five days later, maybe more, when I'm lying in bed, pretending to be asleep.

Missouri keeps calling my name. "Sierra? Sierra?" She won't stop.

"I hear you, Missouri," I snap. Then I feel bad. Maybe she's in trouble or needs something. I sit up. "Are you okay?"

"I'm okay," she answers. "It's *you* I'm troubled about."

I lie back down. "If you don't want anything, I'm going back to sleep."

"I *do* want something," she says. "I want you to go back in there, turn on the light, and look in the mirror."

I feel anger building inside me. I'm not used to anger. "That's not going to happen." If she thinks she can help with one of her God-made-you-beautiful-on-the-inside talks, she can forget it.

"The swelling's gone way down. You need to see for yourself. I told you yesterday and the day before."

She did. That part's true. But I don't believe her any more than I believe Nurse Miller. I roll over and wrap the covers around me.

"You don't believe me." When I don't respond, she starts all over again. "Sierra? Sierra? Sierra?"

I pull the pillow over my head. When I quit squeezing my ears, I hear her, still calling to me. "In case you forgot, I threw up the last time I looked at me."

"You won't this time." Her voice is calm, and that makes me angrier.

"*Please* leave me alone!"

"I will . . . but you'll have to make me a little bet first."

"A bet?" I roll over in bed so I can look at her. The light squeezing through her window hits her face. For an instant she looks young, like a little girl.

"Mmm-hmm. You take one more look in that mirror—"

I start to protest, but she keeps talking.

"—and if you aren't glad you did, I'll shut up about it." She stops talking, as if to prove her point.

"You promise?" I sit up now and dangle my feet off the bed. At least that doesn't hurt the way it used to.

She presses her lips together and pantomimes zipping them shut. I can't help grinning because it's exactly what Jacqueline and I used to do.

I know Missouri won't leave me alone unless I do this. I swallow. "Okay."

"Wait. I'm not done. A wager goes two ways.

If you're not glad you looked in the mirror, then I'll keep my mouth shut about it. But if you *are* glad, well, you owe me a Sunday."

"A sundae? Like hot fudge?"

She laughs so hard that she lapses into one of her coughing fits. "Oh, child, I couldn't have asked the Lord for a better roommate. You owe me one Lord's Day! A Sunday morning."

I remember that Jacqueline lost some bet with Missouri too—a Sunday morning, which I figured meant going to church with Missouri. I almost join her laughing, until I remember what I have to do for this wager.

It's a no-win situation.

"Sierra? Sierra?"

"I'm going." I slip out of bed and wait until I'm sure I'm steady. I haven't had to ring for a nurse to do this since the day before yesterday.

I tell myself that my face can't look worse than it did last time. But my heart pounds as I shuffle toward the bathroom.

"You want me to come along?" Missouri asks, getting out of bed.

"No," I answer.

She meets me at the foot of her bed anyway. I wonder if somehow this is all a trick, a moral lesson. She'll get me in there and read me *face* verses from her Bible.

I step into the dark bathroom and stare at the floor. I want to get it over with, but I'm a take-off-the-Band-Aid-slowly kind of girl. I raise my eyes from the floor, to the toilet, all without turning my head toward the mirror. The monster is waiting for me there.

"It's all right, child," Missouri whispers. She's right behind me. "You'll see."

Slowly I turn. This is what I think. It's an old Three Stooges' line. I love the Stooges.

Then I do turn slowly.

When I glimpse the image in the mirror, the first thing I think is this: *Sierra, there you are.*

I look like I've been in a fight. And lost. But it's me now. Sierra. I can make out my face's real shape, oval. I don't have much of a nose, but it's there. I can see it, still sunken into my too-fleshy cheeks. But it's *my* nose.

"I have a nose," I mutter.

"You have a right fine nose," Missouri agrees.

I blink back tears and stare. The whites of my eyes are still red, but there's green where the green should be. They're *my* eyes. I recognize them.

I lift my bangs to see the scar, then spread the wisps to cover that part of my forehead. My hair is awful. It looks like it's been run over by a lawn mower. I know that if I hadn't seen the monster before, *this* face would have scared me. But the person I'm looking at is me, Sierra Reynolds. And seeing her, seeing *me,* feels a little like coming out of the black cave for the second time.

I stare past myself to Missouri's reflection in the mirror. She's grinning, and her eyes are misty and soft.

"Thank you, Missouri."

"Thanks nothing," she says. "You lose. You owe me a Sunday morning."

16

The next morning Nurse Miller whisks in with breakfast and starts the day way too early.

"I can't stand my dirty hair one more day," I complain as soon as I finish my toast. I touch one of the clumps that hangs by my left ear. "Can't I wash it or something?"

"Now that's what I call a good sign," Nurse Miller replies. "Missouri, did you hear that? The girl finally cares about her hair."

"I heard," Missouri answers.

"So?" I press.

Nurse Miller jots something on my chart, then comes at me with the blood-pressure cuff. "As it happens, we have a beauty salon right here in the hospital. I'll have the girl come up and wash your hair for you."

An hour later the beauty salon comes to my hospital room. This is no ordinary salon. The stylist, a girl named Twila, is no ordinary stylist. She chews gum as if she wants everyone to watch the way the pink blob in her mouth mixes with her saliva. She carries with her a basin under one arm and a bag of supplies under the other. She also brings ingenious torture techniques that put Bev, the Nazi physical therapist, to shame.

It takes Twila over an hour to clean my short hair. When she's finished, I feel worse than I do after physical therapy. She's jostled everything in my head and started it throbbing. But my hair is clean.

I fall asleep almost immediately. Only it's not a deep sleep. Images flash through my mind. I keep going back to the football stadium. We're cheering in the crowd.

Then I'm at a gross stained sink, washing my hands. I recognize this place as the stadium john. I hear voices. Two girls. They're talking about *me*. But in my dream, I don't know if I'm dreaming or remembering or if it's happening right now.

"When are you going to tell her?" one of the girls asks. She's loud, almost shouting at the girl in the next stall. I can't see who she is. "I know you don't want to upset Sierra. But she's a big girl," she continues. "She can handle it."

And I'm thinking, *Tell me what? Handle what?*

In the next stall someone stirs. I can't see who it is. But I recognize the shoes—Steve Madden Gatsbys. They're Kenzie's. I should know. I convinced her to buy them.

I jerk awake so suddenly that the bed shakes. I almost expect to be in the john at the football stadium.

But I'm in the hospital.

I hear voices. Missouri's and my mother's.

"She looks much better," Mom is saying. "Oh, you're awake." Mom gets up from the chair beside Missouri's bed and walks over.

When she gets to the bed, she actually looks at me. Then she touches my hair. "Missouri told me you got your hair washed. That must feel so much better."

I try to smile. I'm still shaken from the dream, if that's what it was.

"Are you all right, honey? Is it the pain?"

I shake it off. "No. I'm fine. Just a bad dream." I scooch up in bed. My head feels light. Probably the lack of gunk. Or the aftereffects of wash torture.

Mom frowns and tilts her head, like she's at the art museum, with one of her fine arts committees. "Why didn't the stylist at least even up the sides?"

"No one wants to see a pair of scissors in that girl's hands," I observe. "I really do need to do something about my hair though. It's so horrible. Wish I could just fix it before Ryun comes back."

Mom grabs her purse and puts on her coat. The coat is new. Or at least I've never seen it before. It reminds me that it's winter. I forget in here. "Wait right here," she says.

"Really? And I was just about to go out clubbing."

I think I must doze off, because the next thing I know, Mom is making another entrance. This time, she's carrying a grocery bag.

"What's that?" I ask her, sitting up again.

"You'll see. Can we get you into the chair?"

I don't have anything else to do. I slide my legs off the bed, then sit there a minute before I move to the chair.

Mom reaches into the bag and comes out with a towel that she wraps around my neck. She reaches in again and pulls out three pairs of scissors and a pair of thinning shears, with tiny teeth. Then she brings out a handful of combs and a spray bottle of clear liquid.

"Mom, you're scaring me."

"Don't be silly." She sets hair spray on the bedside table and spreads out the scissors and combs.

"What is all that stuff?" I ask.

"Tools of the trade," she answers.

"Tools of *what* trade?" My mother has never had a trade.

"Don't get smart," Mom warns.

There are a hundred responses to this. Jacqueline has used them all. I glance at Missouri, who raises her eyebrows.

Mom sets the wastebasket behind me.

"Okay," I say. I figure I've gone along with about all I can here. I take the towel off my neck. "I think I see what you're trying to do, Mom. That's really nice of you. But I'll just wait for a real beauty shop. I could wear a scarf until then."

Mom takes the towel and returns it to my neck.

"I'm cutting your hair, Sierra." She rolls up the sleeves of her coral silk blouse and picks up a long-tailed comb. Hovering in front of me, she stares at my hair, measuring each side with the tail of the comb. She runs her fingers through her own hair. Then she moves behind the chair.

"Mom, get serious! You can't cut hair."

"*Who* can't cut hair?" She combs the back of my head. "I've cut hair." She reaches for the scissors.

"Come on. It doesn't count if I was under two years old and didn't know a bad haircut from a good one."

"Well, I didn't cut your hair before you were two years old or after. But before you were born, I cut a lot of people's hair."

I wince as I hear the scissors snip, snipping behind me. "Yeah? Whose hair? When?" I'm thinking skin-heads, but Mom has probably never seen one.

"I put myself through college by cutting hair."

"Good for you!" Missouri chimes in.

"You're kidding. I never heard that before."

"Well, your father didn't think it fit the image of a psychiatrist's wife to work in a beauty parlor." She sounds amused.

It is pretty amusing.

"Besides, I didn't actually get certified. I just had a knack for cutting hair—a good *eye,* people used to say. I could see what the hair should look like. Then I just cut it until it matched the picture in my head. Any-way, mostly I cut for college students. A few profs too. Kept me busy enough all four years at State."

"I had no idea." I'm speechless.

"There's a great deal you don't know about me, Sierra."

Now I'm afraid she's going to slip into martyr mode. I can't imagine there's much I don't know about her. But I'm not about to ask.

I wish I had a hand mirror so I could see what she's doing to the little hair I have left. Imagine me wishing for a mirror. Missouri would get a kick out of that. She's sitting on her bed now so she can watch the show.

"How's it looking, Missouri?" I ask.

"Those scissors are moving so fast, I can't rightly tell," she answers.

"Great," I mutter. I could pretend I'm sick and make Mom stop. On the other hand, how much worse could my hair look? I'm not about to give the hair Nazi another chance. I grip the arms of the chair and wait.

Thirty minutes later Mom packs up her tools, whisks the towel from around my neck, and asks, "Well, what do you think, Missouri?"

Missouri hobbles over and stands next to my mother. She comes up to Mom's chest. "Why, I do believe you missed your calling. It's perfect."

"Perfect, huh?" I narrow my eyes at the old woman. "Are you being straight with me?"

"I'm willing to wager another Sunday on it," she says.

Mom looks puzzled. "Might as well take a look." She pulls out a hand mirror from her bag and turns it over to me. The rat. She's been hiding the mirror on purpose.

I hold up the mirror and try to examine my hair, without letting my face get in the way. It's short, shorter than I've ever had my hair. But the bangs are wispy now instead of clumpy. They still hide the scar on my forehead. She's made everything pixie short, but layered, so it shows more gold highlights. At the sides, the hair curves naturally around my face, covering some of the swelling.

I can feel way too much neck, but the Band-Aid over my scar is still covered, barely. My fingers trace the layers of hair. I have to admit, it looks stylish, professional.

"Not bad," I say, handing back the mirror.

"High praise," Mom says, but she's grinning.

"It might keep me from frightening small children," I observe.

"And old women," Missouri adds. Then she laughs so hard that Mom calls for the nurse.

After Mom leaves, I'm about to fall asleep in the chair, watching *Jeopardy!* reruns with Missouri, when I hear laughter in the hallway. It's not the nurses at the nurses' station.

I know those laughs–Kenzie and Ryun. They get louder with the footsteps. Then they shush each other and enter the hospital room as if it were a church.

Or a morgue.

Kenzie and Ryun step into the hospital room at the same time.

Seeing Ryun's brace again makes me shudder.

"Hey, your hair looks good!" Kenzie exclaims.

I smile at both of them and wonder what Ryun thinks of my short hair. He loved it long. "Would you believe my mom cut it?"

"No way!" Kenzie replies.

They hang together near the door, as if they're ready to escape should the need arise.

"Come on in, you guys! I've missed you like crazy."

"Yeah. I'm sorry we didn't get over yesterday," Ryun says, coming closer, still limping. He's not looking at me. He pops a breath mint.

The last thing I want is for them to feel like they

have to see me out of duty. "I know how busy you are with practices and classes and everything."

The silence is awkward. The only noise is a TV commercial for cat food. We all stare at the screen, as if we don't want to miss this important cat news bulletin.

"I miss Paddywack," I say, the cat commercial making me think of my little dog. "Jacqueline promised she's taking good care of him." I turn to Missouri. I can't remember telling her about my dog. "Paddywack is our Chihuahua. He's the cutest little thing. Follows me everywhere."

"I like dogs," Missouri says.

I get up from the chair. "I'm okay," I say, when Kenzie takes a step, like she wants to help me. I want to show them that I can walk again, that I'm coming back. "Ryun, why don't you drag the chair over to my bed. Kenzie, you can sit on the bed with me."

I make it and grit my teeth so I won't wince as I pull myself to a sit-up position in bed. I quickly cover my feet and legs.

Kenzie sits on the edge of the bed and swings her long legs.

Ryun pulls the chair over and sits down. He shoots me a quick smile, then glances at Kenzie. Again.

"Any news on a scholarship yet?" I ask. I'm terrified that he'll tell me he can't get a scholarship now.

"Johnny Moser–," Ryun begins, "you remember him, that assistant coach at Duke. You met him at a couple of tournaments."

I nod. I do remember him.

“Anyway,” Ryun continues, “Moser says they want me at Duke. I’m just waiting for the call.”

“That’s great, Ryun!” I want to ask him if it will matter to Duke about his leg. But he seems so sure of himself, I feel relieved. Ryun will get his scholarship. He deserves it. “I’m so proud of you.”

Ryun shrugs and looks away.

I don’t really know if he’s angry with me about the accident. I want him to tell me it’s all going to be just like it was, that his leg will be perfect. *We’ll* be perfect. I wish just once he would come without Kenzie.

Then I feel bad. Kenzie doesn’t have a car, unless she borrows her mom’s old van. And I do want to see her too.

“I really appreciate you guys coming over. How are classes, Kenzie?”

“Okay,” she answers. “Wish I’d gotten econ over with before this year though.”

“Pretty good friends, don’t you think, Missouri? To come and see me in the hospital?”

“I should hope so,” she says slowly.

They smile at her. I’ve introduced them at least twice.

I feel like I’m clawing sand to come up with conversation. When Lady Smooth comes in to check on Missouri, I’m grateful for the interruption.

“Nurse Miller, you know my friends, right?”

“We’ve met. Glad you came by.” She hands Missouri a paper cup with a pill in it and waits until she swallows it.

I turn to Kenzie. “Did you know Mrs. Miller’s son is Drew Miller? He’s in our English class.”

"Yeah?" Kenzie says. "I know Drew."

"Sure." Ryun twists in the chair to face Nurse Miller. "I thought Drew should go out for ball."

"He did. He played varsity until we moved back here," Mrs. Miller explains.

"So why didn't he go out here?" Ryun asks.

"He's decided he wants to be a doctor," she says, placing two fingers on Missouri's wrist to take her pulse.

"A doctor?" Ryun turns and raises his eyebrows at Kenzie. She shrugs.

"Yeah. He doesn't talk about it much. But he studies all the time. Now if you'll excuse me." She pulls the curtain around Missouri's bed. I can see their shadows.

Kenzie starts in on her mom's latest attempt to grow winter squash indoors in the winter. I'm glad to have the silence filled. She can talk about anything for all I care.

Ryun stares at Kenzie as she talks. His lips curve at the corners. I watch him, watching her.

Kenzie glances at Ryun at the end of every sentence. He's her punctuation. I don't want to give a word to what I'm feeling.

What am I doing? I'm being stupid. This is my boyfriend. And my best friend. They saved my life. They may have gotten closer since the accident. That's good. I want them to be good friends.

"Are you?" Kenzie's asking me a question, but I haven't been listening.

"I'm sorry," I say. "What?"

"Are you better? Do you know when you're getting out of here?" she asks.

"Nobody's said yet. I can't seem to shake my fever. They won't let me out of here until my temperature is normal. I know that much."

Ryun looks past me. "I hope you get home for Christmas. It would be lousy to be stuck here through the holidays."

Kenzie leans over and punches him on the arm. "Ryun! That's two weeks away. She's not going to be here that long."

He pretends the punch really hurt. They laugh. "Good," he says, sobering up.

I fake a laugh too. "They better not try to keep me here over Christmas. And my family better not cheat and get a fake tree this year."

"They wouldn't dare," Kenzie says, turning to Ryun. "They don't want to upset Sierra."

Her words make me stop breathing for a second. It's like they're a rerun. I've heard those words before or part of them. In my head. *"Don't want to upset Sierra."*

"You okay?" Kenzie asks.

I make myself smile. "I'm just tired."

Ryun springs up. "We'll let you sleep." Then he leans over and kisses the top of my head. "I'm sorry," he whispers.

I pull back so I can see his face. "Stop saying that. You have nothing to be sorry about. You and Kenzie saved my life. *I'm* the one who's sorry."

"Let's not go over this again," Kenzie pleads. "We're all sorry. Okay? Let's just get on with it."

She jerks her head toward the door, a not-so-secret gesture for Ryun to leave. They move toward the hall.

"Thanks again for coming," I say.

Kenzie turns around. "Seriously, cool hair, Sierra."

"Thanks, Kenzie." And I mean it. She's a good friend to say so.

Someone brings in our food, Missouri's and mine, on trays. It looks like mashed potatoes every night. But they're trying to fatten me up. So I get chocolate pudding and, tonight, what looks like a bunless hamburger.

When we're finished, instead of turning on the after-dinner game show, Missouri walks over to my bed and sits in the chair. "Is it coming back, child?"

I know she means my memory. "I'm not sure." I'm glad for the chance to talk about it. Inside my head the pieces of memory get diffused with bits of my imagination. They're hard to sort out. I tell her about the thing I remembered from the stadium john, the fragment of a conversation that I might, or might not, have actually overheard.

I'm struggling to find the words to describe my amnesia. "It's like when my sister and I used to paint by numbers. You know, those sets you buy? You can paint all of the number fours and the number eights, and still the picture doesn't look like anything. That's what this feels like. I'm painting in numbers, but nothing holds them together. I don't get a picture."

She nods, and I feel like she understands. She knows what I'm feeling, although I don't know how she could.

"I want more pieces," I say, as if I'm begging *her* to give me some. "I need more pieces."

Missouri watches me. Her hands are folded in her lap, onto her nightgown. Her eyes stare into mine as if she's reading one of her Bible verses. "Jesus," she says, her eyes open. "Help Sierra remember what she needs to remember. Then help her forget what she needs to forget." I guess it's a prayer, kind of.

She gets up so slowly that I'm afraid she'll crash back down into the chair.

I think about asking her to stay. I know she would. But I don't want her to talk to Jesus anymore or about Jesus or to find more verses from her used Bible. So I watch her shuffle back to her bed.

■ ■ ■

The next day Nazi Bev is crueler than ever. We take it out into the hall. I use a walker, and I have to rest in the lounge at the end of our floor before walking back to the room.

I've just about given up on the possibility of Ryun dropping by on his way home from school when in he walks.

I'm so happy to see him, so secretly thrilled that he's come alone.

Then Kenzie walks in behind him. The flash of anger I feel when I see her surprises me. Kenzie is my best friend.

"Hi, guys," I say, hoping I'm smiling warmly at both of them. Ryun's cheeks are red from the cold outside or the warmth of the hospital.

"We wanted to see how you're doing," Ryun says, not looking at me.

"Take off your coats," I urge.

"We can't stay," Kenzie says.

Ryun nods at her, then explains, "Yeah. I need to get to work."

Kenzie smiles. "You look good."

Ryun comes to my bed and kisses the top of my head. "Sorry we can't stay and talk and stuff." His gaze darts around the room.

Kenzie looks nervous.

They're making *me* nervous. Part of me wants them to leave. But that doesn't make sense. I hate it when they're not here. I'm so mixed-up. I feel like screaming.

Kenzie tugs Ryun's arm, as if to pull him toward the door.

The gesture jars me. Ice water shoots through my spine.

And just that fast, I know that I'm right. My best friend and my boyfriend. I'm on the wrong end of a country-western song.

"We should go," she says. And the *we* means something, something huge, something unfair.

Ryun looks at her the way he used to look at me—expectant, familiar. What they have isn't friendship. It's more than friendship. I can see that.

They leave, and I imagine them walking out of the hospital, their arms around each other. I picture them getting into Ryun's car. He opens the door. She slides in. He helps her fasten her seat belt. The engine starts. They're off on a romantic sunset drive together.

Or maybe not. Maybe they're going out for burgers at Riley's. I speed up the image, making them go faster and faster, pressing Ryun's foot to the floor. Kenzie reaches for his arm again, just like she did in my hospital room. Only now I imagine Ryun, jerking his hand away, shocked at Kenzie's move. The car drifts off the road. He pulls it back, but it's too sharp. The car flips over.

And *bang!* Missouri and I have two new roommates.

That part about the car flipping? I'm wondering if that's my subconscious trying to work its way up. Because the car I'm picturing isn't Ryun's car. It's the Chevy. Dad's '57 Chevy. And the sign in the background isn't Riley's. It's Route 58, where Sergeant McCarthy said the car went off the road. The scene of the accident.

I don't sleep at all that night, or at least it feels as if I don't. My brain is swirling. Pieces of memory are coming at me so fast, I have to dodge. I let them swirl, until they settle into the right slots on the puzzle board. The picture is coming together.

All the while Kenzie's refrain plays in my head—*"Don't want to upset Sierra."*

And I'm back in that bathroom at the football field. I'm leaning on the sink because I'm afraid I'll collapse if I don't. The voices from the stalls are loud, piercing. Kenzie and a friend. I think the friend is Holly, but I'm not sure.

"I know you don't want to upset Sierra," the friend says. "But she's a big girl. She can handle it."

"Tell Ryun that. He's so afraid of hurting poor Sierra," Kenzie complains.

"So you're just going to keep seeing each other behind Sierra's back?"

"I don't know what we're going to do," Kenzie answers.

At the sink I stare at my hands as if I've never seen hands before and can't figure out where they came from.

"It's just that," Kenzie continues, "Ryun and I connect on a deep level, deeper than he and Sierra ever could."

This can't be happening. Not to me. Not with my

friend and my boyfriend. I think I'm going to be sick, physically ill. I grip the sides of the sink.

"What do you mean?" the friend asks.

"Ryun is so real, so deep. He's just not rah-rah like Sierra. Don't get me wrong. I really like Sierra. She's a lot of fun. Ryun really likes her too. That's what makes this so hard. Neither of us wants to hurt Sierra's feelings, you know?"

"You have to tell her. Get it out in the open."

A toilet flushes.

Somehow my legs move without orders from my brain. I'm practically running for the door. My hands open it. I'm outside. Cold air slaps my face. I'm sweating.

People are on their feet, cheering.

I replay this scene so many times during the night that I hear it and see it exactly the same way. Every word is in place, every picture.

At first, that's as far as the memory goes. I get outside the john and feel the cold wind. Did I wait there outside the bathroom? Did I ambush Kenzie? Did I hit her? scratch her eyes? pull her hair?

I could do it now.

Then I remember. I didn't wait by the john. My legs walked back to our bleacher seats and sat me down next to Ryun. He was cheering, like everybody on our side of the stadium. Kenzie came back and sat on the other side of me. Her elbow touched my arm. I smelled smoke—someone behind us had been smoking. And perfume. Not Old Spice.

Ryun left and came back with three Cokes. One for me. Two for them. I thanked him.

I *thanked* him.

Kenzie cheered in the right spots. She leaned over and made comments about other kids passing in front of us. I was in awe of how she could be like that, so completely at home with two faces.

I could never, ever have pulled that off. I couldn't have. Not to anybody. Never to a friend.

But the memory stops there. I get to the same point, after the Cokes, in the middle of the game, and the movie stops. A blockade is set at that spot in my brain. I can't get over it. Can't go under it. Can't get around it.

I have to get through.

I fast-forward to my hospital room. Kenzie and Ryun coming to visit. Smiling at each other.

Maybe I never told them what I overheard. Maybe they still believe they're doing what they're doing secretly, behind my back. Do they laugh about it? Are they glad I'm here, my back so far away that they can do whatever they want behind it? She can touch his arm. He can glance at her. They must think I'm the dumbest person on earth.

Maybe I am.

I want to remember. But the memories are circling me, teasing, staying just out of reach.

Maybe that's the wrong image. It's more like pieces of memory shrapnel are embedded in me, and some are working their way up. I try to tear at them, to pull them out. Dig, dig, dig. But all I'm doing is making holes.

■ ■ ■

The next day I don't get out of bed, except to go to the bathroom. With the lights out. Missouri sits beside my bed and waits. She doesn't say anything. I realize that I haven't spoken to her for hours. Maybe longer. I'm losing track. I've heard so many voices inside my head that I didn't stop to think that one of them might be hers.

"You're remembering." That's all she says.

I'm lying on my back, staring at the smooth white ceiling.

"Are the memories so bad?" she asks quietly.

I think I nod.

"Accidents are violent things," Missouri says.

I roll over so I can face her. "I don't remember the accident. I'm trying to, but I can't."

"Then what?"

"I remember what happened before." I lie on my back now. The ceiling hasn't changed. I can see the crack lines along the wall. If I squint at the ceiling long enough, it becomes a movie screen. I see myself. And Kenzie and Ryun.

Missouri doesn't move. She doesn't ask me questions.

I think it's that, more than anything else, that makes me want to talk. I roll over on my side again. Her eyes are still aimed at me. The weathered face is more familiar to me than my own.

"I need to talk, Missouri."

"I need to listen." She smiles.

"You have to promise me you won't tell anyone. Not anyone." Again, I'm not sure why this is so important. Except for Missouri, nobody knows that I've gotten any of my memory back. I don't want anyone else to know. If everything is out in the open, it can't be put back, back the way it was, the way it should be.

There's a power in knowing that they don't know what I know. And this feels like the only power I have left.

Missouri does her zipped-lips gesture for me.

"I need to start at the beginning of that night." I say it as if apologizing.

"I have no place else to go." She settles into the chair.

I start with getting ready for the game. I start with thick-soled, purple Skechers, a matching sweater, and new jeans. Jacqueline is hassling me about something. I think I'm trying to tell her she needs to go to school football games, even if they do bore her.

"Dad's already gone," I continue. "He has work at the office. I'm a little mad at him because I wanted him to see me in the new shoes. But he's given me the keys to his classic Chevy, so it's impossible to stay mad for long."

I walk Missouri through the whole evening. I take her with me into the john to wash my hands. I let her overhear what I overheard. We run out of the john together and feel the cold wind on our cheeks. We sit down beside Ryun and feel Kenzie returning. And watch the players move on the field.

"You didn't say a word to them?" It's the first time Missouri has spoken since I started my story.

I shake my head.

"Not even after the game?"

"I can't remember after the game," I explain.

"Did your team win?" she asks.

I think it's a dumb question. What could it possibly matter? "Yes," I answer.

She grins. "Then you do remember something after the game."

She's right. "I don't know how I knew that. I can't remember the game ending or the Hornets winning." But I do know.

I think of the memory flash of Route 58, Kenzie, and Ryun. Me at the wheel. I tell Missouri about it. "I was driving fast. I remember that. But I know I hadn't been drinking. We had Cokes at the game, and that was it. I guess we might have gone somewhere after the game, but I doubt it, not after what I heard."

"Maybe you've remembered enough for one day," Missouri suggests. She sighs. "Don't you want to tell your mama about this?"

"No! And you promised you wouldn't say anything."

"I'll keep my word," she assures me. "What about Nurse Miller? You could tell her. She wouldn't–"

"No." I'm more sure than ever that I don't want anybody else to know. "She could let something slip to her son, Andrew." I could see it getting back to Ryun.

"A stranger then. I'll bet they've got people at the hospital to help you get the rest of your memory back."

"A shrink? No, thank you. I live with a shrink." I could never talk to Dad about this. "I just want to know more before somebody gropes around in my head. I haven't remembered anything about the accident anyway. That's what everybody's waiting for. Maybe when I remember that, the accident. Then I'll tell people. Just not now."

We're quiet for a while. Then Missouri asks, "What if your friends come visit you again?"

I haven't thought about that. I don't know what I'll do the next time I see them. "Missouri, how can I ever face them again? How can I be in the same room with those . . . those traitors? What am I supposed to do now?"

Missouri doesn't answer for a long time. Then she says, "There's nothing much you can do, except forgive and forget."

I laugh. "Forgive and forget?"

"Mmm-hmm."

"Forgive and forget? You couldn't have picked two things further from my mind. Not even if you tried. I never forget anything. Okay—with the exception of this accident. And forgive? Have you been listening to what I've been telling you? Didn't you hear what Kenzie and Ryun have been doing to me? My boyfriend and my best friend?"

The anger rises in me all over again. It's as fresh as the first minute when I put things together. "I will never forgive them for what they did to me. I couldn't forget, even if I wanted to."

Days pass. Ryun has surgery for a partial ACL tear. But I only know this because Nurse Miller gives me reports. Kenzie only comes to my room once, and I pretend I'm asleep. She doesn't wait long before leaving.

Ryun calls, but he uses his surgery or his crutches as an excuse to stay away. *My* Ryun, my old boyfriend, would have come to see me if he had to crawl.

I'm in a constant state of nausea. Mental nausea.

During the day, I do what's expected. Jacqueline stops by every day after school. Mom visits more than Dad. My parents don't seem to notice that they're conversing with a shell of a human being.

Drew drops off my lit book and offers to go over his class notes with me, but I'm not up to it.

Nothing else about the night of the accident is coming back to me, not when I'm awake or when I'm asleep—I'm not sleeping well. So my mind keeps replaying the memories I do have—the bathroom scene, the football game, the flashes of us in the car. These film clips don't get old or worn. They're as sharp as the first time I remembered them. The hurt, the pain, is as sharp too, as fresh as if the crimes had just been committed.

■ ■ ■

The next afternoon I'm sitting up in bed, trying to read Hemingway's "Hills Like White Elephants." I've been over the line a dozen times because the words won't travel from the page to my brain. Nurse Miller has cracked the window open, just enough to let fresh air squeeze in. And I hear tires squeal outside. A car takes off too fast, burning rubber.

I feel that squeal inside my chest. My book crashes to the floor.

"Are you all right?" Missouri asks.

I don't answer because I'm still hearing the squeal in my head. And I'm seeing the green Chevy.

I'm driving. I know I'm going too fast. But I'm so angry. My foot presses the accelerator. I'm screaming: "How could you do it? How could you betray me? Seeing each other behind my back!"

Ryun is sitting next to me. Kenzie is on the other side of him, hiding behind his shoulder. I'd like to choke her.

"I can't believe this! You were supposed to be

my best friend!" I cry. "And you try to steal my boyfriend?"

"It wasn't like that," Kenzie says.

"Wasn't it? Then how was it?" I'm driving faster and faster. I hear the squeal of tires as I take the turn onto Route 58.

"Sierra, slow down!" Ryun shouts.

"Don't tell me what to do!" I yell. "I loved you! How could you do this to me? I would never have done anything to either of you."

"Slow down," he says. "Stop the car. We'll talk about it."

But I don't slow down. I press the accelerator.

Then it's over. The car fades. The picture breaks up in my head.

Missouri is standing beside my bed, studying me. "What did you remember?" she asks.

So I tell her. "It had to be right before the accident," I say, after I've given her every detail, just as it came to me.

I'm so angry. Angry at myself for driving fast like that. It was stupid. I know that. But I'm angry at them even more. If they hadn't been so cruel, so deceptive, none of us would have been where we were. It's their fault too.

And yet here I am, in this hospital bed, scarred for life. And they're out there somewhere together, probably laughing at all they've gotten away with.

And I know I can't go on like this much longer.

The day drags on. I can't help myself. I keep trying to imagine when they were sneaking around to be with each other. Cheating. Was it the time I called Kenzie to run to the mall with me because Chinese Laundry Shoes was running a big sale? She stammered around and said she had to help her mom. Was she really meeting Ryun?

Or maybe the night Ryun broke our date to the movies. He'd coughed over the phone and said he had such a sore throat. I'd been so sympathetic. Was he really sneaking out to be with Kenzie? Where did they go? What did they do?

I think it can't get any worse. Nothing I can remember could possibly be worse than discovering betrayal.

Then that night something happens. I'm in the chair next to Missouri's bed. She's watching a game show, and I'm staring at the screen, not taking it in really. But a commercial comes on. A car commercial. Kids are driving through a tunnel, singing.

And suddenly I see a different car than the one on the screen. I see the Chevy. I'm there. I'm shouting. I want to get out of the car. I don't want to be there.

"Stop! Let me out of here!" The car keeps going. It swerves. I'm crazy. So angry. I can't think of anything except getting away. Getting out. I reach for the door. I'll show them. I'll show both of them. I don't care. I don't care what happens to me. I have to get out.

There's shouting. Kenzie and Ryun yelling at the same time. I don't listen. I can't hear. My ears are electric wires with a current racing through them.

I reach for the door. Someone grabs at my arm. My hand is on the door handle.

"No!" I yell this. The cry carries. It's here in the hospital room.

Missouri gets out of bed and stands in front of me. Her hands press on my shoulders. "Sierra? What is it, child? What's the matter?"

I see the picture. It's frozen in front of me in living color. I'm reaching for the door. But it's not the driver's door. It's the passenger door. My hand is on the door handle of the passenger door.

"Missouri," I whisper, because the sandpaper in my throat has come back. It's closing my air passages. "I was trying to get out of the passenger side."

The realization moves over me like a fast-moving storm cloud, changing the atmosphere, the very air in our room. "The accident. The car. I wasn't in the driver's seat. I wasn't the one driving."

"Sierra! Sierra! Answer me!" Missouri's face is close to mine. I think she's been shouting at me.

But I'm back inside the Chevy. In the passenger seat. "I wasn't driving," I say again. I focus on her eyes. "I remember now."

"Are you sure, child?" Missouri asks. "Are you sure it's a real memory? I thought you remembered driving."

I try to pull the pieces together. They're so close now. I can see my hand reaching for the car door. I can feel the car moving. Other hands, other arms, reach for mine to stop me. "I was next to the passenger door. I see it, Missouri. The highway and the trees blurring past us. I was screaming at them."

"At who? Your friends?"

"Kenzie and Ryun. I was so angry. The car was close to the shoulder. And I wasn't driving it."

"Then who was?" she asks.

I picture the hands again. I know Ryun's hands, his long fingers and big knuckles. But it's Kenzie's hands I'm seeing. Her nails painted red. Her rings. She's trying to keep me from opening the car door.

"Sierra?" Missouri takes hold of my arms. "What is it?"

"Ryun's hands," I say, staring past her. Because I'm seeing Ryun's hands now. One is reaching for me, reaching past Kenzie to get to me. And the other hand is on the steering wheel.

"Ryun was driving." I hear my own words as if someone else is saying them, someone far removed from all of this. Someone detached, cold. With a heart of steel.

"Are you sure, child?" Missouri asks.

"I'm sure." And I am. I know what happened now. It's not so much that I'm seeing it. It's that I remember. It's all there. "I *was* driving. After the game, I drove out to Route 58. Ryun wanted to get pizza. But I couldn't stand it, having him sitting between Kenzie and me, knowing what I knew.

"So I told them I knew what they were doing behind my back. Ryun started to deny it, but Kenzie said she was glad everything was finally out in the open." I turn and stare at Missouri. "Can you believe that? She was *glad!* My best friend was *glad* I knew she was cheating behind my back with my boyfriend. I screamed at them. How could they betray me like that? And the angrier I got, the faster I drove.

"Ryun was sitting next to me. He kept yelling for me to slow down, to pull over so we could talk. I took a curve too fast. The tires squealed. And when I had control again, I pulled over and stopped the car. I remember getting out and slamming the door as hard as I could, then running to the ditch. I'm not sure if I thought I was going to be sick, or what.

"Ryun ran after me. He tried to put his arm around my shoulder, but I shook it off. We argued. Finally he convinced me to get back in the car. He'd taken the keys—I guess I'd left them in the ignition. And he wouldn't give them back. He insisted *he* was driving until I calmed down. I stormed back to the car. But no way was I going to sit between Ryun and Kenzie. So I made Kenzie scoot over, and I sat in the passenger seat.

"We hadn't gone very far when Kenzie said something about how I should just accept this and get over it. She said horrible things. 'Grow up, Sierra.' That's what she said. 'Ryun and I want to be together. Just move on.'

"So I said, 'Fine! I'll move on! I'm getting out of here.' And that's when I reached for the car door. I know it sounds crazy, but I couldn't stay there next to *her*. I had to get out."

Missouri's grip on my arms hasn't eased off. She's leaning on me. "Do you remember what happened next?"

"We struggled. I guess Ryun lost control of the car. The car went one way, then swerved the other way. I think I remember knowing we were going to crash. And then there was a deafening noise, like a bomb going off. And everything stopped. Everything was black."

I stare at her and see my image in her eyes. "That's it. I don't remember anything else until I heard voices here in the hospital."

"You don't remember being pulled out of the car?" Missouri asks.

I shake my head. I know what the police said about Kenzie and Ryun pulling me out of the car before it exploded. I don't believe it. Not anymore. Not now. They're no heroes. They lied about that, just like they lied about everything.

Missouri lets me go. When she straightens up, she wobbles and grabs her hip. I reach for her, to catch her. But she sits on the bed before I can do anything. "I'm all right," she says. "Sierra, don't forget that whatever went on in that car, your friends did risk their lives to pull you out."

I grin at her. She's so good. So naive. She still believes the hero story the papers conjured up. "If they pulled me out of that car, it was for one reason. One reason only."

She frowns at me. She still doesn't get it.

"They needed a fall guy. Don't you see? They needed everyone to think I was driving. They had to get me out of the car. I wasn't behind the wheel." It makes so much sense. A part of me, a part that isn't here, wasn't there, sees this.

"Oh, sugar. Don't be believing that."

I smile at her. Missouri could never understand what I understand now. I almost envy her.

"You need to call your parents." She reaches for the phone.

"I'm not calling my parents," I say calmly.

"They need to know your memory's back. They need to know you weren't driving the–"

"No, Missouri. And you promised. You can't tell them either. I'll lie and say it was all a dream. And I won't tell you anything again."

"Child, I gave you my word. I won't be breaking it. But you got to tell somebody. How about that nice policeman? He left you his phone number, didn't he?"

I shake my head. "Not yet. It's okay, Missouri. When the time is right, I'll tell the police everything. Just not yet." Something is settling over me, a calm, an assurance. A power. I remember Mrs. Albertson, my sixth-grade teacher, telling us, "Knowledge is power." She was right. Knowing what I know *is* powerful. And knowing that *they* don't know that I know feels like an ultimate power.

"Well, what are you two up to?" Nurse Miller comes into the room. She's carrying a tray of Missouri's medications. "You look like you're plotting an overthrow of the hospital. Should I be worried?"

"You caught us," I say, laughing. I'm good. I'm convincing. "We want your job."

"Well, you can have it." She sighs. "At least tonight you can. That Mr. Reins down the hall is the most cantankerous man I've ever known. He's so feisty. Can't believe he's not well enough to go home."

I laugh.

Missouri hasn't said a word.

"You all right, Missouri?" Nurse Miller asks.

"She's exhausted," I explain. "It's not easy plotting the overthrow of an entire hospital. It was all Missouri's idea, you know."

"I always knew you had it in you, Missouri." Nurse Miller moves to the other side of the bed.

The hurt that was in me, the strength of it, has transformed into something else. I'm not sure what yet. But my brain is percolating.

After the nurse leaves, Missouri picks up her old Bible and stares at the pages. I don't know if she can see the words or not.

It's the time I usually go to sleep. But I'm not sleepy. Instead, I do the physical-therapy exercises beside my bed. One set. Two sets. Three sets. The exercises hurt more each time I repeat them. But the hurt builds into something else, like adding logs to a fire.

I work my feet, my ankles, my legs, and my hip. I need to be strong. I have to be in good shape. Great shape. I need all the strength, all the fire, I can build.

I am going to get even.

On Christmas Eve Ryun limps in to visit me first thing in the morning. Kenzie's not with him.

Twenty-four hours earlier I would have been filled with joy to see Ryun, to know that he'd come alone.

Now I'm filled with another emotion, and it's left me calm and in control. "Ryun!" I call. "Where's Kenzie?"

Out of the corner of my eye, I see Missouri look at me as if she doesn't recognize me, this roommate of hers, a changed person.

I *am* changed. I have a purpose. I have knowledge.

"Come and sit, Ryun." I pat my bed. "How's the leg? Does it hurt?" It hasn't even been two weeks since his surgery, but he's getting around without crutches.

Ryun glances nervously around the room. There's no Kenzie to look to. Poor Ryun. He eases himself down on the foot of my bed as if he's afraid he'll break me. "It's okay."

All at once I feel like two different people. One Sierra wants to cry for Ryun, to hurt because he's hurt.

But the other Sierra, the one I'm listening to, knows that he has hurt me much more than he could ever be hurt. He deserves this. He deserves more.

"I got the call from Duke," he says, grinning as if he's ready to burst. "It's official. I'm going to Duke. Full soccer scholarship." He runs his fingers through his hair.

"They called you?" I know I need to sound more enthusiastic, but I can't stand how unfair it feels. He's done this to me—bruised my ribs, dislocated my hip, banged up my face. He's made me take the blame for what *he* did. And now he gets to go off to Duke University, scholarship in hand, as if nothing's happened?

"Yeah," he continues. "I would have told you sooner, but . . . well, you know."

"That's really great, Ryun. But what about your leg? Aren't they worried you won't recover all the way?" I soften my voice and add quickly, "I mean, *I* know you will. You'll work hard and be terrific. I was just afraid . . . well, that maybe they'd be worried or want to wait and see before they forked over $30,000."

"I didn't tell them about the accident or my leg."

Of course. I should have known. Why would Ryun be honest with them? I say, "Ah" or something like that.

"Yeah. I figure, 'need to know,' right? Even if I end up sitting out the early tournaments and some school games, no big loss. I'll be back in shape by spring. Duke won't know the difference."

"Well, congratulations. Really. Your mom must be so proud of you."

Ryun's mother lives for her son. I've met her only a couple of times. Ryun is so totally American, with no Korean accent at all, that the first time I met his parents, I was surprised. His dad speaks English, but with a thick accent. His mom doesn't speak it at all.

For the first time, I wonder what Ryun's parents would do if they knew their son had been driving and that he'd made sure his girlfriend took the blame for the accident.

"Are you okay?" Ryun asks. I think he's been talking to me, but I missed what he said.

"Yeah. Sorry. It was great of you to come by on Christmas Eve," I say warmly. "You must have last-minute shopping to do."

He shrugs.

"Any cool Christmas plans?"

I can tell he's flustered. It's almost funny. Ryun flustered? He's the one so in control of our relationship.

Except that's all changed. Just like that. I wonder if he can sense it.

"I–my family, we're not doing much this year."

Inside my head, behind this face that's smiling at Ryun, I see him exchanging gifts with Kenzie.

"I picked up something for you," he says. He takes a book out of his backpack and drops it onto the bed. Not wrapped. It's P. D. James' latest mystery.

"Thank you. That's so sweet. You know I love mysteries." Does he? I'm not sure. "I'm afraid I haven't gotten anything for you. No Christmas shopping this year." I give a soft laugh. The truth is that I already have three Christmas presents for Ryun. I bought the first one nine months ago. I got him a Duke sweatshirt off the Internet, as soon as I found out that's where he might want to go. Got myself one too.

I finger the pages of the thick novel. "I'll have lots of time to read this, I guess."

Ryun almost looks at me. "You're different."

"Hmm. Couldn't be the face, could it?" I say it as a joke. "Or my hair?"

"I didn't mean that," he says quickly. "I mean . . . *you*. Like you're okay again. In a good mood."

"I'm sorry." I touch his arm. "Was I in a bad mood before? I didn't mean to be."

He squirms. "No. I didn't mean that. I just mean—"

"No. You're right, Ryun. I guess I have been in a lousy mood. I may not graduate. All the school I've missed." I don't think I've considered this before. I don't think it's true. I'll get a tutor. I'll talk to my teachers. I'll graduate.

My words hit the mark though. Ryun looks pained. "Man, Sierra. You have to graduate."

I shrug stoically.

"I'm sorry," he says.

"You say that a lot for somebody who has nothing to be sorry about." I smile at him and squeeze his arm.

He studies his Nikes.

"Listen, Ryun. It was nice of you to come by. Really. Tell Kenzie hi for me." There's not a note of sarcasm in my voice. I should join the drama club.

Ryun stands up and buttons his coat. He heads for the door, his leg dragging a bit.

"And, Ryun?" I stop him in his tracks. "There's one more thing. One thing I just have to say."

Missouri sits up straight now. She's watching us. I can feel her stare.

"In case I didn't say it before, when I was in the bad mood, thank you. I'm really grateful to you and Kenzie. I will never forget what you did."

He turns and actually looks at me.

"Saving my life like that," I continue. "I owe you both so much."

"I—you don't . . ." He sighs. "I have to go. Good-bye, Sierra." Ryun walks out.

I lean back in bed, my arms behind my head, and replay the entire visit, every word.

It was the most satisfying conversation I've had in weeks.

I can hardly wait to see Kenzie.

23

Kenzie doesn't come by the hospital all day. I'm wondering if she senses something. Or maybe she's with Ryun. I imagine the gifts they're exchanging for Christmas. I picture them sneaking out of their houses, meeting up in the city, a coffeehouse maybe. Kenzie gets there first. She waits, anxious, fingering her gift for Ryun, hoping it's good enough. She checks out the room, making sure nobody they know will catch them. Then, through the ice-frosted window, she sees him. He's carrying a gift so large he struggles with the weight of it.

"Sierra?" Missouri sits in the chair beside my bed. I didn't hear her walk up. She's wearing a white blouse and a gray wool skirt that's a size too big for her. Her black shoes must be half as old as she is, but they look unused. The heels could be building blocks.

"You look nice," I say.

"When's your family coming by?" she asks.

I glance at the alarm clock my mom left in the room. I'm surprised to see that it's Christmas Eve for real, that the whole afternoon has gone by. The blinds are open, and it's dark outside.

"Later, I guess," I answer.

"I don't like leaving you. Maybe the doctor would okay a trip to church with me. I get special permission, you know. They didn't let me go when I was in the main hospital, after I broke my hip. But we manage here in the rehab wing. Drew and his mama are coming by for me a little before seven. I could let it count for a Sunday. Pay off that bet you owe me."

I shake my head. "No, thanks. Not tonight. I don't think I'm up to it, even if the doctor says I can go, which I don't think he will." I will never be up to going to her church, but I'll keep my word and go. Once. Just not tonight.

They bring each of us a tray of better-than-usual hospital food—a slice of turkey, with mashed potatoes and mixed vegetables. But it still tastes like hospital food. They must have a secret sieve that drains out flavors. Missouri hardly touches her meal, but the night-duty nurse doesn't comment on it as she clears away the tray.

"Merry Christmas!" Andrew Miller, dressed so sharp he could operate, glides into the room. He's carrying two poinsettia plants and sets them on each of the bed tables.

"Thanks, Drew," I say. "You shouldn't have gotten me anything." I mean it. It may be the only thing I've said all day that I do mean.

"This is from the church." He strides over to the bed and pulls something out of his inside overcoat pocket. The long black coat goes great with his leather loafers. He tosses a small package on the bed. It's wrapped, with a lopsided bow that he must have tied himself. "*This* is from me."

"No way!" I pick it up. "Tell me it's not our friend Grady."

"I set Grady free. Remember?"

"Can I open it?"

"And spoil that beautiful wrapping job? Huh-uh!"

"If you don't open it," Missouri interjects, "I will."

I remove about 22 pieces of tape and pull out a disposable camera. "Drew, thanks!"

"I know you must have a dozen high-tech digitals at home. But I thought you could snap a few hospital shots before you leave the place."

I raise the camera and snap one of Drew.

"Not what I had in mind," he complains.

"It's a great gift. Thanks." I get out of bed. It's easier now, and I wear my own nightgowns. "Missouri, prepare to say *cheese.*"

I take two shots, under protest, of Missouri in her skirt and blouse. I want to save the rest to get her in the tiny flowered nightgown. And I want her in the morning, when she first wakes up, and one of her face reflected in the TV as she watches her game shows.

Drew's off-duty mom comes in to help get

Missouri to the car. Lady Smooth looks even more elegant in her church clothes. They wheel Missouri out, bundling her like a papoose.

About a half hour after Missouri leaves, Mom, Dad, and Jacqueline come in. They try so hard to make it seem like a regular Christmas Eve that I'm pretty sure each of us is just waiting for it to be over.

■ ■ ■

On Christmas morning I actually wake up before the nurse comes in to take my temperature. I start to holler "Merry Christmas" to Missouri, until I see that she's still asleep. It's a first, my waking up before my roommate.

I watch her, but I can't see the sheet move. A stillness creeps through the room. I want to see the sheet move, her arm twitch. But nothing stirs.

I throw back my covers and jump out of bed so fast, the room spins. "Missouri?" I cry, fear shutting off my windpipe so it comes out a whisper. A million thoughts bounce off the walls of my mind, most of them tethered by *shoulds*. I should have talked to her more. I should have told her how much having her to talk to has meant to me. I should have told her that she was my angel, pulling me out of the cave when I was unconscious.

I stand beside her bed. Then I reach down and touch her forehead.

Her eyes fly open.

"Missouri!" I drop to my knees. My hip stabs my ribs, as if the bone has flown loose and lodged in my side. I don't care. "You're okay! Oh, Missouri, I thought—" But I can't finish.

She turns her head and squints those heavenly brown eyes at me. "I haven't gone home yet, child."

"I'm sorry." My chest heaves as if I've been running. I push myself to my feet, using her bed to help.

Missouri scoots up in bed, her gaze never leaving my face. "I love you, Sierra. Merry Christmas, sugar." She tilts her head toward the white ceiling and shouts, "And happy birthday to you, dear Jesus!"

Breakfast shows up late, but it's worth waiting for—biscuits and margarine, not just jelly, scrambled eggs, and cream of wheat.

The phone rings. I reach for the phone by my bed, but it's Missouri's phone ringing. She answers it, and I can tell it's someone from her church, calling to wish her a merry Christmas. She hangs up, and it rings again. For the next hour, it's nonstop Christmas calls for my roommate.

I try not to let it, but a sadness creeps in. I'm pathetic. Sitting in a hospital bed on Christmas morning. No phone calls. While my 101-year-old roommate can't get off the phone.

It doesn't matter. I've told myself that Christmas is just another day. I'm not quite ready to say that I don't believe in God anymore. It just doesn't seem to matter. What I do know is that if there is a God, he's really dropped the ball in the justice department. I'm going to have to take care of that one on my own.

The phone rings, louder this time. Startled, I glance at Missouri. She's talking on *her* phone. I pick up mine. In spite of myself, I think, I'm hoping it will be Ryun. Maybe he'll confess everything, beg me to forgive him, to take him back, to let things be the way they used to be.

"Hello?" I say. My voice shakes.

I hear someone take a breath on the other end of the line. Somehow I know it's Kenzie.

"Uh–merry Christmas, Sierra." I'm right. It *is* Kenzie.

In the background, I hear whispering. I picture Ryun there with her, their heads pressed together against the receiver.

But it's a girl's voice I hear in the background, something like, "Kenzie, go on!"

"Kenzie? Is that you?" I sound so cheery, so grateful for the call.

"Yeah. We–Holly's here and Carin–we wanted to know if it's okay to stop by for a few minutes. Wish you merry Christmas and all."

"That's so nice of you guys! This is a pretty depressing place today," I warn her. "Are you sure?"

"Of course we're sure!" Carin hollers. It must be *her* ear next to Kenzie's at the receiver. I picture the perky blonde, who was *my* friend long before Kenzie came into our group.

"Thanks, Carin!" I exclaim. "I'd love to see you, even for a few minutes."

"We'll be right over," Kenzie promises and hangs up almost immediately.

I'm not sure why she hangs up so fast. I can't

read Kenzie, not yet. I thought I knew McKenzie Parker, but I was wrong. The Kenzie I knew, the Kenzie who had become my best friend in just a short time, never would have done what she did—dated my boyfriend behind my back, lied to the police about me.

And I want to know Kenzie. I need to know her, what makes her tick, what drives her. It's vital that I learn what Kenzie cares about, what's important to her.

So I can take it away.

"Friends stopping by for you?" Missouri asks. She's moving slowly toward the bathroom.

"Something like that."

She glances suspiciously over her shoulder at me. "That girl? Kenzie? She stopping by?"

"Yep. A couple of other girls too."

"I got me a bad feeling about this," she says.

"What do you mean, Missouri? I'm glad they're coming. You're the one with all the Christmas calls." I give her my best smile.

She doesn't return it. "The longer you put off truth and forgiveness, the harder they bite on you."

I don't answer. But I think about it. I think about what that means to Kenzie. And I hope it's true—that in the end, the truth will bite her harder because I'm taking my time with it. I know that's not at all what

Missouri is saying, but I believe it. *Revenge is a dish that's best served cold.* I can't remember who said this or where I heard it. But I am counting on it.

I watch Missouri make her way to the bathroom. She favors her good hip, and I know I have to be careful so I don't limp like that. It's minutes before she comes out of the bathroom. But she takes up the conversation where she left it. "Seems to me Christmas is a good time to think about forgiveness. Mmm-hmm." She sits on her bed, as if she doesn't have the strength to lie back down.

"Forgiveness? Missouri, you haven't lost *your* memory, have you? Don't you remember what I told you about Kenzie? And Ryun? They don't deserve to be forgiven."

"Well, sugar, who does? Mmm-hmm. Who does?"

I think she's about to launch into a Christmas sermon, when I hear laughing—no, giggling—in the hall outside our room.

"*You* go first!" someone whispers.

Kenzie enters the room, as if she's been shoved in. She stumbles. I see that she's wearing brand spanking new Steve Madden Kinkos.

"Cool boots, Kenzie!" I say, by way of a greeting. The boots are distressed leather on top, with a sole I wouldn't wear to my funeral—3-inch heel, too thick, with a rubber cap and rubber lug sole. She got the brand right, but she still doesn't get it. "You've got to see if they have a purse to match."

Kenzie glances at her bag, which she probably thought *did* match, until I was kind enough to clue her in.

"Merry Christmas," Kenzie says halfheartedly. She spreads out a navy T-shirt on my bed. Tiny white letters spell *If you can read this, BACK OFF! You're too close.*

"You know, for when you go back to school. So nobody bumps you in the halls?" She shrugs.

"Thanks, Kenzie. You are *such* a great friend." I picture her buying the stupid T-shirt in the mall, with my boyfriend watching, admiring how thoughtful my best friend is.

Carin's still standing in the doorway, like she's afraid whatever's wrong with me is catching. But Holly walks right up to the bed and stares at my face. Holly is a cheerleader I've hung out with for a couple of years. She helped make over the "new Kenzie."

I'm almost sure it was Holly in the john, talking to Kenzie that night.

"Oh, Sierra!" Holly whines, her lip curling up like her eyelashes. "I would have come by sooner. But, well, you were unconscious. Kenzie said your face was swollen and you cut your hair, but I had no idea. Does it hurt?"

"My face?" The old Three Stooges' joke pops into my mind—*Does your face hurt? Because it's killing me. Nyuk, nyuk, nyuk.*

"Well, yeah. And everything else too," Holly adds.

"Give her a break, Holly," Kenzie says.

"No, that's okay." They're so pretty. All three of them. And now I'm not even *cute.*

I have to focus. I don't care how I look to them or to anyone. In fact, the worse I look, the better.

When the truth comes out about what Kenzie and Ryun did to me, people will remember me this way.

"It hurts," I admit. "Not all the time. My eyes water too much. I guess my hip is the worst. I bruised a couple of ribs, which only hurt when I laugh." I try to smile.

"Man, you're brave. I don't think I could handle it." Holly backs away from me. I can see her shoes—square-toed Nine West Anakins. Pea green. These girls need me more than I need them.

Kenzie jerks her head for Carin to come in the rest of the way. It reminds me of Kenzie's secret signals with Ryun in this very hospital room.

Part of me wants to kick Kenzie and Holly out so I can have a good talk with Carin. She and I became shoe friends in sixth grade. I'd never noticed her earlier because she was in another class. Then, about a month into school, she came up to me at lunch and asked if I had a different pair of shoes for every outfit. The way she asked it I knew she wasn't trying to mock me or anything.

We talked shoes every lunch period after that.

Carin steps closer. She has a plastic bag full of magazines.

"Those for me?" I ask, reaching for the bag.

She quickly hands them over. "Sorry. Wait till you see the *In Style* though—whole section on shoes of the stars."

"Thanks, Carin."

"So how *are* you, Sierra? Really?" She isn't looking directly at me.

"I'm okay," I lie.

“That’s super! That’s the spirit.” Carin could burst into a High High cheer at any moment. “You’ll be out of here and back to normal in no time.” She risks a glance at me. “Your hair looks so cute!” She turns to Holly to back her up. “Don’t you think Sierra’s hair rocks? I may have to get *my* hair cut.” She fingers the long blonde curls, which she wouldn’t cut under penalty of death.

“It’s really nice,” Holly says.

Hearing Holly’s voice, I know I’m right. She *was* the one in the john, talking with Kenzie. The thought makes my skin freeze.

Carin sits on the bed and crosses her legs. She’s wearing Stuart Weitzman Pauline boots that had to cost $250. Brown, pointed toe, ankle-high. I’d have gone for the knee-highs, but they’re definite quality.

“Wow! Love your Stuart Weitzmans! Did your parents get them for you for Christmas?”

She sticks out her foot to admire her new boot. “Yep. Al and Kathy came through for me this year. Did you open any of your gifts yet?”

I start to say no. Then I change my mind. “Well, only one.” I try to form my swollen lips into a shy grin. “But it was the most important one. From Ryun.”

“Ryun? That is *so* great of him!” Carin exclaims.

“He’s been wonderful through all this,” I say. “He would have spent the whole day with me, if I’d let him. You know how he is. But he was here so late last night. I wanted him to spend Christmas with his family. They’ll really miss him when he’s at Duke.”

Kenzie shifts her weight.

"You are so good!" Carin exclaims. "So what did he get you?"

"Ryun was here last night then?" Kenzie asks.

Carin and I both turn to look at Kenzie. She smiles, tight-lipped.

He didn't tell her. She didn't know that he was coming to see me yesterday. I can see this, and it's like a gift to me.

"You know," I say slowly, addressing all three of them, "it sounds crazy. But Ryun was able to make last night the best Christmas Eve I think I've ever had. This accident is bringing us closer together than ever."

My words strike Kenzie hard. Her face looks as if I've landed a spear in her gut.

Carin touches my hand. "That is so beautiful!"

Holly clears her throat.

I can feel Kenzie's anger. It feeds my own. How can she be jealous of *my* boyfriend? How can she possibly resent it that he stopped by to see me? I picture them arguing about it, Kenzie demanding to know why he didn't tell her. What did she expect? She should know, better than anybody, the kind of betrayal Ryun Lee is capable of.

"So? Tell all!" Carin says. "What did Ryun give you?"

I can't just say he gave me an unromantic novel. "Okay. One gift I *can* show you. But one I can't."

"I *love* this!" Carin exclaims.

I catch a look from Holly to Kenzie. I'm right. Holly knows. She was there in the bathroom. I want to know how long she's known that my best friend and my boyfriend were sneaking around behind my back. I can tell by her eyes and the way she twists her body toward the door that she wants out.

For a second I'm amazed I can read these three *friends* so well. Before the accident, I couldn't. As far as I knew, we were close loyal friends who would do anything for each other. Being betrayed has done something to me. It's opened my senses, knocked everyone off pedestals, and sent them tumbling, unguarded, in front of me.

I show them the mystery novel. "Isn't Ryun thoughtful? He knows me so well. I love mysteries. And what better gift could there be than something to read here? Plus, the card was so sweet." I pause as if I'm reading the words in my head. As if there had been a card.

"And the other present?" Carin coaxes. "You *have* to tell. Right, girls?"

"That's up to Sierra," Holly suggests.

I look to Kenzie, but she turns away.

"Okay. I'll hint. Let's just say it's red. And I've got it on right now." That should fire up the argument a bit. I pull my robe around me modestly.

"Victoria's Secret?" Carin squeals.

Before I can answer, Holly says, "I really have to get home. My mom's freaking that I cut out of Christmas so fast. Great seeing you, Sierra."

Carin pouts. "I didn't even get to ask you what it's like to have amnesia. I mean, can't you remember *anything?* Well, obviously you remember *some* things. You knew us and everything."

"Doctor Snyder said it's traumatic amnesia," I say

truthfully. "I remember everything up to the night of the accident and nothing from then on, until I woke up here."

"That must be so *weird!*" Carin exclaims. "So, like, will it come back?"

I shrug. "Sometimes, I guess, the memory comes back. But other times, it never does."

"We gotta go," Kenzie says. She does a little wave thing with one hand.

"Yeah. Merry Christmas," Holly says. She and Kenzie are to the door now.

"Thanks for coming," I call. "And for the shirt."

Carin gets up. "When can you come back to school?"

Doctor Snyder has already told me that he thinks I'll be good to go for at least half days after Christmas break. I shake my head. "Could be a long time yet. I just hope I don't have to repeat my senior year without you guys."

Carin slaps her hand over her mouth. Her eyes tear up at the thought. "We won't let that happen! If you have to have another senior year, we'll stay an extra year with you!" She scurries to catch up with Holly and Kenzie.

When they're gone, I realize that Missouri is humming. I recognize it, a Christmas carol, "Hark! the Herald Angels Sing."

I glance over at her. I can tell by her frown that she has been listening to every word. "Don't start, okay, Missouri?"

"I was just thinking, child. And praying." She goes back to humming.

I can't help following along in her song, my mind supplying the words to her tune: *"Hark! the herald angels sing, 'Glory to the newborn King; Peace on earth, and mercy mild . . .'"*

She stops, leaving those words hung up in my head. I think about how different her Christmas and my Christmas are. Everything about her cries *peace.* I know she's not afraid of death. I smile over at her. I think I love this woman now. But the last thing I want is her peace.

Missouri sighs. "Peace on earth." The way she says it makes it a wish or a prayer.

But for me, if I still prayed, peace on my earth is about the last thing I'd pray for.

It's still morning when Jacqueline bursts into the room. "Merry Christmas, Sierra and Missouri!" she shouts. She's wearing *my* long cashmere coat, which is too big for her. "Look what I brought you!"

She unbuttons the coat and out hops my little black Chihuahua onto my bed.

"Paddywack!" I reach for my dog. He backs up but dances and wags his tail. Then he leaps onto my lap and trots up my stomach to lick my chin. "I've missed you, baby!"

"Jacqueline!" Mom walks in, apparently surprised to see Paddy. "I can't believe you brought that dog into the hospital!"

"Ah, it's nothing," my sister responds, as if Mom has paid her a huge compliment.

"Can you see him?" Jacqueline asks Missouri.

"His name is Paddywack. Sneaking him in is my Christmas present to Sierra."

"Cute little thing. He looks a little like a rat, doesn't he?" Missouri observes.

I have to hold my dog in the air to keep him from licking my face. It feels so good to hold him, like a piece of my old life is still here. Paddywack hasn't forgotten me.

Dad breezes in, takes off his overcoat, and smoothes his hair. "Merry Christmas, Sierra."

"Merry Christmas, Dad!" I call.

He stares at Paddywack, then glares at Jacqueline.

She returns his glare with a sweet smile. "Yes, indeed. Merry Christmas, Dad!"

He comes over to my bed. He and Mom are both carrying shopping bags.

"Hey! Presents?" I ask. "For me?"

A nurse comes in. Nurse Miller has the day off. This nurse doesn't look much older than me, and she's not hiding the fact that she'd rather be just about any place else. Without a word to us, she pulls Missouri's privacy curtain and starts in on her.

"You okay, Missouri?" I ask.

"I'm fine," she answers.

Mom sets her bag on my bed and pulls out two gifts that could only be shoes.

"I love the shape of those boxes," I say, taking one onto my lap. Paddywack scratches on the Christmas paper and helps me unwrap the box.

When I lift the lid from the shoe box, I smell leather. They're the boots I've been wanting all year.

They've been front and center in the Nordstrom window. Stuart Weitzman Pauline boots, just like Carin's, only these are tall and metallic plum.

"They're exactly what I wanted!" I exclaim.

"No kidding?" Jacqueline comments. "You only wrote down the name, brand, color, and style number."

"I'm glad you like them, honey," Mom says, handing me another box.

"Thanks, Mom and Dad." I know Dad didn't set foot in the ladies' shoe section of Nordstrom. But they're from him too.

Dad walks to the other side of the bed and sits at the foot. Dr. Richard Reynolds is a force, even in a hospital room with a bunch of women. If I had to use one word to describe him, it would be *distinguished.*

"Open another one," he says, waving at the box Mom has placed on my lap. The way he says it makes me think he isn't going to stay long. I wonder if he's had another emergency. Crazy people get even crazier on Christmas. I can't remember a Christmas when Dad has been able to be home all day.

I open the second box. It's a pair of Aldos, tan, with cork heels, something Aldo must have come up with after a night of too much sangria. Not one of his best creations.

"Thanks, Mom. They're really nice."

"You hate them." She reaches for the shoes and puts them back in the box. The martyr is lurking.

"I don't hate them. I'm just trying to think what I have to wear with them."

"We can return them," she says stoically. "It's not

a problem. It's hard to pick out shoes for you, when you're not around."

I'm thinking that I'm not gone on purpose and it's not fair to make me feel guilty because I don't like the stupid old-lady-tan Aldos.

"Before this gets ugly," Jacqueline interrupts, "try this box."

I open the remaining two pairs of shoes. One pair is perfect–charcoal Manolo Blahnik. They sell for even more than the Weitzman boots. The other pair I'll return as soon as I get out of here.

The young nurse whips back Missouri's curtain. We all jump, even Paddywack, who barks at her.

"You can't have a dog in here!" the nurse protests. "It's against hospital rules!"

Jacqueline looks puzzled. "Are you sure? Because I read all the rules, and I didn't see that one. Which rule is it?"

Now the nurse looks flustered. "Well, I have never seen a dog in the hospital. I'm sure they're not allowed."

"Because you've never seen one?" Jacqueline persists. "Have you ever seen an Albanian monk here?"

"No. That's not the point. Everybody knows you can't have a dog in a hospital. You just can't. It's . . . they're not sanitary." Her lips tighten, and she stands a little straighter, as if proud to have scored this point.

Poor nurse.

"Did you know that *not* having a dog is actually bad for you?" Jacqueline inquires. "Studies have shown that people who own pets have better mental and physical health. Didn't they teach you that in nurses' training?"

"No, but–"

"A dog's mouth and saliva are germ free, compared to a human's mouth. Do you kiss?"

"What?" The nurse's face flushes.

"Plus," Jacqueline continues, "man's best friend keeps you gainfully employed. About 830,000 people a year require medical treatment from dog bites."

Dad stands up. "That's enough, Jacqueline. I'll take the dog home. Thankfully, we drove separately. I'll just drop the dog off before heading to the office."

"You're going in to the office?" I ask, trying not to let him see how much I want him to stay longer.

"Can't be helped." He reaches for Paddywack.

The little dog growls and snaps at him.

"Paddywack!" I scold. I pick him up and hug him, rubbing my swollen cheek against his soft hair. "You be good for Daddy."

Dad puts on his coat. Then, cautiously, he takes the dog and tucks him under one arm, like a football. "Sorry I have to leave, honey. I'll try to stop back tonight. Okay?" He balances Paddy and kisses the top of my head.

I watch Mom watch Dad leave. She hasn't said anything, but her eyes look sad. I can't stand feeling this way, like things are happening behind my back.

"So what else is in those bags?" I ask, sounding 100 times more enthusiastic than I feel. I want to pretend that this is a wonderful Christmas scene, a family rallying together, making a memory in a hospital room. The old Sierra could have pulled this off. She would have seen it just like that. She would have snapped a picture and demanded we all "make a memory!"

This Sierra, the one I'm becoming, can't. She sees tension and sadness. She sees too much of what Jacqueline sees, has maybe always seen. And she wonders where her father will really go after he drops off her dog.

Mom pulls more gifts from the shopping bags—earrings, a new watch, a necklace I'll return. I get the usual hospital presents—two nightgowns, a robe, and a pair of old-lady slippers.

Even Jacqueline has come through with more presents—a subscription to *Health Magazine,* a book on "strenuous activities to avoid and why." But she also gives me a pair of funky pink flip-flops that I might actually wear.

"And I got both of you this!" Jacqueline tosses me a package, about the size of a book, but soft and lightweight. Then she delivers an identical package to Missouri.

Mine is a small red pillow.

"Why, it's lovely," Missouri says, as she takes out a gold pillow.

"These hospital pillows are bad for you," Jacqueline explains. "Too puffy. A person can suffocate. And if you don't suffocate, you can still get a migraine headache from a big pillow."

Missouri and I thank my sister for saving our lives and keeping us headache free.

Jacqueline hands one last gift to Missouri, then takes it back and rips off the wrapping paper. "It's a sun hat," she explains, setting the floppy yellow straw hat on Missouri's head. "At your age, the sun is very bad for your skin. You can wear it when you go wading in that fountain down there."

Missouri laughs. I feel awful that I didn't even think about getting her a present.

Mom and Jacqueline bundle up and get ready to leave. "We'll come back tonight," Mom promises. "We'll try to sneak you in some Christmas cookies. I made those almond ones you love."

I thank them.

When they're gone, Missouri and I both turn off our lights and go to sleep.

When I wake up, Missouri is on the phone.

"Thank you kindly," she's saying. "I think I'd best stay here this evening after all." Pause. "No. Nothing's wrong. I guess last night's Christmas Eve service tuckered me out more than I knew. It was a wonderful service. I'll miss y'all tonight. But I'll be praying with you." Pause. "Well, same to you. Merry Christmas." She hangs up the phone, and I think I see her wince when she reaches over.

"Oh, dear," she says, catching my eye. "Did I wake you, child?"

"I was awake. Are you okay, Missouri?"

She sighs. "My, yes. I'm just a little tired. I'm not as young as I used to be." She winks over at me. "You won't mind me sticking around tonight instead of going to the church, will you?"

"Don't be silly." Truth is, I'm glad to have her stay. But I know how much she was looking forward to the Christmas service at her church. She must be feeling pretty bad not to go. "I'll even read something for you, if you want."

"Why, that would be the nicest Christmas gift you could give me." She lies back on her pillow and closes her eyes.

The young nurse, muttering about being shorthanded, brings in our Christmas dinners. From the looks of the meal, the kitchen must be shorthanded too. We turn on a Christmas special and watch while we eat, although Missouri barely touches her food.

Before I'm finished with the day-old chocolate pudding, Mom and Jacqueline are back. True to her word, Mom has smuggled in a plate of Christmas cookies. I eat three of the almond crescents. Jacqueline passes the plate to Missouri. She takes one cookie to save for later.

"Is Dad driving *his* car?" I ask, glancing at the door for the tenth time.

"I wouldn't count on your father being able to get away in time tonight, honey." Mom fusses with my hospital table. She waters the plant Aunt Vin and Uncle Earl sent. She waters our poinsettias.

"Dad's not coming?" I ask.

"You know how much he wants to be here. He would be if he could."

Mom's words echo in my brain. I've heard these exact words so many times before. I've always believed them. My dad is important. People depend on him. So why am I not buying this now?

"He's still at the office?" I ask. "Didn't he go back home?"

Before Mom can think of an answer, Jacqueline plops on my bed. "Guess what Dad got himself for Christmas."

I shrug. I'm still watching Mom, wondering what's going on in her head. I used to think that my mother didn't have a worry in the world. I thought she carried on so much about little things and complained so much about Jacqueline because she didn't have anything else to complain about.

"A new car." Jacqueline answers her own question. "And not just any old new car. He found another '57 Chevy! Can you believe it? He claims this one is in better condition than the other one. I said, 'That's not saying much, because the other one is a pile of ashes on Route 58.' He didn't laugh. Dad needs to work on his sense of humor. I got him a joke book for Christmas. Anyway, he believes classic cars are serious business." She lowers her voice in an impersonation of Dad. "'It's an investment, Jacqueline.' The car is light blue, where the other one was green. But otherwise, they're twins."

“What did *you* get for Christmas, Mom?” I ask.

“Pearls. I know they’re kind of old-fashioned. But you still can’t beat a nice string of pearls when you really want to look elegant.”

“Picked them out herself,” Jacqueline says, raising her eyebrows at me.

My stomach wants to reject the cookies and the pudding. This family isn’t the one I had before the accident. It can’t be.

“Shhh!” Jacqueline springs up from my bed. “Hear that?” She turns to Missouri. “Missouri, do you hear that?”

From down the hall comes a jazzed-up rendition of “It Came upon the Midnight Clear.” It gets closer and louder, with a chorus of voices holding the melody, and a clear, soulful, female voice taking the lead.

Jacqueline races to the door and waves. “Hey, Karissa! Cool!” In the doorway, Jacqueline sways and moves to the music.

“Who is it?” Mom demands.

Jacqueline turns around. “Karissa!”

“Who’s Karissa?” I ask Mom.

Mom shrugs.

Jacqueline steps back, and in come about a dozen people, all dressed up, smiling and laughing. They’ve stopped singing, but their voices still fill the room. They’re all African-American, and I’m guessing they’re from Missouri’s church. I figure that the slim pretty girl who stops by Jacqueline must be Karissa.

“Lordy, Lordy, Lordy!” Missouri exclaims. She holds her face in her hands and shakes her head.

Then I see Drew and Nurse Miller standing in the middle of the crowd. Mrs. Miller is wearing a red dress and has her hair down. "Merry Christmas, Sierra. Mrs. Reynolds. Hope I don't lose my job over this production."

The tall man beside her puts his arm over her shoulder. He looks like a football player. "How are you doing, Jack?" he asks my sister.

"No way! You're married to Nurse Miller?" Jacqueline sticks her hands in her overall pockets, then turns to Mom and me. "Mr. Miller is my social studies teacher!"

"I know." I haven't told my sister about this discovery.

"And mighty proud of it," he answers. "You staging any protests against the hospital or anything? 'Cause I'd like to know what I'm getting myself into."

"You will be the first to know," Jacqueline promises. "I'm thinking about breaking my sister out of this joint before she catches any deadly viruses. But no firm plans yet."

"Good to know," he quips.

A middle-aged man steps forward. He looks like a cross between a lawyer and a has-been basketball player. "Hello. I hope we're not interrupting anything." His voice sounds like quiet thunder. "I'm Reverend Joshua Brown of the Redeemer Church. This is my wife, Althea. Missouri is one of our oldest members." He smiles at her. "By that, I only mean you've been coming to our church longer than most, Missouri."

“Reverend, don’t you know by now you couldn’t offend me if you tried?” Missouri says.

He turns back to us. “When we heard Miss Missouri wasn’t up to coming to our church tonight, a number of us decided that we would come to her.”

“I thank you!” Missouri says. “Lordy, Lordy, thank you!”

“It wouldn’t be Christmas at the Redeemer without Missouri,” Mrs. Brown says. She and a couple of the other women walk over to Missouri’s bed and kiss her on the cheek.

“You must be Sierra.” Reverend Brown walks over and extends his hand. I shake it. “We feel as if we know you. Missouri has spoken of you so freely. You’ve been a godsend to her.”

I can’t think of anything to say. I want to know what she’s said about me.

“So are we singing, or what?” Drew asks.

His mother elbows him.

Jacqueline sits back on my bed, as if she’s getting ready for the concert. “This is so tight!”

I glance at Mom, who has a forced smile. She looks like she’s a second away from jumping out the window.

The reverend guy pulls out a Bible. It’s only half the size of Missouri’s, but it’s too much for my mom.

She grabs her coat and slips it on. “It’s very nice to meet you. All of you. So nice of you to come by on Christmas. I’m sure they . . . we . . . it’s greatly appreciated. I wish I could stay. But Sierra’s father is at home. Well, he’s probably on his way home.” She starts for the door. “Come on, Jacqueline.”

My sister doesn't move. "I want to hear this."

Mom smiles at her, then at the group. "We need to get home, honey."

"Thanks. I'm good." Jacqueline smiles back at Mom.

Christmas tension hangs in the air.

Karissa turns to a heavyset woman next to her. "Mom, what if we dropped Jack off on the way to church?" She smiles at my mom. "Would that be all right with you, Mrs. Reynolds?"

"Well . . . ," Mom starts.

Karissa's mother puts her hand on her daughter's shoulder. "It's no trouble, Mrs. Reynolds."

Mom turns to Jacqueline. "Is that what you want?"

"Cool."

"Well, thank you, Karissa."

Karissa introduces her mother. Mom thanks her too. Then she leaves, wishing us all a merry Christmas.

As soon as Mom's gone, Reverend Brown takes over. Instead of letting the choir sing, he says the usual Christmas things about the baby being born, and Jesus showing up in a place where nobody expected a king to be.

I feel a little tricked, since it's turning into a sermon. I'm thinking I might try to talk Missouri into letting this count as the Sunday morning I owe her. But I don't hold out much hope that she'll go for it.

The reverend hands his Bible to Drew, who reads the regular Christmas verses about Mary and the angel and the trip to Bethlehem and the wise men and shepherds. In a couple of places, a few of the women say, "Mmm-hmm." Or, "That's right." So it's a little uncomfortable, but not too bad. Mom couldn't have handled it.

Finally that part's over, and they start the Christmas carols. They sing without stopping for breath. They're good. Really good. In a different way from Baker Avenue choir. Our church choir is good, but in a rehearsed way, with tenor and alto coming in at the exact right moment. These singers make me sway, like Jacqueline. You can't help it. Their voices blend together and then break apart, harmonizing so that I forget they're singing without a piano.

Jacqueline's friend Karissa takes the lead on half the songs. She has an amazing voice. She could make it as a singer. Her notes wind and dive and soar on "Peace Like a River," Missouri's favorite hymn. The other voices paint a deep soft background for her melody. I watch Missouri, who listens with her eyes closed, her chin lifted, as if she's gazing through her closed eyelids to heaven.

They feel something. All of them. They *mean* the words.

As I listen, I can sway with the music. I can feel the soul. But not the words. They mean nothing to me. Maybe they never did.

It's not until the next morning that I see the card on my bedside table. It's a Christmas card. I open it, wondering if someone left it last night or this morning.

A slip of paper falls out. I pick it up. On one side are the letters *IOU*. On the other side is written: *English lit tutoring*. It's signed *Andrew and Grady*.

Nurse Miller rushes into the room with our morning meds.

"Mrs. Miller, did Drew leave this last night?" I ask.

"No. He asked *me* to leave it for you when I came into work this morning. Anything in it?"

"Tutoring lessons. It's a great gift. I'm afraid I'm going to need a lot of help. Tell him thanks, will you?" I stuff the paper in my gown pocket and spend the rest of the day wondering what it will be like when I go back to school.

I am supposed to be released the next day. But my temperature shoots up over 100 again. Dr. Snyder says I can't leave until my temp goes down or at least until they figure out why it went up. He orders another MRI and a sonogram, but both come back negative.

I'm disappointed, but I handle it. My mind is busy. When I'm not planning subtle and not-so-subtle ways of getting even, I replay events and conversations in my head. I've always done this, replayed things in my mind. Maybe that's why my memory has been so good. Only now, the scenes I'm replaying don't make me sentimental. They make me cold. And resolved.

■ ■ ■

Ryun doesn't stop by the week after Christmas. But he sends flowers. Kenzie calls, and I'm quick to let it slip that my boyfriend sent me beautiful flowers. I don't tell her that the card says, *Get well soon. Ryun.*

■ ■ ■

My temperature goes back to normal, and I'm finally released on New Year's Eve. Mom and Jacqueline are coming to pick me up because Dad had to go into the office for an emergency. Thanksgiving to New Year's is Dad's busiest season. He's always told us that.

While I'm waiting for Mom, I say good-bye to Missouri. I'm excited about going home, but it's hard to leave this woman. It almost frightens me, in a way, to be leaving her. "You be careful, Missouri," I say, taking her hand. Her fingers are so bony that I'm afraid they'll break. But she squeezes my hand harder than I squeeze hers.

"*You* take care, child," she says, her gaze boring through me. "You remember what we talked about. Don't forget you owe me a Sunday. And don't forget about Jesus."

Part of me will even miss Missouri's Jesus. "Yes, ma'am." I grin at her. "But I thought you said I *should* forget. 'Forgive and forget'?" We've gone back and forth like this so often that it hardly feels like a disagreement.

"Mmm-hmm," she says, my hymn-hummer again. "You just got to mind what you choose to forget and what you choose to remember."

She coughs hard. I still don't know what exactly is wrong with Missouri. Nobody has logged more time in this hospital than Missouri and I have. Her hip hasn't healed all the way yet. When I asked Nurse Miller how Missouri could stay in the hospital so long, she just said that the hospital was the best place for Missouri, and she had enough wrong with her to keep the insurance companies from complaining, since this wing of the hospital qualified as a rehab care unit.

I get her some water, and she finally stops coughing.

Mom enters the room with a flourish. "Sorry we're late. It's snowing. Traffic was terrible."

"*And* bad for you," Jacqueline adds, strolling in behind Mom. She's wearing horrible green rubber boots that I've never seen before and would like never to see again. I hope she didn't get them for Christmas.

"Did you know," Jacqueline says, as if we're all in the middle of a conversation, "that the surgeon general is going to put a warning sticker on the windshield of every car? Just like he did on cigarettes—and none too soon, if you ask me. So the sticker's going to warn us that car exhaust contains chemicals that give us heart attacks, asthma, cancer, bronchitis, anemia, immune-system disorders, and mood changes. Which is kind of a weird one to put in there. I think he should add a line about car exhaust being the number one source of carbon dioxide, which is the chief cause of global warming. But maybe that's just me."

Jacqueline walks over to Missouri and scoots onto her bed. "So, Missouri, maybe now you can get a cute guy as a roommate. You think? Although when Sierra's boyfriend, Ryun, was in here, they made him room with Mr. Reins down the hall."

Mom leaves to chew out the hospital administrators for not having our bill ready. Then she returns to the room to tell us all about it. "You'd think they could at least have everything in the computer, wouldn't you? How hard can that be?"

"Maybe they were too busy saving lives or something," Jacqueline suggests.

Mom sighs.

"So, Sis," Jacqueline says, gathering my few belongings into a plastic bag Nurse Miller gave her, "want to stop at Eden's Pond and go ice-skating on the way home?"

"Jacqueline!" Mom scolds, as if we're not supposed to let me know that I'm not able to ice-skate at the moment. "Don't start."

I grin at my sister, and she looks surprised. I know she's just being funny. Before the accident, I guess I automatically sided with my parents in Jacqueline disputes.

Before the accident.

I've been thinking of everything in those terms—B.A., "Before Accident," and A.A., "After Accident." It feels like the world split in two then. And B.A. keeps getting farther and farther away.

"What should I do with these flowers?" Jacqueline asks.

She's holding the purple-and-white bouquet from Ryun. I've already given Missouri the roses from Dad, my poinsettia, and the plant from the yearbook staff. Ryun's flowers are still beautiful—daisies, with little purple flowers. "Throw them away."

Jacqueline frowns over at me. Then she shrugs and chucks the flowers into the wastebasket.

Nurse Miller comes in with a silver wheelchair. "All aboard!"

"I don't need that thing," I object.

"Regulations," she answers.

I step into it. "Guess I know by now there's no arguing with Lady Smooth."

"You got that right!" Missouri agrees.

"Can I drive?" Jacqueline asks.

"After the tales my husband has told me about the infamous Jack?" Nurse Miller answers. "I think I better handle these wheels, if you don't mind."

"Good idea," I mumble.

"Come on," Jacqueline begs. "I promise to be a better driver than my sister."

"Jacqueline!" Mom says again, horror in her voice.

This time I don't smile. Not because of Jacqueline, but because, still, when I think about the deceit—the fact that my *friends* told everyone that I was driving—I get a physical reaction. My stomach burns. It's burning now as I picture Ryun behind the wheel and Kenzie next to him.

"Ready?" Nurse Miller is behind me, pushing the wheelchair.

"Ready," I answer. As we reach the door, I turn to take one last look at my roommate. "Bye, Missouri! I'll come back and visit, okay?"

"You better, child!" she shouts. "And don't you be forgetting. You owe me a Sunday!"

I'm wheeled past other rooms that look just like mine and Missouri's. Other nurses shout good-byes as we move down the hall to the elevators. We share an elevator with a man about Dad's age. He's on a stretcher, probably headed to OR. His nurse doesn't look as kind as my Lady Smooth. I hope he has a wife who's sticking by him.

The second I'm wheeled outside, a gust of wind slaps me and freezes my nose hairs. I want to drink it in. It's crisp and fresh. And I wonder if air always tasted this way. How could I not have noticed that, B.A.? I've never been a nature girl, like my sister. In fact, there's always been something sad about beautiful sunsets and fields of flowers if I see them alone. Like they didn't matter because Ryun wasn't with me.

"Are you warm enough?" Mom asks as we move toward the curb. She tucks in the blanket over my lap.

I nod.

A skinny, white-haired man drives Mom's Volvo to the curb and steps out. He's a volunteer valet. His name, Charles, is pinned to the lapel of his jacket.

Jacqueline runs up to him and shakes his hand. "I'm Jack," she says. "Thank you for bringing our car around, Mr. Charles. It's a nice thing you're doing. It's bad for older people to sit around the house after they retire. You'll live longer."

Charles grins at my sister. "I do believe you're right, young lady."

Nurse Miller helps me into the backseat, as if I'm 102, which is about what I feel like. "You call me or the doctor if that temperature goes up again, hear?" She leans in and hugs me. "You call me for no reason at all, if you feel like it."

"I will," I promise. "Thanks for everything . . . Lady Smooth."

Mom and Jacqueline get in the front.

Nurse Miller stands beside the car, holding the

back door open a minute. "Don't forget to come back and see Missouri. And me!"

"I won't," I promise.

She shuts the door and then waves at us as we drive away, until I can't see her any longer.

"Isn't it nice that you were able to get out for New Year's Eve?" Mom remarks as she turns the corner.

I let that sink in for a minute. I can remember every New Year's Eve. I know which friends I celebrated with. I remember every New Year's Eve date, each pair of shoes worn, every last party. I have pictures of all of them.

Not this year.

"Very cool," Jacqueline says. She turns in the seat to face me. "You're out just in time to make your New Year's resolutions."

I smile back at my sister. "It's good to be out," I say at last. "But I've already made my New Year's resolution."

Jacqueline's eyes narrow. "Yeah? Like what?"

"That's for me to know and you to find out." It's a stupid thing we used to say when we were little kids.

But it works. Jacqueline makes a face, then turns back around in her seat and leaves me alone.

I *have* made my New Year's resolution. One. Only one.

I am going to get even.

The short trip home from University Hospital takes more out of me than I thought it would. Mom and Jacqueline hover next to me as I walk in from the garage. I have to use the crutch Dr. Snyder sent with me. It's awkward. I can't imagine getting around the halls of High High with the thing.

There's one step from the garage into the kitchen. We stand back so Mom can unlock the door. The second she gets it unlocked, out jumps my Chihuahua.

"Paddywack!" I cry.

Little Paddy dances around my legs and scratches my ankles. He lunges at my calves with a force that almost topples me. I ease down to my knees, feeling a stab of pain in my hip and a tightening of my ribs. But I have to hold my dog. He leaps into my arms.

"You're a traitor!" Jacqueline declares.

Startled, I look up at her. For a second I think she knows. I think she knows everything I'm thinking of doing.

But she frowns down at Paddywack. "That little dog followed me around like a girl's best friend the whole time you were in the hospital. He even slept on my bed! Now look at him. What am I, Paddywack? Chopped liver? No. Chopped liver, you'd come to."

My dog won't stop licking me. I have to tilt my head so he can only reach my chin. "I love you too, Paddywack," I coo.

With the help of the doorframe and the edge of the kitchen counter, I manage to get to my feet again. My ribs ache and make it hard to take full breaths.

I glance through the open kitchen into our living room. I guess I expected it to have changed while I was gone. But it's the same. If they had a Christmas tree up, it's down now, although the mantel and dining table still hold a few Christmas decorations.

Our house is like most in our end of the suburbs—pricey because of location and because everything is so new out here. Dad makes sure we have "investment" art on our walls. The color scheme in the living room, beige with bright red accents, is taken from an original painting by Eduardo Sanchez, an up-and-coming artist. I don't think any of us actually likes the gigantic painting that fills one whole wall with geometric shapes in red and beige. But Dad says it will be worth millions one day.

We have no stairs, except a small drop-off that leads from the kitchen to the family room. My room is off the living room, with a bay window that faces front. Jacqueline's is down the hall on the other side of the bathroom we fight over. And Mom and Dad's bedroom is at the far end of the hall.

I let everybody else carry in my hospital stuff, while I sit on my bed and glance around this room that doesn't even feel like my room anymore. It's a B.A. room, filled with B.A. memories that seem to belong to another person. Two entire walls are covered with collages and framed photos of my friends and me. Opposite the bay window is an 8x10 of Ryun and me at our fall formal. I can't stop staring at this picture. I loved him. I know I did.

He has his arm around me. I'm staring up at him, starry-eyed. He's looking to the left of the camera, a half smile on his face.

Who's he looking at? What's he smiling about? Why couldn't I see this before? I am totally in love with him, and he's looking somewhere else?

My gaze takes in a collage of photos, all from overnights with my friends. Kenzie shows up in almost every picture. I'm the one who got her invited to those parties. At least at first I was.

In one corner I have class pictures from kindergarten through junior year. I look so happy, standing in almost the dead center of every photograph.

Mom comes in and sets down a pile of cards and letters on my dresser. "We've been saving your mail for you, Sierra. You don't have to open them all at once. Aunt Maureen and Uncle Tom sent flowers.

I have them on the dining table, but we can move them in here if you like."

"That's okay," I answer. I feel too tired to even open my mail.

Paddywack slides into my room—my bedroom has hardwood floors—and stands on his hind legs, scratching the side of the bedspread until I lift him up. He curls up into a ball on my lap. If he were a cat, he'd purr.

"You really do look tired, honey." Mom closes the blinds on the bay window. "Why don't you take a nap? I took the phone out of your room, so it won't wake you. Your dad will be home in time for dinner. I'll make stir-fry, your favorite."

"Thanks, Mom. A nap sounds pretty good."

As soon as she shuts the door, I get up, go to my desk, and pull out paper and pen. I'm too tired to sit at the computer. But I have a New Year's resolution to fulfill. And I can't wait any longer to get started. I'll write a draft longhand, because I know I won't be able to sleep until I at least put my plan into action.

I'm beginning with Ryun. He's the easiest. I know what he wants. And I know how to keep him from getting it. Ryun Lee loves soccer. That scholarship, his ticket to Duke, to soccer fame, means the world to him. He would do anything to keep that scholarship.

And I will do anything to take it away from him.

I sit back on the bed and think. It would be so easy to tell the truth in this letter. I could come right out and condemn Ryun. I could tell the scholarship committee that Ryun Lee is a coward, that he's letting me take the blame for an accident he caused. I could tell them he's a liar, that he told the police I was driving so he wouldn't get in trouble. So easy.

But I don't want it to be easy.

> *Scholarship Committee/Duke University,*
>
> *My name is Sierra Reynolds, and Ryun Lee is my boyfriend. I know you're considering him for a soccer scholarship. I'm writing to ask–no, beg–you to please let him keep his soccer scholarship, in spite of his injury. You see, the car accident that shattered Ryun's leg and caused his ACL tear was all my fault. I couldn't stand it if my carelessness ended his soccer dreams. The surgery will help. The doctors all say so. And knowing Ryun, I'm sure that his disability will inspire him to work harder than all your other players.*

I reread what I've written. It's good. I've learned deceit from the best. Who would have thought I had it in me? Not me. Certainly not Ryun.

But as I read it again, I realize I can't send it. I would love to. It's not that. I can picture the whole thing–the committee convening again, deciding to investigate. Ryun getting a visit from them. The look on his face when they tell him they're taking back the scholarship. It would all serve him right.

But I can't send the letter. I can't leave a paper

trail. Sooner or later even Ryun would figure it out. And I'm afraid it would be sooner. *Revenge is a dish that's best served cold.*

I crumple the paper into a wrinkled ball and toss it into the wastebasket under my desk.

I'll find a better way.

I guess I do fall asleep. I wake up to loud voices. It takes me a second to remember where I am. I glance across the room, expecting to see Missouri.

But I'm here in my own bed. Not in the hospital.

Paddywack is curled beside me. When I sit up, he wags his tail.

I walk to the door and crack it open to hear what's going on. They're in the living room—Dad, Mom, Jacqueline.

"I said *no!*" Dad shouts.

"It's not fair!" Jacqueline shouts back. "We're just going to the movies! It's New Year's Eve, in case you hadn't noticed."

"It's also the first night your sister is home," Dad says.

I make myself stand up straighter, even though it hurts every muscle in my body. Bev has drilled into me the fear of being a hunchback for the rest of my life. I shuffle out to the living room, with Paddywack tagging along behind.

"I did tell her she could go with her friends," Mom says.

"Well, I'm telling her she *can't!*" Dad snaps. "Not on her sister's first night back. Is it too much to ask you to give up one night for Sierra?"

"It's okay," I say.

They turn and look at me, as if I've caught them. Jacqueline's wearing a purple felt hat, turned up on one side. Dad still has his jacket on. His briefcase is on the floor by his feet.

Dad rushes over to me. "Sierra! Good to have you home, honey. Here, sit down." He guides me to the couch. It's hard, beige, modern, sort of like an upholstered church pew. It will be easy to get up from.

"I'll go get your medication," Mom says, rushing away to the kitchen.

"See?" Jacqueline demands. "Sierra doesn't care if I go out."

"*I* care!" Dad insists.

The doorbell rings.

Jacqueline crosses her arms and narrows her eyes at Dad.

"Get the door, Jacqueline," he says evenly, in his calm psychiatrist voice. "Make your apologies. And tell them to go away."

"Dad, it's really okay if–," I start.

Dad interrupts. "This is not about you, Sierra." I think he may be right. It's past being about anything, except winning the battle. He glares at my sister. "The door, Jacqueline."

The bell rings twice more, as my sister takes her time answering it. She talks with her friends for a couple of minutes, leaving the door open, another thing Dad hates.

I can feel the outside cold. The glimpses I get of her friends include lots of goth black clothing, pierced ears and noses—and hats. The tallest girl has burgundy hair that's not natural, like Jacqueline's, but is just as wild as hers.

Jacqueline slams the front door. Then she marches down the hall. I can hear her bedroom door slam. I think I feel the floor shake.

I watch the news with Dad. Every time the phone rings I wait to hear, "Sierra, it's for you!" I hear it only once. Carin calls to see if I'm coming back to school on the third. I tell her I doubt it.

But I *am* going back then. I'm just not letting anyone know. About the only thing I learned from Mr. Rausch's history class is that winners throughout history have known the art of the surprise attack.

Dad leaves for an emergency at about 10 o'clock. Mom and I try to stay up to see the ball drop in Times Square, but we're both too tired. We give up around 11 and say happy New Year, then go to bed.

The last few nights in the hospital, I dreamed about getting a great night's sleep in my own king-size bed, curled up on my feather bed, under a down comforter. But my first night in my own room, I can't sleep. I doze off, then wake to a *boom* in my head and a panic, as if the accident is happening all over again. I can't remember where I am. And when I do, I want to see Missouri.

About 1 a.m. I get out of bed. Paddywack follows me to the kitchen. The refrigerator hums, and I think of Missouri again, my hymn-humming roommate. I hope she's okay. A car moves up our street. Then it's quiet again as I drink a glass of orange juice. I miss the night music of the hospital.

On the way back to my room I glance down the hallway at Jacqueline's room. I'm not sure why I do it, but I go to her door and listen. I can't hear anything. I open the door a crack. I see her form on her bed, under her window. I tiptoe to the head of her bed and look down at her.

There's nothing but a pillow, turned the wrong way. I pull back the covers. Jacqueline isn't there. She's stuck pillows under the blankets to make it look like she's in bed, but she's gone.

I think about waking Mom and Dad. But then I imagine the scene. They'd both be more angry than worried. I'm not sure I want to start off the New Year like that. My sister is a free spirit, but she's more levelheaded than most kids her age, than most kids *my* age. She's already announced that drugs are always bad for you—and that includes alcohol—and sex is unhealthy unless you're married. Jacqueline is as immune to peer pressure as she is to parental pressure.

I head back to my room. When I hear a car

drive up and a door slam, I peek through my bay window. I see Jacqueline climb out of the backseat of a Toyota. I turn off my light and wait until I hear her in her bedroom. Then I follow her, easing the door open.

Jacqueline's just climbing into bed. "What are you doing?" she snaps.

I turn on her bedroom light and shut the door behind me. "Where have you been?" I know I sound like Mom or Dad. "You weren't in your bed."

She takes the offensive. "What were you doing in my room? You had no business coming in here, Sierra!"

I don't fall for it. "I mean it, Jacqueline. Where were you? We can call in Mom and Dad right now and let *them* ask you, if you'd rather." I score with this.

Jacqueline sits in her bed and tugs the covers up to her waist. "I went to the movies. We greeted the New Year. And I came home. Happy New Year."

"You can't just sneak out like that. What if something happened to you? Mom and Dad wouldn't even know where to go looking."

"What's the big deal? Even *you* said you didn't care if I went out."

"But *they* cared. And you can't just go sneaking–"

"I can't? Why not? Everyone else around here does." Jacqueline spits out these words. I've seen my sister angry before. But this is something else. Bitterness? I'm not sure what to call it.

"Don't get crazy, okay?" I'm not sure where

she's going with this. "Nobody's sneaking around, except you."

She laughs, but it's a dry harsh laugh. "I may be the little sister, but *you* are the young one. You never see anything."

"What are you talking about?" My stomach is heaving. I think I need to sit down, but I don't want to.

"Dad."

I feel like bolting from the room.

Jacqueline shakes her head at me. "Where do you think he goes all the time? There aren't that many crazy people in the world. I'll bet he had another *emergency* tonight. Did he? He did! I can see it in your face. If you want to talk about sneaking, go talk to Dad." She rolls over so her back is to me.

"Dad has patients who need him. He's an important man. You know that. He's not sneaking. He's–"

"Fine. Whatever you say, Sierra."

I don't want to have this conversation. I don't want these thoughts to be in her head. In mine.

"Well . . ." I try to focus, to get control. "This isn't about Dad. It's about *you*. Don't do that again–sneak out of the house."

She wheels around and pulls herself up to sit in bed again. "Then don't *you* sneak into my room again!"

Jacqueline throws back her covers and gets out of bed. She walks straight to her desk and pulls something out of her drawer. She turns and throws it at me, then climbs back into bed. "Guess my privacy isn't the only privacy invaded, huh?"

I reach down and pick up the ball she's thrown me. It's a wad of paper. I start to smooth it out and realize it's *my* paper. It's the paper I wadded up and threw in my wastebasket, the letter to the scholarship committee.

"Jacqueline!" I crumple the paper in my hand, turning it back into a ball. "What are you doing with this? How dare you rummage through my wastebasket!"

"Take it easy," she answers. "It wasn't in your wastebasket. It was on your floor. You're still a lousy shot."

"Don't try to be funny. This is serious. You'd better–"

"So why are you writing Ryun's scholarship committee?"

I have to think. Fast. "I'm not. That's why it was in the wastebasket."

"On the floor actually." She's cool now. Relaxed. Jacqueline at her best. "So, why *were* you writing that committee? They don't even know about

Ryun's injury, do they? I can't imagine Ryun telling them."

"That's what I decided." I stare at the paper ball, trying to think of what to say next. I've watched too many people lose the battle of wits to my sister. "I was just feeling so guilty, afraid Ryun might lose his scholarship to Duke because of me. So I thought if I wrote the committee and told them it was my fault, maybe it would help. You know?" I glance up at her. Her head's cocked to one side. She's listening. Judging. "If they knew Ryun and how hard he'll train to get his leg back to perfect condition, I don't think they'd worry."

"But they'd have to investigate, wouldn't they?" she asks.

I shrug. "That's what I started thinking. It would be pretty stupid to write that letter and start them wondering, especially if they don't even know about the accident." I smile at her. "So I trashed that idea. Or at least I tried to. Why were you in my room, anyway?"

"I wasn't spying or anything. I couldn't find my gloves. I'd dropped them into your hospital sack. You guys were still eating dessert by the TV. I just saw the paper on the floor and picked it up." She stares at me a minute, and I'm afraid she can see through me. "Are you going to tell them?"

"Who?"

"The Pope and Queen Elizabeth. Mom and Dad! Who do you think? Are you going to tell them I snuck out?"

I wait a few seconds before answering. "I won't tell, *if* you promise not to sneak out again, Jackie."

"Whoa! What did you call me?"

"I–"

"You called me 'Jackie'! I heard it. You have never called me anything but Jacqueline, not ever!"

"Did I?" But I can replay what I said. I called her "Jackie." I have no idea why it came out.

"You should get your head banged one more time," she says. "Then maybe you'd call me 'Jack.' I don't really like 'Jackie' much better than 'Jacqueline.' " She pronounces it "Ja-a-ah-que-line."

I can't help grinning. The kid could make a living as a comic.

"You know how you said you were sorry you didn't get me anything for Christmas?" she says.

"I will. Just give me a few days."

She shakes her head. "I want it now. Call me 'Jack.'"

"You're kidding, right? You want Mom and Dad to kill both of us?"

"You don't even have to do it around them. Go on. Try it. Call me 'Jack.'"

I sigh. "Why is it so important?"

She shrugs, but I can tell it matters to her.

"Okay. Here goes. Hi-jack."

"Very funny."

"Sorry." I try to be serious. "Merry Christmas, Jack. Happy New Year, Jack."

"Not bad." She rolls over in bed. "Now try, 'Good night, Jack.'"

■ ■ ■

New Year's morning, Drew calls. "Missing that hospital food yet?"

I ease myself down on the couch with the cordless, and Paddywack hops onto my lap. "I'll say. The food out here actually has smell. And taste. Very disturbing."

He laughs.

"Drew, are you sure you want to waste your time tutoring a semidropout?"

"I've tutored before. It's the best way to study for finals."

"So you're actually using me and my ignorance to help you study for finals?" I ask.

"That about sums it up."

"Good. Then it's a deal. Might as well wait until I get back to class and see how far behind I really am. Maybe Ms. Rowe will let me skip some of the long short stories?"

Drew laughs. "Wouldn't count on that one. Just let me know when you're ready. Will you be in school Tuesday?"

I'm not sure why it's harder to lie to Drew than it has been to lie to all of my girlfriends. "I don't know. Dr. Snyder said I should start out with half days. I'll probably do mornings. I don't have much in the afternoons anyway."

"Are you up to coming to church this morning? Missouri claims you owe her one."

I'd totally forgotten it was Sunday. I don't think I can face Missouri's church. "Not this time, Drew.

I won't go back on my bet though. I promise. Next week. Okay? I'll call Missouri and tell her. She'll forgive me, don't you think?"

"Missouri? She'd forgive you if you burned the church to the ground."

Mom and Dad get ready for Baker Avenue, second service. "You're sure you don't mind staying home alone?" Mom asks for the eighth time.

"Of course not. Go." I look around for other signs of life. "Is Jacqueline going?"

"Who knows what that girl is doing?" She checks the wall clock, then glances back toward her bedroom, where Dad is still getting dressed. In our house it's Mom who usually waits for Dad, instead of the other way around. "Jacqueline left over an hour ago, with that girl Karissa. If your sister is not back in time, we're leaving without her."

I have a feeling my little sister will not be back in time.

Mom and Dad return at high noon. On the dot. That's the best thing about Baker Avenue. The pastor never goes overtime. Jacqueline still isn't back.

"Everybody asked about you, honey," Dad says, stepping in from the garage.

"Did you drive your new car?" I tease.

"No. Do you want to take a look at it?"

I don't. "Sure," I say.

The car is covered with a canvas tent. Dad carefully folds it back. It takes minutes.

"Isn't it something?" He stares at the Chevy, then runs his finger over the white streak along the side.

I shudder. I see the other car, the green '57 Chevy. I'm slamming the driver's door and stomping to the side of the road. I feel the nausea. My anger and hurt choke me. I can see Ryun, coming over to me, insisting that he'll drive, that I should get in and quit acting like a child.

". . . guy had to sell it. So really, it's a good investment." Dad hasn't stopped talking about the car. *This* car. "What do you think?"

"It's great, Dad. I think I better go back inside."

It's midafternoon when Jacqueline strolls in, whistling. I think it's the same song Missouri used to hum, "Peace Like a River."

I meet her in the living room. Mom's in the bedroom, and Dad's gone. "Jacqueline, Mom and Dad are really–"

"Excuse me?" she interrupts. "Are you addressing *me?*"

I get it. "Sorry, *Jack.*"

She grins. "That's more like it." She eyes me, head to toe. I'm still in my robe. "You didn't go to church with them?"

"I slept in."

"You decide if you're going back to school yet?" she asks.

I think about telling her that I am. But she'd only wonder why Ryun wasn't coming to pick me up. "Hard to say. I'll see how I feel."

She takes up whistling where she left off and disappears into her room.

That evening I'm in my room when the doorbell rings. A minute later Mom opens my door. "It's Ryun!" she whispers.

In spite of myself, in spite of everything Ryun has done to me, all the lies and betrayal, I can't stop the fluttering inside my chest.

This is leftover B.A. emotion, I tell myself, as I walk out to the living room. Ryun is sitting on the couch, playing with Paddywack, who looks overjoyed to see him.

I take a deep breath and say, in my best B.A. voice, "Hi, Ryun! How are you?"

"I'm good. How are you?" He peels off a breath mint, sticks it in his mouth, and stuffs the roll back in his pocket.

I sit beside him. It's unsettling to have him this close. I can't help wondering why he's really here. How worried is he that I'll get my memory back?

Mom brings him a mug of Mexican hot chocolate, which she thinks he loves because he complimented her the first time she served it. Then she leaves us alone.

"You look better," Ryun says. He leans over and kisses my cheek. "That doesn't hurt or anything, does it?"

"Nope." I want to be in control of my emotions, but I'm not. "How was New Year's Eve?"

"Okay," he answers. "I meant to call you."

And you didn't because you were out celebrating

with Kenzie. "Just as well you didn't," I say. "I fell asleep really early."

"Well, I was thinking about you the whole time." He clears his throat.

If I don't keep talking, he could get suspicious. B.A., we used to talk for hours. "So, Ryun, tell me everything about that call from Duke. Wish I could have been there."

It's the right lead-in. Ryun launches into a blow by blow of the phone conversation.

"Johnny Moser," he begins. "You remember him from tournaments, right? Duke's assistant coach? He said I—"

As he talks, I react to everything he's saying—how Johnny Moser went to bat for him before the selection committee, how much they all want him at Duke. But in the corners of my brain, I'm trying to come up with a way to get that school to take back the scholarship.

We talk a little about classes.

"You want me to come by for you Tuesday?" Ryun asks.

This surprises me. But in Ryun's mind, we are still boyfriend and girlfriend. I forget that I'm not the only one pretending here. Of course he should pick me up for school, at least until I can drive myself again. But I'm not ready for that much pretense. Not quite yet.

"I doubt I'll make it the first day, Ryun."

"Yeah?"

When he says he needs to go, I walk him to the door.

“I wish you were coming back to school Tuesday,” he says.

I almost believe him.

He leans down and kisses me.

“Bye, Ryun,” I manage.

I watch him get into the car and drive away. My hands are shaking. And I know I have to be careful. I’m not as strong as I thought I was. I can’t spend as much time with Ryun as I used to. It’s not going to be easy to keep my boyfriend while I orchestrate his downfall.

After Ryun leaves, a loneliness sets in, sharp as pain.

I pick up the phone and dial Missouri. Her number is just one away from my old hospital number, so I know it by heart. I hear three rings before she picks up.

"Hello." Her voice makes me smile.

"Hi, roommate. Thought I'd better check and make sure you're not throwing a big party in my old room."

"Sierra! How are you, child? Lordy, it's good to hear your voice."

"I miss you, Missouri," I admit. "Are you feeling okay?"

"Sugar, I miss you too. And I'm feeling just fine. Got to church this morning too."

I feel a pang of guilt. "Sorry I didn't make it. Did Drew tell you? I'll come next Sunday. Okay?"

"Why, that would be wonderful. I'll hold you to it, child."

"And I'll come visit you really soon too. Drew is going to tutor me in English class. He said he'd take me to the hospital to see you."

"That would be so nice," she says. "Mmm-hmm, I'd like me a visit from my miracle child."

She's never called me that before. "Well, I don't feel much like a miracle," I admit.

There's a pause on the other end of the line. Then she asks, "Sugar, have you told anybody yet?"

I know right away what she's asking. "Nobody except my old roommate."

Mom comes out to the living room. "Did Ryun leave already?"

I nod at her, then tell Missouri, "I have to go. I'll call you tomorrow, okay?"

"Watch over my miracle child," she says. I know she's not saying it to me. It's a prayer.

■ ■ ■

Monday morning I call Missouri first thing. We have a long talk. I can hear the hospital noise in the background.

When we finish, I turn on the TV and watch cartoons, something I haven't done for ages. Then the Three Stooges marathon comes on, and I watch the whole thing.

The doorbell rings, and Mom answers it. I can tell by her voice it's not anybody she's expecting.

I click off the TV and turn around to see Sergeant McCarthy step inside.

Fear paralyzes me. Maybe they looked at the evidence again. Maybe he's here because he knows. Maybe he knows I have my memory back.

"Sierra?" Mom's leading him to me. "Look who's here."

"Hey, Sergeant McCarthy." I have to clear my throat. It's closing, like it did in the hospital.

"You're looking much better," he says. He grins and holds out a bouquet of flowers.

I'm thrown. I don't know what I expected. Handcuffs? Not flowers.

Jacqueline comes out of her room and bursts into the living room. She's wearing a headset, and the music's so loud, I can hear it. "Wow!" She pulls the headset off. Some rapper is shouting now. Probably something awful about killing policemen.

"Turn that off, Jacqueline," Mom says.

Jacqueline has already dialed it down. "Are those for me?" she asks McCarthy. She puts her hands on her hips. "Did Officer Williams send them for me? He's so shy. Couldn't bring them himself?"

"Jacqueline!" Mother scolds.

McCarthy laughs. "Sorry. Not this time." He hands the flowers to me. They smell like spring. "These are for you, Sierra. Glad you're feeling better. Happy New Year."

"Thanks. Really. I can't believe you came all the

way over here just for this." I hand the flowers to Mom, and she carries them to the kitchen.

Jacqueline's already on the phone.

"I don't live that far from you really. I'm on my way home. Thought I'd check up on you. You haven't gotten your memory back?"

I have to be careful. This is a policeman. Even the new A.A. Sierra doesn't feel like lying to a policeman. "Sometimes I hear this big *boom!* Yesterday morning it woke me up. I guess it's how it sounded when we crashed. I don't know."

"Well, you hang in there." He pulls out a card from his wallet. "I'll jot down my home number, in case you ever need me. I'm two blocks over on Walnut Drive." He writes his number on the back of the card and hands it to me.

I take it. "Thanks. And thanks for the flowers."

Mom walks Sergeant McCarthy to the door. The visit has taken so much out of me that I want to go straight to bed.

I wash my hair, which takes a lot less time than it used to. Then I set out what I plan to wear to school. I know Mom and Dad will try to talk me out of going, but I'll win.

It feels like that night before the first day of school—every first day of school—when I'm excited, scared, curious, and apprehensive, all rolled up into one. Ryun would pick me up if I asked him, but I won't. Still, I remember other mornings when he'd swing by for me. On Saturdays he'd take me to the mall. He wouldn't even complain when I wanted to look into every shoestore window or try on $500 shoes. I miss *that* Ryun.

B.A. Those days are gone.

■ ■ ■

Tuesday I wake early and get dressed with as much care as if I were running for homecoming queen. I choose a green sweater I bought last fall. I have to wear black pants that are now a size too big for me. My black BCBGs look perfect with the pants, though.

In the bathroom I take out my makeup. It seems weird that I haven't touched my makeup kit for over a month. But one look in the mirror, and I put everything back in the cabinet. My eyes are too swollen for eyeliner or mascara. And my puffy face is too red for base makeup. I don't need blush. That's for sure.

It's okay, I tell myself. *You want to be pitiful. You got it.*

Jacqueline flings open the bathroom door. "Hey! You're dressed."

"Jacqueline–"

"Jack," she corrects.

"*Jack,* didn't anybody ever teach you to knock?"

"Sierra, didn't anybody ever teach you to lock?"

I brush past her to the hall.

"Are you going to school?" she shouts after me.

"Yes!" I shout back.

I was right. Mom and Dad do put up a fight. I was right about my winning too. As a bargaining chip, I agree to let Mom drive me and pick me up.

And I'll only stay a half day. Dad ends up telling me how brave I am to go back to school already.

In the car I try to collect myself. But it's not easy. My hip hurts more than it has since I've been home. I try to brace myself for the expressions that are going to come as soon as kids see my face. I didn't have to go in this way, all alone. I could have called Carin and asked her to come by. Or Ryun.

But it's better this way. In the long run.

"Why didn't you wear your new boots, Sierra?" Mom asks, as if I've hurt her feelings for wearing non-Christmas-gift shoes.

"I still have a little swelling in my right ankle. These are comfortable. But I'd rather wear the boots."

"Trust me," Jacqueline adds. "Nobody will be looking at your feet."

"Jacqueline!" Mom gives me a reassuring smile. "Honey, you call me if you want to come home before noon. I'm going to the gym this morning, but I'll leave my cell on."

"I'll be okay. My last class before lunch gets out at 12:10. I'll just meet you in the parking lot."

Mom pulls into the lot, which is already full of seniors. But I'm the only senior driven to school by her mother.

Jacqueline hops out of the car and opens my door. She hands me my crutch. "Want me to walk in with you, One Foot?"

I take the crutch and pull myself out of the car.

A knife blade sticks into my hip, or that's what it feels like. "I'm good," I say, using one of her lines.

She grins. "Well, I'm just a parking lot away if you need me." Then she dashes off and joins a crowd of kids who could perform in the do-you-know-where-your-kids-are? public-service announcements. One has blue hair and a giant hoop in her nose.

It's cold, but the snow has melted. Mom gets out of the car and comes over, but I wave her off. "Thanks. I'll see you about 12:30. Bye." I know she's watching me. She's not the only one.

I hobble toward Highview High. The big brick building is a sprawling city, with a population of 2,000. Most of us come from suburbs, although a few, like Kenzie, live on the outskirts, where the houses are remodeled and people have gardens.

"Sierra!"

I've been staring at the sidewalk, so I won't put my crutch in a crack. I look up to see Alyssa. She's with three other girls, all of them on yearbook staff with me.

They jog toward me. I grip the crutch, as if it can keep me upright, in case they run over me.

"Oh, Sierra!" Alyssa's nose turns up. "I didn't think you'd be back yet! Your face! It's so—here, let me help. What can I do?"

"Your hair is so short," Stella, a sophomore, observes. "But you're skinny! Man, I wish I could lose that much weight."

They flank me on both sides until I make it inside the building.

"Thanks, guys." I'm out of breath. "Have you seen Ryun?"

Alyssa frowns. "Hey, why didn't Ryun come with you?"

"Is he here?" I ask.

"I saw him," Julie offers. She's a redheaded junior who works twice as hard on the yearbook as Alyssa does. She's wearing killer Doc Martens. "He and Kenzie were standing by the senior lockers."

"Really?" I'm just right—puzzled, not accusing.

"Why didn't Ryun pick you up?" Alyssa won't let it go.

"I—I'm not sure," I answer.

I catch kids giving me double takes as they rush by. Some of them slow down, stop. I am a traffic accident on the side of the highway.

"Come on. We'll find him." Alyssa takes my arm, and I let her.

We turn the corner and walk down the north hall. Ryun is standing in front of his locker, and Kenzie is leaning on the locker next to his—*my* locker.

If I had any doubts, any second thoughts about what I'm going to do to these two traitors, I don't have them now.

"There they are!" Alyssa shouts. "Ryun! Look who's here!"

Ryun turns and squints our way. Smiling, I wave my crutch.

"Sierra?" He moves to the center of the hall. Kids flow around him as if he's the river boulder. He starts toward us.

Kenzie waits a few seconds where she is, then walks after him.

We have an audience now. Kids back up, making way for Ryun and me as he walks closer and closer. I hold out my arms. The crutch slides to the floor. And he comes to me. We hug. I have to fight off the memory of how much Ryun's hugs used to mean to me B.A.–a lifetime ago.

"You came?" He picks up the crutch. "I thought you weren't."

I know Alyssa's listening. "Really? Well, here I am. It's okay. I'm just trying a half day. Mom's picking me up before lunch."

I take Ryun's hand and wait until Kenzie joins us. Then I interlock fingers with my boyfriend. "Hey, Kenzie! How did you get here?"

"I—uh—" Kenzie glances at Ryun, the way he looked to her in the hospital. "Ryun gave me a lift."

Out of the corner of my eye I see Stella and Alyssa exchange looks.

I turn to Ryun. "Thanks for taking good care of my friend."

The buzzer sounds.

"Kenzie, would you mind grabbing my notebook out of my locker?" I tuck the crutch under one arm. Then my boyfriend and I walk, hand in hand, straight past Kenzie.

Walking into my first-period class, leaning on Ryun, I can almost believe that nothing has changed. We sit in the same seats, next to each other. Kenzie trails in and takes the chair on the other side of mine.

But everything *has* changed. This class used to be warm and friendly. I felt safe here, surrounded by friends I trusted. Now, sitting between Kenzie and Ryun, the only thing I feel is betrayed. And the room is nothing more than a staging ground.

"Welcome back, Sierra!" Ms. Rowe smiles at me, without looking away. I have to hand it to her for that. I haven't always been her most attentive student.

"Thanks, Ms. Rowe. Good to be back."

A few of the kids murmur greetings, but nobody gets too close.

"Your hair looks great!" Carin whispers. She's in the seat behind me.

I look around until I spot Drew. He's wearing new Nikes and a Nike cap backward. "Hey, Drew!" I call. He feels like the only real thing in the room.

"'Bout time you make a school appearance," he says, grinning.

I ask about his mom and Missouri. We talk for a minute over Carin's head. She glances from one to the other, like she's watching a tennis match.

"Tutoring tonight?" Drew asks, as Ms. Rowe tries to quiet us.

"You're on."

"What's that about?" Ryun asks. If I didn't know better, I'd think he was jealous.

"Drew offered to catch me up in this class," I explain.

He shrugs.

I used to think I knew Ryun so well. But I don't know what he's thinking. Maybe I never did.

I try to listen to the discussion on a Raymond Carver short story, "What We Talk About When We Talk About Love," but my mind won't focus. Ryun is so close. The last time I sat in this chair, I believed that Ryun and I were in love.

Kenzie's doodling in her notebook. What's she feeling, having me sit this close to Ryun? I want to feel better because I'm making her feel worse. But I don't. She can't possibly feel worse than I do.

I should tell everything right now. Raise my hand and say that I've learned a lot about love the past month. And a lot about betrayal.

But I won't. Not yet.

The class ends. Chairs squeak as kids race out.

Ryun slips his backpack over his shoulder. "Need me to run interference to your next class?"

"That's okay." I turn to Kenzie. "Kenzie and I have econ."

Kenzie squirms in her chair, then stands up. "We better go."

I pass her my books and grab my crutch. I catch a longing look between Kenzie and Ryun, but it's nothing that would hold up in court.

We stay to the left as student masses rush through the halls. I force myself to talk naturally. "So, Kenzie, what have you been up to?"

"I've been spending a lot of time at Little Lambs."

"Yeah? Tell me about that."

Her face softens as she talks about the day care and the kids there. "There's this one kid, who's only seven. But he's catching on to the guitar so fast, like the music's already in him, waiting to come out."

I make the appropriate *mmms* and *ahs*. But I'm thinking that Little Lambs means a lot to Kenzie. She needs these kids to idolize her. They probably think she's wonderful. Maybe they trust her as much as I did.

And maybe I should do something about that.

We take our usual seats in econ. "Kenzie," I say, while the room fills, "I want to talk to you about Ryun."

Her eyes widen. But it's not fear. It looks more like hope. In that second I can tell how much she wants me to know about Ryun and her. She *wants* it out in the open.

"I'm going to need you to help me with Ryun, until I'm back to normal. I don't want him to miss out on any of his senior year, just because his girlfriend has to take it easy."

The sparkle fades from her eyes, and her shoulders sag. It's not the conversation she was hoping for. "Whatever," she finally answers.

For the rest of my morning classes, I'm so tired that I might as well have stayed home. The last hour before lunch is yearbook staff meeting. It's about all I can do to hobble in and sink into my chair at the big round table in the art room.

"You made it," Alyssa observes. She places a stack of layouts in front of me, then says, "Would you mind moving? Julie's been sitting there. She and I need to edit layouts."

I am where I always sit. "I'm too tired to move." If she wants my chair, she'll have to carry me out of it.

Alyssa stares at me a second. Then she lets it go. "Well, I guess Ryun seemed pretty happy to see you."

I nod.

"He is one in a million to stick by you like this. Not that you'd have to be one in a million to stay with you," she adds quickly. "It's just—well, you know how hung up on looks most guys are."

My stomach twists, and my hip throbs. So, good ol' Ryun gets yet more credit for sticking with his ugly girlfriend. I'm not sure how long I can keep this up.

"Sierra! Good to have you back." Mrs. Wilcox lumbers into the room and collapses into the chair next to me. She's wearing clogs and is dressed like a gypsy in an orange multilayered skirt and a white puffy-sleeved blouse, both designed to hide the fact that she weighs over 200 pounds. Her gray hair is streaked with white, and her lipstick is as red as ever. "We've missed you." She and I aren't buddies or anything, but I've always gotten along okay in her classes.

"I've missed you too. Thanks for the flowers. Sorry I let you guys down. How's the yearbook coming?"

"Right on schedule," she answers.

"That's great." But it doesn't feel great. I think I honestly believed that if I weren't there to hold things together, the whole yearbook would fall apart. "Did anybody get good pictures of the Christmas dance?"

She smiles and reaches behind her to the photo drawer. "Julie took these." She places a dozen snapshots in front of me. "We're running all of them."

I finger the pictures. They're good.

I want to go home. I don't want to be in the art room. I don't want to work on the yearbook. Two months ago, B.A., this yearbook committee was the second most important thing in my life, right behind Ryun Lee.

"Julie, bring over the rest of the layouts so Sierra can take a look," Ms. Wilcox calls.

Julie carries over several boards, set up with page layouts. She's angled the photos so they all lead to the center, where High High's insignia shows up in gold.

"Looks good," I admit.

I watch as they pass photos back and forth. I listen as they talk about events to cover, pictures to take. I don't contribute anything. I might as well be in another room, in another school.

And every time they talk over my head and I feel left out, I blame Kenzie. I blame Ryun. It's as if every hour shows me one more thing I've lost because of their betrayal.

Carin and I meet up in the hall, and she walks me to the door before lunch so I can wait on Mom.

"How was it being back?" Carin asks. "Were people nice to you?"

"Sure."

There's an awkward silence. I get the feeling she's dying to cut out to the lunchroom.

"Hey! Greg and I are going to the basketball game Friday night," she blurts out. "Maybe we can double with you and Ryun."

"Sure," I say, before I remember I'm just a pretend girlfriend.

"I'll have Greg work it out with Ryun," Carin says. She waves at Alyssa, who's motioning for her to come to the cafeteria.

"See you tomorrow," I say. And I make my way, alone, to the parking lot.

Mom pops out of the driver's door as soon as she sees me. Then she badgers me with questions all the way home.

As soon as I make it inside the house, I shed my crutch and go straight to my room, where I collapse on my bed.

I don't wake up until my sister storms in from school, slams the front door, and yells, "I'm starving!"

I crawl out of bed and realize that I'm starving too.

Jacqueline is already making herself a sandwich. "Want one?" she asks.

"Sure," I answer. I don't even care what she puts into it. I drop into a chair at the kitchen counter.

"I'm in a big fat rush," Jack says, smearing mayonnaise on bread. "We have to make at least 20 signs."

"What for?"

"Teflon." She slaps unidentified meat and cheese on the bread and hands me the sandwich on a paper towel. One less plate to load and unload from the dishwasher. "You should check. I'll bet the high school uses Teflon cookware too."

"So?"

"So, Teflon puts chemicals into the environment, chemicals that take centuries to break down. Who knows what the long-term effects will be? We might all spawn a generation of mutants with giant Teflon heads and no brains at all!" She takes a huge bite out of her sandwich. "A bunch of us are protesting *and* boycotting. No more cafeteria for me."

She pours us both a glass of milk and sets mine in front of me.

"Thanks, Jack," I say, almost too tired to lift the glass.

"Cool."

"What?"

"You called me Jack, like for real."

"We have a deal, right?" But it *is* the first time I've called her Jack without thinking.

About seven, Drew shows up, carrying a stack of books. He follows me to the dining room and sets down eight books on the mahogany table we use only for special occasions.

I eye the mound of books. "Am I that far behind?"

He laughs. "No. But we have a term paper, so I checked these out for you."

The front door opens, and Jack comes in with two of her friends. The friends have different hair colors—green and burnt orange—but they're dressed like twins in black pants, black shirts, big necklaces, and multiple earrings.

"Hi, Drew!" Jack calls, leading her friends through the living room.

"Hey, Jack!" he answers. "Heard about your Teflon protest."

"Good. Word must be getting around." She and her buddies thunder down the hall and into Jack's room.

"Your father must be a very patient man," I observe. I pull out my English notebook and catch Drew staring at the cover. I'm totally embarrassed.

All over the yellow notebook cover, I've scrawled: *Sierra Lee. Sierra and Ryun Lee. Mr. and Mrs. Ryun Lee.*

I flip back the cover and turn to a clean sheet. The B.A. Sierra was an idiot.

■ ■ ■

The next day at school, things go a little better. The crutch isn't so awkward. I don't feel quite so stiff. My hip hurts the whole day, but my ribs are better. After school, Drew comes for another tutoring session. Then we go visit Missouri at the hospital.

When we get there, we ride the elevator and step off on my floor. But it all feels like an old movie, something I saw a long time ago.

"You okay?" Drew asks.

Without realizing it, I've stopped in the middle of the hall and am leaning on my crutch. I walk on now. "Yeah. It's just weird seeing this place as a civilian."

"I've never been here as a patient," Drew says.

I hear Lady Smooth's voice as we come up the hall.

She squints. Then she comes running up the hall and throws her arms around me. "How are you, Sierra?"

"Hello to you too," Drew says, like he's left out.

His mom pulls off his cap and smacks his arm with it. "You didn't tell me you were coming by!"

"We miss you around here, Sierra," Mrs. Miller says. "Missouri's going to be so pleased to see you!"

She turns to Drew. "Glad you stopped by. I've got some boxes you can help move."

"Might have known," Drew says, following her past the nurses' station.

I make my way down the hall. It's funny. I was there so long, but I'm having trouble finding my room.

Then I hear her. She's humming.

I stop outside the room. It's the "Peace Like a River" song. I stand and listen, feeling more peace than I've felt since I left the hospital.

Finally I walk in. Missouri stops humming. When she smiles, it's like the sun coming up. I cross the room and hug her.

She hugs me back. A skeleton couldn't have less meat on its bones than she does. "Well, Lordy, Lordy, I thank you for bringing my girl back to me."

"I miss you," I whisper. Finally I let her go and sit on the bed. I glance across the tiny room at the empty bed, where so much happened to me. "No new roommate?"

"I've had two roommates. They just don't stay long," she answers. Missouri narrows those eyes at me and stares, as if she can see through to the other side. "You haven't told a soul, have you, sugar?"

I shake my head. "But it's okay."

"Mmm-hmm."

"I know," I say. "It's not how you'd handle things. But it's how I have to deal with this. Trust me. It's all working out."

"Hmm." Missouri takes my hand in both of her

bone-thin hands. "God loves you, Sierra. And he forgives you too."

I pull my hand away. "Forgives *me? I* wasn't the one driving. Remember?"

"I remember," she says, putting her hand on mine again. "But we all need forgiving. There's no peace, but with forgiveness."

"Hey, what are you two up to?" Drew asks, pulling over a chair and reaching for Missouri's old Bible.

For a while, the three of us talk and laugh about nothing.

"Guess what Jack's into today," I say.

"I can't imagine," Missouri admits.

"She's petitioning the school on behalf of the 'alphabetically challenged' students."

"The what?" Drew asks.

"My sister claims that she's alphabetically challenged," I explain. "I guess the *A*s got to go first one time too often."

Missouri laughs so hard her eyes water. "That child is a gift!" she declares.

"Now that's one movement I can get behind," Drew says.

"You're an *M*. You middle people have nothing to complain about," I insist.

"Not true," Drew explains. "Every now and then, a teacher will realize the plight of those end-alphabetically challenged, and they'll reverse the alphabet, let the *Z*s go first. That still leaves us middlers in the middle. We never get to go first."

We talk more about little things. Then Drew

opens the old Bible and reads a bunch of psalms to Missouri.

I don't pay much attention to the words. But I can't take my eyes off Missouri's face as Drew reads to her. She soaks up the words, like they're water and she's in the desert. I wish I'd brought my camera.

When it's time to go, I promise her I'll see her in church Sunday.

■ ■ ■

On Friday I don't feel well. I blame Bev, the Nazi physical therapist, who tortured me for 60 minutes Thursday afternoon. Mom takes my temp at 99 point something and goes ballistic. She calls Dr. Snyder, but he says it's nothing to worry about. Still, she doesn't want me to go to school.

I don't fight it. B.A., I couldn't stand to miss one single day of my senior year. Not anymore. It's getting harder and harder to act like Ryun's girlfriend. I see him only a few minutes in the morning, and I'm positive he doesn't have a clue that I'm acting. Kenzie and I are playing "keep away" from each other.

What's hard is the way I feel all the time. If I'm not burning with anger, I'm hurt. If I'm not hurt, I'm empty and lonely.

It also occurs to me that being sick will give me a good out for the basketball game. Carin has everything lined up for our double date. But I'm not sure I'm ready for an entire night as Ryun's girlfriend.

Ryun calls me after school and plays the caring thoughtful boyfriend.

"You can still come to the game though, right?" he asks.

I hear music in the background—hard rock, which he *never* plays with me. He's in his car, on his cell. "I better not."

"Shoot! Are you sure?" He's ticked off—not that I'm not going, but that maybe he can't.

"You go on, though," I say.

"Yeah? Are you sure? Because I could come by and keep you company or something."

I'm tempted to call his bluff. But I don't. "Seriously, I want you to go."

"Okay then. Well, take it easy." He sounds relieved. Jazzed. He hangs up so fast that I'm left holding the receiver, listening to the silence. It's like he can't wait to get me off the phone.

I recall other times I felt like this—something nagging in the back of my head, telling me there was more to Ryun than he let on. Like the time he canceled our trip to the mall because he said he had to take his sister somewhere. I was totally understanding, even though I'd waited all week to pick up new Skechers. But something inside was trying to tell me that Ryun didn't have to drive his sister anywhere. There was more to the story.

B.A., I could just talk myself out of those nagging thoughts with no effort at all. Now, A.A., I can't. And this time I do something about it. I dial Ryun's cell.

His voice mail clicks on, and I hang up. He's on the phone. He must have dialed the second we hung up.

It doesn't take a genius to figure out who he's talking to.

I dial Kenzie's number and get a busy signal. I'm right.

I wait 10 minutes and dial Kenzie's number again. They're still talking.

A cold anger builds inside of me. I dial again. And again, until Kenzie finally answers.

"Did you forget something?" she asks.

"Kenzie?" I say.

"Oh. Sorry. Sierra?" She fumbles the phone. "Uh . . . how are you? I mean, you weren't in class. Everything okay?"

"I'm okay. Needed a day off."

"That's good. So, you going to the game?" she asks.

She knows I'm not. I can tell. Ryun called her the second I got off the phone to share the good news. A part of me wants to change my mind, to say, "Yes. *I'm* going to the game with Ryun. Better change your little underhanded plans." But the other part of me, the part that's willing to wait, says, "No. I think I'll stay home and rest up. Want to join me? You could spend the night. We haven't had much time together lately."

"That sounds really good . . . but I was thinking I'd go to the game. Holly wants me to watch her cheer. Another time?"

"Okay. Say hi to everybody for me."

We hang up. And I know. She and Ryun will find a way to get together tonight. They think they can do whatever they want behind my back and get away with it.

That power returns. The power I felt in the hospital the day I decided not to tell anyone my memory was back. Things have changed for Ryun and Kenzie, and they don't know it. But *I* know. And before long, everybody else will too.

The minute I hang up with Kenzie, the phone rings.

It's Carin. "Good! You answered. Are you okay?"

"Just worn-out."

"Honestly," Carin says, "you should have heard the rumors flying around about you, just because you missed school! Everything from a heart attack to . . . well, anyway. Glad you're okay."

"I was going to call you. I can't make it to the game tonight."

"No fair!" she says. "We'll miss you guys."

"Ryun's still going."

"He is?"

"Yeah, I . . ." Then I get an idea. "I really feel

awful about backing out on Ryun. Will you and Greg keep an eye on him for me?" Maybe I can at least wreck Ryun's plans to hook up with Kenzie. It's not much, but it's something.

"Sure. Hey! Tell you what I'll do. I got a mobile camera phone for Christmas—you know, one that sends picture messages? My sister, Marla, got one too. You can use hers, and I'll send you live shots of Ryun at the game! Finally, something to use this phone for. So far, Marla just calls me to see if she's wearing the wrong shoes, which she usually is."

I smile to myself. This is great. Ryun and Kenzie will *have* to stay away from each other.

"Plus," Carin continues, "you can tune in Kelsey, Sarah, Megan—a bunch of us got camera cells for Christmas. Mick and Eric too."

"Appreciate this, Carin." I just wish I could tell her how much.

Carin and Greg stop over before the game. I open the door. Greg's twice as tall as Carin and twice as skinny. He's wearing black-soled Tigers with a brown belt. Embarrassing. Carin's wearing Sanibels, just about the only style Birkenstocks I'd personally wear.

"Great shoes, Carin," I say, backing up so they'll step inside. It's dark already and cold.

"We're in a hurry," Greg says to my feet. I'm used to it by now.

Carin digs into her bag and hands over the cell. "When it rings, push this. The image shows up here."

"Thanks. Next best thing to being there, right?" I smile bravely.

"You are such a sport!" Carin squeals. "Isn't she, Greg?"

"Yeah," he agrees. "We're going to be late."

After they leave, Jack comes out of her room. "Who was at the door?"

"Carin and Greg."

She comes up and takes the phone out of my hands. "Why did they give you a phone?"

It rings, and Jack almost drops it.

I laugh and take the phone. When I punch the button, a picture comes onto the screen.

"Can you see me?" Carin's voice is loud. The screen shows her chin and neck.

"Quit fooling around." This must come from Greg, although I can't see him. "I told you we'd be late. Now we'll have to sit on the visitors' side. I hate that."

Ryun and I always hated that too. I tried never to be late for our game dates.

The phone cam moves to show Greg, smoking, behind the wheel.

"Greg," Jack says. I'm not sure she's ever met Greg. "Can you read? Check the warning, albeit incomplete, on your pack of cigarettes. I won't try to talk you out of smoking because I figure anyone who's stupid enough to inhale smoke–in spite of research proving that cigarettes cause cancer, loss of bone mass, heart disease, ulcers, aneurysms, not to mention loss of teeth, hearing, and impotence–"

"Hey, who is this?" Greg whines.

"—is probably too stupid to quit anyway," Jack continues. "But you, Carin. Did you know that a woman exposed to secondary smoke may have trouble becoming pregnant? And if you do give birth, your baby may be underweight and suffer lung disease and asthma?"

"Pregnant?" Carin cries. "Who said I was pregnant? I am *not* pregnant!"

Jack groans and walks away.

"Sorry, guys," I say, trying not to laugh. "That was Jack, my little sister, the one leading the great Teflon protest at school."

"Hey, I saw those posters," Greg says, throwing his cigarette out the window. "What's the matter with her, anyway?"

"Have fun at the game," I say, changing the subject. "I'll leave the cell on."

Mom is off on one of her art gallery fund-raisers. Dad is out of town for the weekend. So somehow Jack and I end up watching a movie together. I can't remember the last time we watched anything together. It's a really old monster flick, so bad that we laugh nonstop.

Jack dashes to the kitchen to make popcorn when the phone rings, our real phone.

"I'll get it." I take the receiver back to my spot on the couch. "Hello?"

"Sierra, how *are* you?"

"Okay. Alyssa? Why aren't you at the game?" I can count on one hand the number of times Alyssa has phoned me.

"I *am* at the game! But I just had to call and see if you're all right."

"Yeah. Thanks." I remember what Carin said about rumors going around at school. Maybe Alyssa bought into one. "I had a tiny fever. I think I was just tired."

"I mean now. Tonight." Alyssa's voice turns patronizing. "How are you, really?"

"I'm fine. What's going on?"

"Hasn't Carin called you? She said you had her sister's phone. I just figured . . ."

"What are you talking about?"

"She hasn't! Sierra, I'm sorry. Uh–nothing." I hear someone besides Alyssa in the background. "I shouldn't have called you. I'm . . . I'm sorry."

"Wait a minute–"

But she's already hung up.

"That was weird," I say, when Jack brings over a bowl of popcorn.

The phone rings again. I start to get up to answer it.

"Carin's phone," Jack says.

I grab it and punch the button. "Hello?"

"Sierra?" says a soft voice. There's a roar in the background, crowd noise.

"Who's this?"

"Uh . . . it's Megan. I just . . . I mean . . . I thought maybe Carin . . ."

"Megan, will you tell me what's happening?"

"You haven't talked to Carin? Call Carin, Sierra. And you didn't hear it from me." She hangs up.

"Megan who?" Jack asks.

I stare at the stupid phone. "Okay. That's it. I'm calling Carin. Something weird is going on."

It takes a couple of tries, but eventually I discover the address book and find the number to Carin's cell. I dial, but the line's busy. I keep redialing until it rings through.

"Hello. Eric, is that you?" It's Carin's voice. "Did you get the text message?"

"No. It's me. Sierra. What's going on?"

"Sierra!"

"Carin, I'm getting calls from everybody. What's going on?"

In the background, I hear Greg. "Are you going to watch the game or talk on that phone all night?"

"Carin?" I shout.

"Oh, Sierra. I don't know if you want to see this."

"See what?" I demand.

"Just a minute."

I wait, and a picture comes onto the screen. It's faint, but I can tell it's the Highview gym, packed to the rafters.

"Honest, Sierra, I was just trying to get a picture of your boyfriend for you."

Jack comes back and stares at the screen with me.

I'm getting nervous now. Everybody knows something I don't know. I don't like not knowing.

"Okay. Here I go," Carin says. The picture bounces around.

"Don't go over there again," Greg pleads behind her.

"Are you with me, Sierra? We're in the visitors'

section because we got here late." The picture jostles. "Oops–sorry."

Somebody swears as the phone cam moves through the bleachers.

"Okay. Now. Look."

The picture quits bouncing, and I see Ryun on the screen. He's off in the corner, the far side of the visitors' section. He's a head above the other spectators. Then I see Kenzie sitting next to him, smiling up at him, as if they were the only two people in the gym.

My heart's racing. I can't pull my thoughts together. Other pictures flood my mind–Ryun and me at games, sitting close, sneaking a kiss, holding hands. I never cared about the games, only being there with Ryun.

"So . . . so they're sitting together," I say. I try to get the old Sierra back. She wouldn't be this upset, wouldn't feel like I'm feeling. "They're friends."

Jack is frowning at the screen. "Friends?"

Carin moves closer. The closer she gets, the worse it looks. The worse it feels. There's something between Ryun and Kenzie, in the way they gaze at each other. And then I can see from above . . . they're holding hands. They're leaning into each other, the way Ryun and I used to when we were just about to kiss.

"Have you seen enough?" Carin asks.

"I have to go," I say, my chest burning and my eyes watering. "I'll talk to you tomorrow."

I shut off the phone and let it drop to the couch.

"I can't believe those yahoos!" Jack exclaims.

“You want me to go over there right now? I could knock both of them off that bleacher and—”

“That’s enough, Jack. I’ve got to think.”

“What’s there to think about?” she asks.

But I’m halfway to my room now. I manage to run the rest of the way. Then I throw myself onto my bed. My hip hurts when I land.

But I don’t cry. I refuse to cry. That would be too easy.

They’ll get what’s coming to them. And they have no idea what’s coming. They’ll get what they deserve. I have to hold on to that.

Saturday, the phone never stops ringing. Carin must have sent picture mail, text message, or e-mail to the whole school.

I won't come to the phone for any of the calls. Jack serves as my go-between. I hear her quizzing the callers. Now and then she reports back with some new bit of information. Someone saw Ryun and Kenzie leave separately. Someone else spotted them in the parking lot. Kenzie got into Ryun's car.

It takes me until Saturday afternoon to get control of my feelings. None of this should have come as a surprise. I knew they were seeing each other behind my back. I will not be a victim. Not again.

I have to turn everything around and use it to my advantage. Jack says everybody who calls is up in arms. I should be feeling great about that. It's at least a taste of revenge. But I don't feel great. I don't want the truth to come out–any of it–until I'm ready. It has to be in *my* timing. Not theirs.

About four o'clock, Ryun phones. Mom carries the phone to my bedroom because I still haven't plugged my phone back in. I'm not sure why.

"I don't want to talk to him, Mom." I'm pretending to read on my bed.

Mom has no idea what's going on. All she knows is that polite, well-dressed Ryun still wants to talk to her scarred, damaged daughter. Mom is grateful. She holds the phone to her chest. "Sierra, you can't just refuse to talk to him!"

I glance at her over my book, then continue reading.

She sighs. Then *she* talks to him. "Ryun, I'm sorry. Sierra can't come to the phone right now. Could I give her a message?" She pauses, listens. "Well, that would be wonderful. I'm sure she'd like that."

I shake my head. *I'm* sure, whatever it is, I would *not* like that.

Mom ignores me. "I'll tell her. That's fine then. Thanks for calling." She presses the phone off. "Ryun says he'll drive you to school next week."

She has no right to set this up without me. *They* have no right. What's Ryun thinking? Kids have to be calling him too. Does he think they won't call *me?* That I'm too stupid to know what went on at the game? How dare he assume he can just come by like old times?

Mom keeps talking. "He'll be by for you a little before eight on Monday. And he really wants you to call him back, honey." She sighs pointedly, then leaves, closing my bedroom door behind her.

I think about calling Ryun right then and telling him that I'm on to him. He's not fooling me, not anymore.

But that's exactly what Kenzie wants me to do. And it's not time yet. It's not *my* time yet.

The phone rings. A few seconds later someone taps on my door.

Jack walks in with the phone. "It's Matt Somebody. Isn't he the blond guy who's wanted to go out with you since eighth grade?" My sister hasn't bothered to put the phone to her chest, like Mom did. "Want me to tell him you're asleep?"

I start to say yes. Then I stop. I stare at the phone in Jack's hand. And I make my decision. In that instant I know what I have to do.

A calm comes over me. Finally I feel like I'm taking back control. I've been letting Ryun and Kenzie get to me. Again. But A.A. Sierra is back in control now.

"I'll talk to Matt," I say quietly.

"You will?" Jack's surprised, but she shrugs and hands over the phone.

"Matt?" My voice is calm, friendly. I don't even shoo Jack out of the room. "What a surprise. How are you?"

"Hey, Sierra." Poor Matt sounds nervous. "Was that your sister? She sure hates Teflon."

I laugh. "What can I do for you, Matt?"

"I–uh–Tyler–he e-mailed me a picture, like from the game. He got it from Julie."

"Are you talking about that picture of Ryun and Kenzie?" I laugh again.

Jack frowns at me.

"Well, yeah," Matt stammers. "I thought–"

"Isn't that crazy, Matt?" I interrupt. "The way rumors get started? Gossip spreads so fast at High High. It's unbelievable. I must have gotten a dozen calls last night about this."

"You're not–upset?" Matt asks.

"That my friend and my boyfriend watched a basketball game together? Don't be crazy."

"But–"

"I know, Matt. And I appreciate your call. Really. See you Monday." I hang up.

"Are you nuts?" Jack asks when I'm off the phone.

"What do you mean?" I toss her the receiver.

She catches it. "Ryun? And Kenzie?"

"Not you too," I say. But I can't look at her. "I admit, I was thrown at first. But it's no big deal. Forget it, Jack."

She's quiet for a minute, studying me. Then she shakes her head. "Like mother, like daughter. I thought you'd changed."

It's almost dinnertime when the doorbell rings.

"It's for you, Sierra!" Mom calls.

I stick my head out of my room and see that it's Carin. "Come on back!" I shout.

Carin steps into my room as if *she's* the one who

was caught with my boyfriend. "Sierra, are you mad at me?"

I give her back Marla's camera phone and motion for her to sit beside me. "Mad? Of course not. I was a little peeved at first. You almost had *me* believing something was going on between Ryun and Kenzie."

"Almost?" she repeats.

"You gave Highview the juiciest piece of gossip it's had in a while. I've never gotten so many phone calls. But it's okay."

"It is?"

"Sure. You didn't mean anything."

Carin tucks her legs under her and sits on them. "Wait a minute. Aren't you mad at Ryun and Kenzie?"

"Why? They didn't *do* anything." Saying this takes something out of me, and I have to pick up a pen from my desk, so I can look at it and not at Carin. "They watched the game together. No big deal."

"I'm not getting this. They were–"

"I saw what you saw, Carin."

"Well if I were you, I'd–"

"You're not me. Maybe you've never been in love."

"Have you talked to him?" she asks.

I shake my head. "We love each other. We trust each other. That's all there is to it."

"Wow. I don't know if I could take this like you are." She sounds as if she admires me. She is the exact opposite of Jack. "I mean, Ryun and Kenzie were for sure holding hands. You saw that."

I smile at her, as if I'm the wisest woman in the world. "I don't know how well you know Kenzie. She's got a lot of problems."

"She does?"

I nod, as if she's dragging this out of me. "I don't want this to go beyond the room, okay?"

Carin nods, eager now.

"Kenzie has a drinking problem. Maybe drugs. I don't know. She doesn't talk to me anymore. But she's needy, Carin. And you know what a soft heart Ryun has."

"Kenzie?" Carin's eyes widen. "I didn't know."

"She's always emotional about one thing or the other. I'm sure Ryun was just being nice."

"You think so?" She's weakening. "Because it didn't look—"

"Carin, you really should pay attention to Kenzie. Doesn't she work for that day care at your church, Little Lambs?" I bite my bottom lip. My heart's pounding. This is what I've wanted to do, to say. It's not a total lie. Kenzie drinks sometimes at parties. We all do. For all I know, she might do drugs too. I remember once, when we talked about pot, she said she'd probably try it sometime, just to see.

Still, I feel my face flush. I'm on the verge of nausea.

"Yeah. Why?" She gasps. "You mean you don't think she should work at the Center?"

"I'm not saying that."

"Man, Sierra! My mom is on the advisory board!"

This is no surprise to me. It's what I've been

counting on. "Listen, I don't want to get Kenzie in trouble. But it doesn't feel right to keep quiet about her, not when she's around those little kids so much. It's not like she'd hurt them on purpose or anything. She's probably fine there, as long as they don't leave her alone with the kids. You just shouldn't count on her. You don't know when she's going to be high or tipsy or off on one of her emotional jags."

"Whoa. My mom will absolutely die! I didn't know any of this. But I don't hang out with Kenzie much either."

"Anyway, I feel better not keeping it in." But that's a lie. Like everything else. I don't feel better. "Thanks, Carin."

"For what?"

"For understanding. About Kenzie. And about Ryun. Seriously, don't worry about Ryun and me. No matter what Kenzie was trying to do, Ryun was just being Ryun." That part's true enough. "If I'd been there, Kenzie probably would have grabbed on to me. It's just Kenzie's way. So, can we end it here?"

"Absolutely." Carin gets up and hugs me before leaving.

As I watch her trot to her car, I have no doubt that before she drives home, she'll have half of High High on the phone.

Sunday morning I call Drew and cancel out of church. I really did mean to go this time. But the thought of facing kids from my school there makes me back out.

"Tell Missouri I'm sorry," I tell Drew, after using my weekend fever as an excuse. "And not to give up on me. I'll keep my bargain."

■ ■ ■

Monday morning, I'm nervous waiting for Ryun to pick me up. Jack and Mom leave for school. Dad's already left for work. I practice what I'll say to Ryun about Friday night.

When he pulls into the driveway, I limp out to the car—my first day without the crutch. When I get in, I ask, "Have a good weekend?"

"What?" He glances at me, then backs down the drive. "Yeah, I guess." I catch him sneaking peeks at me.

Seeing Ryun nervous makes me calm. *He's* the one who has something to worry about. I'm not about to make this easy for him.

"I'm starting to get caught up in classes," I say. "Lots of time to study this weekend."

"Uh-huh." He reaches for the roll of mints he keeps in his glove compartment. He pops two of them and offers the roll to me, but I put it back in the glove box.

Ryun listens as I chatter. He answers my questions. But the whole drive to school, he doesn't mention Friday night or Kenzie or the "rumors."

He has to know that I've talked to people, that Carin's talked to me. Does he think I'm an idiot, that he's invisible? Invincible?

In the parking lot, he comes around to open my door. The perfect gentleman. I have to lean on him so I won't slip on the way in.

We walk past Dave and Chad, guys I've known since grade school.

"Hey, Sierra!" Dave calls, ignoring Ryun.

I like this, that even the guys are on my side.

"Hi, Dave!" I call back. "Hey, Chad."

Kids stare at us. They whisper.

I wonder if Kenzie's getting snubbed like Ryun is. I wish I could see it.

Megan storms up to us. "Shame on you, Ryun!" She puts a hand on my shoulder. "Are you okay, Sierra? Do you want *me* to carry your books?"

“I’m fine, Megan. Thanks.”

“Well, I can’t pretend,” she says, glaring at Ryun. “I think it’s terrible what Ryun and Kenzie did to you.”

Ryun runs his fingers through his hair and shifts his weight.

“Megan,” I say evenly, “if you’re talking about the gossip from Friday night and those silly pictures Carin sent to everybody, forget about it.”

Ryun stares down at me as if I’ve just landed a spaceship.

Megan’s mouth drops open. “Forget it?”

“I already talked to Carin. Kenzie and Ryun are friends. They sat together at the game. Big deal. I’m glad Ryun didn’t have to watch the game by himself. Everybody around here should get a life. It’s high-tech gossip. Right, Ryun?” I smile up at him.

“Right!” He grins like he’s won the lottery. In that minute, seeing him glow with the belief that he’s gotten away with one more thing, I think I hate him.

In English, nobody speaks to Ryun. Kenzie walks in as the bell rings. She stares straight ahead, avoiding the glares and whispers.

When she sits down, I turn to her, smiling. “Hey, Kenzie. Did you take notes in here on Friday? Maybe I can get them from you?”

She looks up, puzzled. “Um . . . yeah. I guess.”

“Great. Sorry I had to miss the game with you guys on Friday. Sounds like it was a good one.”

Her head jerks up and she stares at me, her forehead wrinkled. “Yeah.”

I give the same story all day long. High-tech gossip. Ryun and Kenzie are just friends. It's all a big misunderstanding. A few kids buy it. But I can tell that most people don't. And that's just fine with me.

■ ■ ■

The next two weeks fly by. Ryun takes me to school every day and drops me off at home. We manage to exchange small talk. Sometimes I wonder if Ryun sees any difference in the way we are now and the way we used to be, B.A. I am still a convenient, low-maintenance girlfriend.

Drew tutors me on Mondays and Wednesdays. Nazi Bev tortures me on Tuesdays and Thursdays. After I see Bev, I always stop by Missouri's room. I can stay only a few minutes, but those visits feel like coming out of the cave for fresh air. To each visit, I bring a different excuse for why I wasn't in church on Sunday. And Missouri accepts every excuse with a warm smile and, "I'll see you next Sunday, sugar."

Sometimes when I'm with Ryun, I watch him. I feel like a scientist, observing some new species. I notice things I never noticed before, B.A. Like the way he checks his watch when we're together, as if he's got other more important places to be.

Once, when Carin and I are at the mall, we see Ryun with a bunch of older guys. Men, really. I recognize two of them from the adult soccer league Ryun used to play for. I watch him, knowing I've caught him in a lie. He told me he had to work after school, but here he is.

"Let's go say hi," Carin suggests, starting for them.

I grab her arm. "No." I force myself to smile. "Let's follow him."

"Seriously?" Carin and Greg have been fighting, and I think she wouldn't mind meeting some new guys.

"Come on, Carin. Haven't you ever wondered what guys do when they're not with us? Who knows what kind of education we could get! Look! Ryun's leaving."

He heads toward the outside door with two of the men.

I wait until they're almost out, then hurry to the door and watch them get into a red car. "Come on!"

Carin runs to her car, which is in the second row. I get there as fast as I can. Carin's laughing now and into the spy act. She fumbles the key, then gets inside and opens my door.

"Go, Carin!" I cry. "Follow that car!"

Carin takes off so fast, her tires squeal. But she doesn't lose the red car, which stays two or three cars ahead of us.

"You think Ryun sees us?" she asks.

"No way," I answer. "We're too slick."

We follow them to the edge of the city. Half the houses are boarded up. We pass adult bookshops, bars, a strip joint.

"This is getting weird," Carin observes.

The red car turns the corner and pulls up in front

of a bar. A big sign says *CROW BAR,* and poorly painted black crows dot the run-down building.

"Back up around the corner so they won't see us," I command.

Carin does it. "This is pretty sleazy. Now what?"

I don't answer. My perfect-gentleman Ryun, the "Oh-I-would-never-drink! Alcohol-and-athletics-don't-mix" Ryun, seems pretty at home in this dive. I memorize the name of the bar and the intersection, 89th and Lincoln.

"Don't tell anybody about this, Carin. Promise?"

"Okay."

I sit back in the seat and can't help but grin. I feel like I've been given one more weapon. I'm just not sure yet how I'll use it.

But I will.

By February, my plan is rolling forward. I get the okay from Dr. Snyder to drive again. And my first driving mission is to follow Ryun after he drops me off from school. I waste hours in the car, but I catch him going back to that same bar twice, after he's told me he was going to work.

Things at home aren't great. I'm not sure what's changed, unless it's just that *I've* changed. Mom seems so sad all the time. Dad's almost never home. We never talk, not like we used to. Jack and I don't see much of each other either. She's busy protesting with her friends. And every time we are together, she gets in her digs about Ryun walking all over me.

My hip is almost healed now. My face is back

to normal, except for a tiny scar that's hidden by my bangs. I'm *cute* again.

But I don't feel cute. The betrayal still feels fresh. I've replayed those memories over and over. Sometimes I wake up in the middle of the night in a cold sweat.

I'm tired of pretending. Being with Ryun sucks the life out of me. Sometimes he's so nice to me, I find myself almost believing that he cares. Then I do a reality check. It's too hard to go on like this.

So I set Valentine's Day as my personal V-day. I know that I can't keep playing this game with Ryun any longer than that. Valentine's Day is the perfect time for me to get rid of my boyfriend.

A week before V-day we make plans for a romantic dinner at The Lantern, where we had our first dinner together. All week I spread the word that good ol' Ryun and I are planning a romantic dinner on Valentine's Day.

Only I'm planning to stand him up. Ryun has humiliated me for months, dating Kenzie behind my back. Now it's time for him to get a taste of his own medicine. It won't be enough. It won't begin to pay him back for lying to the police about the accident. But it will at least be a start.

The day before Valentine's Ryun is distracted. I might not have noticed it B.A., but he acts weird the whole drive in to school. I'm afraid he's going to break up with me—before I can break up with him. It would be just my luck. And just his. Ryun Lee always comes out on top. I think about breaking up with him as we walk into school, sacrificing my plan to stand him up in front of everybody.

But when I see him looking down every hall, I change my mind. He's not thinking about breaking up with me. He's not thinking about *me*. He's searching for somebody.

It doesn't take much to figure out who he's looking for.

Kenzie.

We see her at the same time, I think. Ryun stands up straighter and waves her over.

Kenzie slows down, then keeps walking to her locker, which is across from ours.

"Kenzie?" Ryun calls.

She takes out a book, then closes her locker. It's a second before she turns around. When she does, I see that her eyes are red. She glances up at Ryun, and her eyes fill with tears. Then she ducks her head and jogs down the hall toward English class.

A part of me wants to run after her. I'm a split hair away from calling to her. We were friends once. In another lifetime. But I don't want to feel. I don't want to feel anything.

Kenzie doesn't say a word during class. And as soon as it's over, she dashes out of the room. Ryun gets up and leaves without saying anything to me.

I turn around and catch Carin before she heads out. "What's up with Kenzie? She seemed really upset."

Carin leans in as if to make sure nobody hears us. "Mom went to the church board and told them . . . you know, the stuff about Kenzie. Nobody did anything for a while, especially since Kenzie's mom is the director of the Center. But now that the church is having this big overnight thing, the weekend after Valentine's Day, the board decided they had to investigate. I mean, what if something happened with one of those little kids?"

I don't know what to say, so I don't say anything.

Carin shakes her head. "It got really ugly. Kenzie's mom threw a fit. The board decided that Kenzie couldn't work at Little Lambs until everything is cleared up. So yesterday afternoon they told Mrs. Parker that Kenzie couldn't come for the Valentine's Day thing."

I tell myself that this is all good news. This is what I wanted. Kenzie can't be trusted. She should never have worked at that center. But I keep seeing Kenzie's red eyes. I think about the kid who liked to play the guitar.

What's the matter with me?

"I better get to class," I say, rushing out, dropping my book. I hustle out of the classroom and bump into somebody.

"Slow down, man." It's Drew. "You want to dislocate your other hip?"

I glance up at him, then look away.

"You okay, Sierra?"

But I see Missouri when I see Drew. I can just imagine what she'd think of me if she knew. If she knew what I'd done.

I will not feel guilty. Kenzie deserves everything I can do to her. And more. Those kids are better off without her. They are. She's a liar. And a traitor.

I race to my locker. Drew's shouting something at me, but I don't turn around.

I round the corner just in time to see Ryun and Kenzie at the lockers. He has his hands on her shoulders. Her back's to me. Their bodies are close. Ryun is so intent talking to her that he doesn't see me. There's something strong between them. Whatever it is, it puts them on the inside, and the rest of the world–including me–on the outside.

I watch them. I am not breathing.

Kenzie pulls away from him and jogs down the hall.

Ryun stares after her.

I have never seen him like this. He has never been this concerned about me, not even when I was in the hospital. Not even when *he* put me in the hospital. Kenzie's just lost a stupid job, and he's this upset? *I* almost lost my life!

On Valentine's Day, Ryun says he has to work before our big dinner. Right.

We make plans to meet at The Lantern at seven.

At lunch Carin can't stop talking. She and I have been eating with Mick, Alyssa's old boyfriend, and a couple of his buddies. Mick and Carin have gone out twice since the big Greg breakup.

"I think it's so romantic that you and Ryun are going back to The Lantern for Valentine's dinner," Carin says. She elbows Mick. "Don't you, Mick?"

"Don't I what?" he asks.

"Don't you think it's romantic that Ryun's taking Sierra to The Lantern tonight to celebrate Valentine's?" she repeats.

"Sure. Cool restaurant," he agrees.

I know of three other couples who will be having Valentine's dinner at The Lantern. They'll have ring-side seats when I stand up Ryun. But it wouldn't hurt to have Carin there too. She'd probably capture the whole thing on her picture cell.

"You know," I say, bumping knees with Carin, "you guys should have dinner there too. It's a really good special, half-price, if you take the Valentine's dinner."

Carin gives me a secret, wide-eyed look. I know she likes Mick, and she's been whining about not having a date on Valentine's.

Mick shrugs, then turns to Carin. "You want to?"

"Really?" she asks. "Sure." She knee-bumps me back.

"Get a seven o'clock reservation," I suggest. "That's when Ryun and I will be there."

At 6:30, a half hour before my big date, I pace my bedroom floor. Paddywack paces with me, his toe-nails clicking. I picture Ryun waiting at the restau-rant. I don't show. Carin and the others watch him. Ryun is red faced, humiliated. Ryun Lee, stood up in front of the world.

But what if I'm making a mistake? Not about breaking up with Ryun. But how I'm doing it. What if they feel sorry for him? What if they actually feel sorry for Ryun?

I picture this too. Carin inviting Ryun to her table. Mick telling him not to let it get to him, that I'm not worth it.

It could happen. Just like that. With Ryun's luck,

he'd come out a hero. Everybody would cheer when poor Ryun turned to Kenzie for comfort from mean Sierra.

How could I have been so stupid? Instead of humiliating Ryun, I've made it easy for him to dump me, with the whole world's blessing. What made me think I was smart enough to beat him?

I cannot let this happen.

Think.

I check the time. Ryun's probably on his way to the restaurant right now.

This is not how I wanted it to play out. Ryun and Kenzie are the ones people should get mad at. Not me.

Ryun and Kenzie.

Ryun. And Kenzie.

That's it. I know where I've made my mistake. I left Kenzie out of the equation.

My bedroom door bursts open, and Jack barges in.

"Jack! Knock!"

She frowns at me. I'm still in jeans. "You're not dressed. Aren't you meeting Ryun for the big romantic Valentine's dinner?" She's being sarcastic. She's sniped at me about Ryun, ever since the night of the basketball game when she saw Carin's picture of Kenzie and Ryun together.

"I'm not going."

"You're kidding."

"Nope. If you'll excuse me, I have to make a phone call." I brush by her.

The number I dial is Kenzie's. I take the phone back to my room and shut the door.

On the fourth ring, Kenzie's mother answers. "Hello?"

"Hi, Mrs. Parker. This is Sierra. Could I speak to Kenzie?"

"Kenzie said she didn't want to talk to anybody."

"Would you tell her it's really important? Please?"

"Well, I suppose."

It's a few minutes, but finally Kenzie's on the phone. "What is it, Sierra?" It's the voice she uses when she talks down to me.

"Carin told me what happened at your church. I think it's awful they won't let you work there."

"Do you?" she asks. I can't tell if she suspects I had a part in it or not.

My stomach is contracting. I have to sit on my bed and lean forward to get it to stop. I remind myself what Kenzie did. What she's still doing by keeping silent and protecting Ryun. "It's probably politics or something," I say. "Don't let them get you down."

"Great advice!" she snaps. "Maybe it works in your perfect little world. But out here, things are tougher."

"Perfect world?" I have to rein in my anger. How dare she call my world *perfect?* "Hey, who's the one who spent weeks in the hospital? And who walked out of that accident without a scratch?"

There's silence at the other end. I'm afraid I've blown it. I've let her see how angry I really am.

But when she speaks again, her voice is softer. "Look, I didn't mean to take it out on you. It's just–

it's not fair. I was really looking forward to tonight with those kids. They're going to expect me to be there. I promised them I'd be there. Instead I'm stuck at home with the earth mother."

"I know. That's why I called you. I knew your plans were wrecked. I–I need a favor."

"I'm not exactly in a good-deeds kind of mood." She has that tone again. I think she still believes I'm the same, sappy Sierra she despises.

"I wouldn't ask you if I had another choice. It's not just for me. It's for Ryun."

"Ryun? Hey, aren't you late for your big Valentine's date?" She doesn't even try to hide the bitterness in her voice.

"That's why I'm calling. I couldn't get hold of Ryun. I'm coming down with something. My fever's back. I can't go to the restaurant. And I can't reach Ryun on his cell."

"So, call the restaurant."

I hate the way she talks to me, like I'm an idiot. "I tried. They're busy. I guess people are trying to get in or something. Listen, Kenzie. I'm sorry to have to ask you this. But I don't know where else to turn. I need you to go to The Lantern. I can't stand to think of Ryun just sitting there, waiting for me. Besides, he's paid for that dinner in advance. He should get to eat it. Go there and take my place. Have dinner with Ryun. Please? I won't ever ask you for another thing. Do this one thing for me. Please?"

"You don't know what you're asking." She muffles a dry laugh. I can picture her, so superior. Even with everything that's happened to me, to *us*, she's sitting there, smirking, smug that no matter what anyone else believes, she and Ryun are together. And I'm nothing.

"Please, Kenzie? Tell Ryun I'm not feeling good. Tell him I begged you to come and have dinner with him. Do it for me? He doesn't deserve to spend the whole night waiting for me to show."

She's quiet for so long that I think she might have hung up. "Kenzie?"

"Oh, all right." And she hangs up.

When I hang up, I really do feel sick.

Thankfully, I fall asleep and don't wake up until I hear Mom banging on my door. "Honey, are you all right?"

Groggy, I stumble to the door. Mom's dressed up in a red sequined gown. She holds out the phone. "Where's Jacqueline?"

"I don't know. I've been sleeping."

"Didn't you go out with Ryun?" she asks.

I take the phone. "Can we talk about it later?"

She nods and I close the door. "Hello?" I say into the phone.

"Did I wake you?" Carin asks.

I'm waking up now. Fast. What I say is important. I can't make any mistakes. "Hi, Carin. Did you have a nice dinner?"

"It was so beautiful!" she says. "I'm sorry you were sick."

"Did you see Ryun before he left?" I ask. This is it. It either works, or it doesn't.

"Before he left?"

"Yeah. Kenzie got in touch with him, didn't she? I couldn't reach Ryun on the phone, so Kenzie said she'd call the restaurant and tell him I wasn't going to be able to make it. She did get him, didn't she? He didn't just sit there and wonder what happened to me!"

"Wait a minute," Carin says slowly. "Run this by me again."

I do. The same lie, word for word.

"That's what I thought you said. Okay. Brace yourself. Because you are not going to believe what Kenzie and Ryun did."

"What do you mean?" I ask.

"Ryun didn't leave. And Kenzie didn't call. She *came.* And she stayed."

"What are you saying?" I'm pretending. But I'm not. The hurt I feel is real. And the loss.

"I'm saying that your Ryun had *your* Valentine's dinner with your supposed friend, McKenzie Parker."

I can see them together, at the little table in the corner, reserved for Ryun and me. I did this. I know that. *I* set them up.

But I feel as betrayed as if I hadn't.

I don't go to school for a couple of days. I refuse to come out of my room. Mom and Jack take turns answering the phone. Mom faithfully reports that Ryun calls four times.

Saturday night, Jack bursts into my room and throws herself on my bed. "Good. You're awake."

"I am now," I snap, sitting up in bed.

"I just want to say that I'm totally behind this breakup with Ryun." She pauses. "You *are* finally breaking up with him, aren't you?"

"Yes." That much I know. I'm not finished with Ryun. And I won't be, not until everybody knows he was the one driving and that he and Kenzie lied about it. But I *am* finished with Ryun the boyfriend. There's no going back on that one.

"Good," Jack says. "Because I never thought he was that great in the boyfriend department."

"You didn't?" I can't think of a single time Jack and I talked about Ryun, B.A.

"Nah. He's too . . . polite. Too smooth. Besides, you hear things." She picks up my pillow and hugs it to her chest.

"What things?" In all the months Ryun and I were dating, I never heard anything bad about him.

"His sister's a sophomore. She's cool. Joon Lee. I can tell she worries about him."

"Jack, why didn't you tell me this before?"

"Because you were still calling me Jacqueline."

"Go on." I probably wouldn't have listened if she'd tried to say anything negative about Ryun before. Now I want to hear it, all of it.

"For openers, Joon said she wished her brother would quit smoking."

"Ryun? He doesn't smoke."

Jack rolls her eyes. "Yeah. He's just addicted to those breath mints."

I start to argue with her. Then I think about how he's always popping those mints. In the car. Between classes. "He smokes! How could I not know that?"

Jack pats the pillow. "I've got a pretty good idea that there's a lot you don't know about that guy. Karissa knows a couple of guys in that city league Ryun plays in. She doesn't like them. I can't get the girl to gossip, but she knows things about Ryun. I'm pretty sure he's the life of the party in that crowd."

"Man, I was an idiot!"

"No arguments here." Jack's grinning so wide I can see her retainer.

I grab the pillow and clobber her with it. "Well, I'll bet I know something you *don't* know about Ryun."

"I doubt it," she says evenly.

"Yeah?" I say. "Did you know he's a regular at the Crow Bar on 89th and Lincoln? He hangs out with these older guys from his city league."

Jack looks impressed. "How do you know?"

"I followed him."

She hits me with the pillow. "You did not!"

I nod. "Tailed him like the criminal he is."

Jack high-fives me. "You go, girl!"

We laugh together, and it feels pretty good.

Then Jack gets serious. "So what was the deal last night? You weren't sick. You never planned to keep that date, did you?"

I shrug. I hadn't planned on telling Jack this much. "Let's leave it here. Okay, Jack? Between you and me?"

She puts down the pillow deliberately and stands up. "For now." And she walks out.

■ ■ ■

I don't go to Missouri's church on Sunday. I haven't seen her all week, since I don't have to go back to Nazi Bev. Drew doesn't even call to see if I'll go to church with him.

At about 10, when I figure I'm safe and the Millers are all at church, I call and leave a message on their answering machine. "Hi, this is Sierra. You're all at church, right? Sorry. I'll make it next week, okay? And, Drew, let's go see Missouri. Bye."

■ ■ ■

I offer to drive Jack to school on Monday.

"That's nice of you, Sierra," Dad says. He sets down the paper and takes a bite of his croissant. "I'm sure your mother and Jacqueline appreciate it."

"No big deal." I take a croissant and sit across from Dad. Jack is flitting around the kitchen. Mom's in her bedroom. "So where were you this weekend, Dad?"

Jack drops the carton of milk. She pulls down paper towels to wipe it up.

"Business conference," Dad says. "Didn't your mother tell you?"

I wonder if every dad refers to his wife as "your mother" and never, ever by her name. "Linda. You can call her Linda."

His chin jabs toward his neck, like a rooster. "I know her name."

"Whose?" I ask.

"Your mother's. What's going–"

"Linda's?"

"You want to tell me what this is all about?" he asks patiently, ever the psychiatrist. He checks his watch, so I'll appreciate how busy he is.

"It's a simple question, Dad. Where were you this weekend? Valentine's weekend?"

"Sierra," Jack calls, "shouldn't we be going?"

"I was in Richmond," Dad answers.

"What conference, exactly, was it, Dad? Who was there, I mean. Because Linda was here. She went to that art gallery show. By herself." I hadn't planned this. But I don't think I can stop. I want him to know that we know. That we're not idiots. "You're gone almost every night. Where do you go?"

"I work hard for this family. My long hours pay for those shoes of yours." He's seething but too much the master psychiatrist to show it.

Jack is pulling me by the arm. "Yep. Long hours. Bad for you, Dad. Working more than 11 hours a day doubles the risk of heart disease. On the other hand, working fewer than seven hours triples the risk. I don't want to be late, okay? Bye, Dad." She hollers down the hall, "Bye, Mom!"

Mom comes out, dressed for the gym, her makeup on.

I feel so sorry for her, I want to cry. Or scream.

Dad picks up the paper. "Don't speed. It's better to be late than to speed."

Jack doesn't let go of my arm until we're outside. She takes the keys out of my pocket and unlocks the car. "Somebody want to tell me what they did with my *other* sister?" she asks, when we're in the car, buckling our seat belts. "On the other hand, never mind. This one is a whole lot more interesting."

I pull into the parking lot and see Alyssa and the yearbook committee waiting for me. It feels like the first day I came back after the accident. I'm not battered physically now, just emotionally.

"Need me to walk you in?" Jack asks, grinning.

"You'll just be a parking lot away, right?"

"You got it." She starts to leave.

"Hey, Jack!" I shout.

She turns around.

"Like your hat!"

Jack grins. Then she tips her hat, a red small-brimmed number, with an "Ants Are People Too" button pinned to the side.

Alyssa runs up before I get to the sidewalk. "Oh, Sierra, we heard. I am so sorry."

I know that Alyssa has had her eye on Ryun

since middle school. The last thing she is, is *sorry.* "Thanks, Alyssa. I really don't feel like talking about it."

"But you're broken up, right? For good?" she asks, double-checking.

"Yep." I push my way through the hall. I'm almost to my locker when I hear footsteps rushing behind me. I know it's Ryun.

"Sierra?"

I don't turn around. "Alyssa, I don't want to talk to Ryun."

"Leave it to us." She and the others circle me while I open my locker.

"Why didn't you call me back?" Ryun asks.

"Leave her alone, Ryun," Alyssa says. "Haven't you done enough?"

"What's your problem, Alyssa?" Ryun moves past her. "We need to talk. People are saying all kinds of things. Like *you're* mad at *me.*"

I slam my locker and face him. "Well, what did you expect, Ryun? You have Valentine's dinner with my best friend? I'm supposed to be okay with that?"

"Well, yeah. I thought–"

"You're really something." It feels good, finally telling him off. "I'm sorry I was sick. I should have known you wouldn't want a girlfriend who's not perfect. But couldn't you at least have waited to break up with me before having dinner, *my* dinner, with Kenzie?"

"W-wait a minute." Ryun's cool is gone. It's wonderful to see this. "She said you *wanted* her to have dinner with me."

I laugh. "Right. Just what every girl wants—her boyfriend to have Valentine's dinner with another girl." I pivot and head for English, flanked by Alyssa and her posse.

■ ■ ■

The rest of the week, it's easy to avoid Ryun and Kenzie. Everybody else seems to be avoiding them too. I don't see them together. But I know they're probably meeting somewhere after school. They might even be enjoying their isolation. They have nobody in the world, except each other. Kenzie's probably ecstatic that she and Ryun are finally in the open, that I'm out of the picture for good.

Well, I am *not* out of the picture.

Not by a long shot.

■ ■ ■

I can't sleep at night. At least two or three times I wake up to the *bang* of the car crash, as loud as if it's happening all over again. I dream of the sky turning over, and I wake up sweating and clinging to my mattress.

It's hard to pay attention in classes. My mind flashes back to the minutes before the crash. I replay every word I heard in the bathroom before the football game, the fight in the car. Nothing is getting better.

The only peace I get comes from visits to Missouri. Drew and I go a couple of times, and I go alone twice.

She never changes. She's never mad at me for missing her church. She doesn't pry into what's happening with Ryun and Kenzie. To walk into that room and see her, or hear her humming, feels like coming out of a blizzard to the fireside.

■ ■ ■

I hear kids talking about Ryun at school. He's not playing soccer for the school team. Kids say he doesn't have to. He doesn't need it. He's already in with a great soccer school. He has his scholarship.

And I know I have to finish my plan to get even. I have to finish and be done with it. Then I get on with life, instead of watching it go on around me. Because Ryun and Kenzie are doing just fine. Kenzie's lost Little Lambs. But she's got what she really wanted–Ryun. And Ryun hasn't lost anything except me. Big loss. He's got his scholarship. He's got Kenzie.

■ ■ ■

The first Saturday in March, I begin *Operation Scholarship*. I start with the Internet and do a statewide search on "soccer + high school + tournaments."

I look until I find one where Johnny Moser, the assistant soccer coach at Duke, is going to be. I met him two times that I can remember at tournaments when Ryun was playing.

Moser shows up in three listings. One of the

tournaments is only an hour away, and it's next Saturday. Perfect. I print out schedules and directions. This will all be over in a week.

■ ■ ■

The week before the soccer tournament, things feel almost normal. The weather has turned, and it feels like spring. Yet every time I see Ryun laughing with his buddies, or I hear about Ryun and Kenzie eating lunch together, I know things are *not* normal. Nothing will be right until I bring Ryun's world down. He has to pay for what he's done to me.

■ ■ ■

Friday, I'm walking Paddywack down our street when I hear a car pull over. Sergeant McCarthy hollers, "Hey, Sierra!"

I tug on the leash and make Paddywack follow me to the police car. "Hi, Sergeant McCarthy." I bend down to see his partner in the passenger seat. "Officer Williams, how are you?"

"Good." He's gazing up at the house though, probably fearful my little sister will descend.

"I'm glad we ran into you," McCarthy says. "I've been meaning to call you. I have some good news. I've been talking to Mayor Cellars. He thinks your two friends deserve a hero's award for saving your life in the accident."

"What?" My heart is racing. *An award? They deserve an award?*

"The mayor is sorry he didn't think of it before now. So we'd like to have a ceremony as soon as possible. You know, with Mayor Cellars presenting the awards–just in time for elections–forget I said that. We want you there too, of course. I haven't told your friends yet. Thought maybe you'd like to do that yourself. What do you think?"

Paddywack is pulling hard on the leash.

"Stop it, Paddy!" I snap. This can't be happening. They can't get an award. An award for betrayal? "Sergeant McCarthy, there are things you don't know about Ryun."

He frowns. "What do you mean?"

"Things I've found out. He's–he's not who you think he is. I don't know if–"

"Officer in the vicinity of Teak and 19th, respond." It's the police radio.

Williams answers. I don't know what they're saying. I can't think. I'm visualizing Kenzie and Ryun on a stage together, smiling, crowned as heroes, with the whole town cheering.

"Guess we have to take that," McCarthy says. "We need to talk. You still have my card?"

I manage to nod.

"Good. Call me." He makes a U-turn and drives off, the light on top of the car swirling red.

I pick up Paddywack and run into the house. I have to think. I have to stop this from happening.

"Was that my police boyfriend?" Jack asks. She's eating a carrot. The crunch is so loud my head aches. "Sierra? What did they want?"

"What do you think they want?" I snap. "They

want to give awards to Kenzie and Ryun for being such heroes."

"You're kidding."

I don't answer. Jack doesn't know the truth about the accident. But she knows enough about Ryun and Kenzie to know they don't deserve medals. I unsnap Paddy's leash and storm to my room.

"Sierra, what are you going to do?" Jack shouts after me.

I slam my bedroom door. What *am* I going to do? How can I watch them be rewarded for betraying me? How could I just be there and let it happen and not say anything–?

Unless . . .

An idea is forming in the back of my head. Why wouldn't I say something? I've guarded what I know so long that it's become second nature. But why should I keep that secret any longer after Saturday? After Saturday, I will have taken care of Ryun's scholarship. Kenzie's already lost the Center. There's no reason that the truth, the whole truth, shouldn't come out.

Why couldn't I use the ceremony to let everyone know the truth? What if it could all–really all–be over?

The more I think about it, the more perfect it seems. People would finally know the truth. I could move on.

It's high time for Sierra Reynolds to get her memory back.

I walk to the kitchen, ignoring Jack's glare as I search through the junk drawer and come up with McCarthy's calling card. I dial the number and am surprised when I get him instead of his voice mail.

"McCarthy," he says. I hear car noises in the background.

"Sergeant McCarthy, this is Sierra Reynolds."

"Great. I didn't expect you to call this soon. I want you to finish telling me about Ryun. What don't I know about him?"

I'd forgotten that I said anything about Ryun. How much of the truth can I risk? "Ryun's been hanging out with the wrong people in the wrong places."

"Who's he hanging out with?"

"Mostly the men on his adult soccer league," I explain. "But he goes to bars with them. I worry about him."

He asks a couple more questions. I give him the name of the one bar I know, the Crow Bar.

"So you're thinking the award ceremony isn't such a good idea?" he asks.

"No! I mean, yes! I *want* an award ceremony."

Jack plunks her plate on the table and glares at me.

I turn my back on her. "I think it's a great idea. It might be just what he needs. I want to be part of it, to say a few words, if that's okay. And I think we should have it at the school."

Jack slams silverware.

"Well, if you're sure you still want to do this," McCarthy says, "the mayor will be glad. I'll call the high school and clear it with your principal. You're quite a girl, Sierra Reynolds."

I feel a stab inside and hate myself for feeling it. Because I think it's guilt. And guilt isn't something I should be feeling.

■ ■ ■

Saturday, I drive to Richmond for the soccer tournament. Mom makes me take Jack, in case I have a relapse or, more likely, another accident. They haven't trusted my driving since the accident.

"I still can't believe you're helping them put on an award assembly for Ryun and Kenzie." Jack pops her gum and slumps farther down in the passenger seat.

"Could we just drop it, Jack?" I beg.

"I know you don't want them to get awards. You even told McCarthy about that bar. I just don't get it."

A truck passes in the right-hand lane. Jack rolls down her window and motions for the trucker to lower *his* window too. He does.

"Jack!" I cry.

She shouts out the window at the man, who looks like he's just escaped from the state prison, "Hey! One diesel truck produces the pollution of 100 cars! Global warming! Think about it!"

The convict honks at her.

Once we get to the soccer fields, I check my schedule and start looking for the right game. There must be dozens of matches going on.

Jack tags along, chattering the whole way. "I never thought you really liked these barbaric sport exhibitions. Didn't you only go to these to watch Ryun score? This many guys in silk shorts. Wrong. Very wrong. Are you looking for Ryun's old team?"

"I'm not sure," I answer.

We traipse up and down the sidelines. Finally I see Johnny Moser, Duke's assistant coach. I recognize him instantly—same buzz cut and wiry build. He's running up the sidelines. Then he stops and stares at the action on the field.

"Let's watch this game awhile," I say, positioning myself a few yards from Moser.

"Why?" Jack glances behind us. "Well, I'm sitting down then." She wriggles her way into a front-row bleacher and starts up a conversation with a couple of parents. "Did you know that soccer players run a high risk of concussion and traumatic brain injury from heading the ball?"

I stay where I am and wait.

In a few minutes Moser moves down the sidelines until he's just a few feet away. He looks at me, past me, then back to the field.

He doesn't remember. He doesn't recognize me.

I'm going to have to make the first move. I turn toward him, lean forward, as if I'm trying to place him. "Mr. Moser?"

He frowns over at me. "Yes?"

"Sierra Reynolds. Ryun Lee's friend?"

I can feel Jack's eyes on me.

"Sierra? I didn't recognize you. Your hair's different, right?" He looks around. "Is Ryun here?"

"He couldn't make it. He'll be sorry he missed seeing you." I walk closer to him. Jack's gaze follows me.

"Yeah. I was pretty disappointed that he didn't get signed up for tournaments," Moser says.

"I've got to say that I really admire you—well, everybody at Duke—for sticking by Ryun like this."

His forehead wrinkles. "Are you kidding? Your boyfriend's a real talent. I think he might even start as striker by next spring."

I smile up at him. "That's so great to hear. That's what I've been telling him too. I'm not sure every coach would be this understanding. I really think his

leg will be better by then. He'll have the surgery over at least."

"Excuse me?" Up to now he's been half listening to me and half watching the game. Now I have his full attention.

"Nobody will work harder than Ryun at physical therapy. You know how determined he is."

"Tell me what the doctors said about his leg again." I can see Moser's wheels turning in his brain. He's going to act like he knows what I'm talking about so I'll keep talking.

I can play this game. "I'm sure you know everything I know. He's already had surgery for the ACL tear, but we don't know what the recovery time will be. We're really grateful to Duke for believing in him. He won't let you down."

"When exactly was the accident?" he asks. His voice is friendly, but his eyes are on fire.

"Before Thanksgiving," I answer. Over his shoulder, I see Jack lurking, listening.

"Listen, I have to run." Johnny Moser's whole demeanor has transformed. He's not the jolly, good-hearted coach anymore. He's angry. Furious. "I'm glad I ran into you."

I watch him walk off the field. My hands are shaking.

"What was that?" Jack asks, staring after Moser as he pulls out his cell and screams into it.

I can't answer her. This is exactly how I'd hoped it would go. I don't know why I feel like this, like I want to run after Moser and tell him I was just kidding. That he should forget everything I said.

"Sierra, what's going on?" Jack demands.

I turn and jog back across the fields toward the parking lot. Jack keeps shouting questions at me, but I don't answer her. I don't say a word until we're both back in the car. Then I can't hold it in any longer. I burst into tears. I haven't cried since I got out of the hospital. And now tears wrack my whole body.

Jack sits quietly until I stop sobbing. "Tell me," she says so low I almost miss it. She takes off her white sailor's cap and keeps staring at me.

"Jack, I want to tell you." And I do. I ache to tell her. "But you'll tell Mom and Dad, and I can't–"

"*I'll* tell Mom and Dad?" She grins. "When have I ever told them anything?"

I grin back. She's right. I've told on Jack plenty, but she's never ratted me out.

"I think I know most of it," she says. "I know you came here so you could let Duke know about Ryun's injury. I'm sure Ryun's lied to them about it. You were planning this all along, weren't you? That's why you were writing that letter to the scholarship committee, the one I found in your wastebasket on New Year's. You *wanted* them to cancel his scholarship, even back then. Why?"

I take a deep breath. "I have my memory back." Then I tell her, blow by blow, the things that only Missouri knows. The argument in the stadium john. The fight in the car. The fact that Ryun was driving and he and Kenzie blamed me.

She listens without interrupting–a first for my sister. Finally she asks, "And you haven't told this to anybody? Ryun and Kenzie don't even know that you know?"

"I told Missouri. That's all."

She smiles, like she approves of my choice in confidantes. "I'll bet Missouri told you to forgive them. Right?"

"Exactly!"

We're quiet for a minute. "They took away everything from me, Jack. I trusted them, and they betrayed me. Then they went on like nothing had happened. They kept dating behind my back, even after I got out of the hospital. And Ryun! There he is, with a full scholarship to Duke and a new improved girlfriend. And now he's being given the mayor's award? He comes away a winner. Nothing touches that guy."

"The Teflon guy," Jack says.

We laugh.

"Now I get it," Jack says, smacking her forehead. "Valentine's. You set them up. And you didn't buy that friendship crap when they were sitting together at the game either." She stares at me, as if she's not sure she knows me. "You're doing all of this to get even? Why didn't you just tell the police the truth in the first place?"

"Because it wasn't enough." I'm not sure I can explain it. "Ryun wasn't speeding. He wasn't drunk. He wouldn't have gotten into any trouble. But he lied. When he told the police I was driving, he didn't know they wouldn't blame the driver for the accident. We didn't know that until later. Don't you see? He and Kenzie didn't care how much trouble *I'd* get into, as long as they didn't."

"So you're getting your own revenge? It's been months. How can you stay mad this long?"

"How can I not?"

Jack almost looks sorry for me. "When's it going to end, Sierra?"

"Thursday," I answer. I start the car.

"Thursday?" Then she gets it. "The award assembly? What are you going to do?"

I stay home from school Monday. Then on Tuesday, when I walk into English class, the principal breaks in over the intercom and asks for Sierra Reynolds to come to the office. I'm careful not to glance at Ryun or Kenzie as I about-face and leave.

When I get to the office, the secretary sends me right in.

Principal Waters motions me to sit across from him. He's the youngest principal we've had in Highview. He's been here only two years, but most kids think he's okay.

"I just wanted to touch base with you about the mayor's assembly on Thursday. Sergeant McCarthy said it was your idea to have it at the high school. We're inviting the middle schoolers." He goes over his plans for the assembly. Then he gets to my part.

"We were thinking you could say a few words at the very end of the ceremony. Does that sound about right?"

I nod.

"Well . . ." He gets up. I do the same. "Thanks, Sierra. Let me know if you have any questions between now and then."

I walk out of the office. My head feels light. I'll just stand up, and in the fewest words possible, tell everyone at the assembly that I was not the one driving. I'll say that my memory has come back, and I'll tell them what I remember. Not all of it. Not the fight. But I'll tell them Ryun Lee was driving. And McKenzie Parker covered it up.

Then it will be over. I don't care what happens after that. I will be finished. And I can go on.

Only it eats at me all day. I want to talk to someone.

I need Missouri.

I catch up with Drew after school and ask him to go with me to see Missouri. We take my car and drive straight to the hospital. I'm going to tell Missouri everything–about talking to Coach Moser, about the assembly. Everything. I *need* to tell her.

The nurses are away from the station when we walk onto the floor.

"I better see if I can find *Lady Smooth,*" Drew says, veering off toward the break room.

I keep going. I want to stand outside and hear Missouri hum. I want to hear "Peace Like a River." I listen hard, pressing my face to the closed cold door, but I don't hear anything. There's no humming. No little Missouri snore. No game-show static.

No dripping. No night music. Nothing.

I open the door.

"Sierra!" Drew calls from the far end of the hall. "Wait!"

I step inside. Missouri's bed is empty. There are no sheets on the mattress.

I hear footsteps running in the hall, entering the room.

I wheel around. Drew and his mother are standing in the doorway.

I can't get my breath. "Where—where is she?"

Lady Smooth comes and puts her arm around me. "I'm sorry, Sierra."

"Where's Missouri?" I'm shaking. I can't see because my eyes are filled with tears. "What did they do with her?"

"She's gone home, sugar," says Lady Smooth.

"Home?" Missouri doesn't have a home. This room is her home.

"She went to be with her Maker, honey. She's gone to her real home."

"No!" I cry. "She can't be dead! I need her. I need to talk to her." I pull away from Nurse Miller, but she comes back and holds me. She keeps talking to me until I stop screaming.

■ ■ ■

I stay home from school the next day and don't get out of bed. It feels as if I'm back in the cave, dark and alone. And I can't stop crying.

Mom brings in food. Jack comes in and tries to cheer me up. But I feel far away from them and from everything, as if I were unconscious.

Toward evening, I pull out the photos I'd taken of Missouri in the hospital. Missouri in her night-gown. Missouri in bed. Missouri in the reflection of the TV game shows. I study her expression. It's the same in every picture—calm, serene, peace like a river.

The last picture I pull out is one of Missouri in her white blouse and gray wool skirt. Drew is helping her on with her coat. They're leaving for church.

Tears well up again when I think about how many times I canceled out on her. I never kept my bargain. I never went to church with her, not even once. It was such a little thing to ask.

There's a knock on my door. I wait for Jack to burst in. But the knock comes again instead.

"Come in," I say, not wanting to see anybody.

Dad walks in. He fills my room with his presence. "Hello, honey," he says. He pulls out my desk chair and turns it around to sit on it.

I can't think of anything to say to my dad.

"Honey, it's hard to lose a friend. And that woman—"

"Missouri," I say.

"Missouri," he continues, "was a good friend to you at a very rough time in your life. But death is a part of life, Sierra. And she was old. She lived a good life. That's all anyone can ask. It's fine to grieve. But you need to pull yourself together. Your mother let you stay home from school today. But you don't need to miss any more of your classes. Do you understand?"

I nod. "Thank you." I feel sorry for him. He didn't know Missouri. I'm not sure if he could know her. When I came home from the hospital and told Mom, she cried. *She* knew what it meant, losing Missouri.

"Good." He gets up from the chair. He smiles. It's a professional smile. I imagine him using it on all his crazy people. "You'll feel better tomorrow. You'll see."

I'm taking a long hot shower when Jack pounds on the bathroom door. "Phone! It's Drew."

It may be the only phone call I'd want to take. "Tell him to hang on, Jack!"

I wrap a towel around me and open the door. Jack holds out the phone and sits down in the hallway, while I talk.

"Drew?"

"How are you holding up?" he asks.

"Not so good," I admit.

"We're having a memorial service for Missouri at our church tomorrow," he says. "I thought you might want to come."

I am so grateful to be invited, it's hard to talk. I clear my throat. "I'd like that. Thanks, Drew."

"It's at 10. I can drive you there from school. We'd get back in plenty of time for the mayor's ceremony."

The mayor's ceremony. My moment of revenge.

Yet the whole day I haven't given one thought to that ceremony. It feels as if all of it must be going on in some other world, another universe.

"Will that work then?" he asks.

"Uh—yeah. Thanks. Thanks, Drew."

■ ■ ■

Thursday morning, it's all I can do to get dressed. I don't think about what I'm wearing. I take the first pair of shoes in my closet.

Ms. Rowe doesn't say anything when I walk into class 15 minutes late.

All around me, I hear the buzz of conversations, people talking about Mayor Cellars coming to the school, about the award assembly. Ryun's joking with Greg about something.

I keep watching the clock. Drew and I have agreed to leave for his church as soon as first hour is over.

The bell rings. I start to get up when Kenzie puts her hand on my desk. "Sierra, I'm sorry about Missouri. I heard, this morning. She was a really nice lady."

I look at her. I don't think Kenzie and I have said two words to each other since Valentine's. In my head I've built her up into this heartless traitor who doesn't care about anybody except herself. I don't know what to do with *this* Kenzie, the one in front of me, who seems to mean what she's saying.

"She was amazing," I say.

Kenzie nods, then gets up and walks out.

The Church of the Redeemer is all the way across the city. Houses get smaller and closer together.

"There it is," Drew says.

I see a white board church that's in strung-out sections, as if it had to be added on to time after time, with whatever materials were at hand. The parking lot is already full. People are pulling in along the street. Drew does the same.

"All these people knew Missouri?" I ask, amazed.

"And loved her," Drew adds.

He nods and says hi to people as we walk in. I see one of the women from Christmas, when they came to our hospital room. She runs up and hugs me.

"Isn't this a glorious send-off!" she exclaims, like we're at a rally. "Missouri must be smiling down! Mmm-hmm!"

She's not the only one smiling. People are shouting greetings across the parking lot. A group of women standing on the church steps break out in a burst of laughter. Someone's telling a story as we pass by, and he can barely get the words out—he's laughing too hard.

I've been to funerals, maybe half a dozen at Baker Avenue. They're the quietest crowds I have ever been part of. *Nobody* smiles. I don't know how to handle what I'm seeing now.

We thread our way through the crowd and inside the church. There's nothing fancy about this church. Square wooden pews, more like benches, fill every inch of space.

"Sierra!" Reverend Brown comes jogging up the

aisle. He waves until he stops in front of us. "So happy you made it!"

"I–I never made it to a service. I kept telling Missouri I would." I'm afraid I'm going to start crying. I would be the only one. And I would never stop.

"Did that old woman win another bet?" he asks.

I'm surprised he knows this. "Yes."

He laughs, a hearty deep bellow, and looks up at the ceiling. "Missouri, God love ya!" He looks back at me again. "That lady brought in more people to this church with her betting than I did with my preaching!"

Drew laughs. And I have to grin.

"First time I met Missouri, I was eight years old," Drew says. "I took a dollar out of the offering plate, and she spotted me. Nobody else. Just this old wrinkled woman."

"What did she do?" I ask.

"She passed me a note. It said, 'Jesus loves you, sugar. Forgives you too.'"

We're quiet a second.

Then Drew says softly, "I put the money back after church."

An organ chord pounds, and music breaks out from all sides.

"Guess I better get moving," Reverend Brown says, hurrying back down the aisle.

Drew and I find a seat in the second row. I've never sat this close in church. The organ's loud, playing a jazzed-up version of "What a Friend We Have in Jesus."

Then voices ring out from the back of the church, and the choir, in gold robes, starts filing in. *Filing* is the wrong word. They sway and move down the aisle in a way that's more like dancing. Their voices blend and split off, taking the song where it hasn't gone before. Their hands clap above their heads, as they flow into the song I know Missouri would have loved: "I've got peace like a river, I've got peace like a river, I've got peace like a river in my soul." I watch them move to the front of the church, maybe 50 choir members.

And there, in the middle of all the dark faces, is one white face. My sister.

"Drew, it's Jack!" I whisper. "What's she doing up there?"

He smiles. "Jack's been in the choir for weeks. Didn't you know that?"

I laugh out loud as I watch her sway and shout out the words. The cuffs of her overalls stick out under the gold robe. She's the only choir member with a hat. A gold hat.

I watch Jack. She's totally into it. And not just the music. She's part of it. There's the same something—joy? peace?—on her face that I see in other people's faces here. That I saw in Missouri's face.

I want that. I think I've wanted it since I first saw Missouri. If she were still alive, if I could talk to her, let her talk to me one more time, she could tell me. I could go to her church with her on Sunday. She could help me get it too.

But it's too late. I waited too long.

"It's a joyful day," Reverend Brown says. "But I admit to a selfish sadness. I'll miss Missouri."

"Amens" and "Mmm-hmms" come from all over the church.

"But joy wins because we know where our friend has gone," he continues.

"That's right!" shouts a woman behind me.

"And where she's gone, there is no more pain, no more sadness, and no death! So let's remember our friend. One hundred and one years, that's a lot to remember. Who wants to go first?" The preacher steps back to make room for the people who line up to tell stories about Missouri.

A woman who looks as old as Missouri talks about the time Missouri lost her six-year-old son to smallpox. I never once asked Missouri about her family. I want to know it all now. I soak up other people's memories.

An old man gets up, not nearly Missouri's age though. "When I was a young man," he says, "I was sorely tempted by the devil."

People say, "Mmm-hmm."

He goes on. "I stole from Missouri. I cheated that woman out of her life's savings. And you know what she did? She forgave me. Said Jesus died for that sin. She told me she knew I'd pay her back when I could. And for interest, I should come to church with her."

Drew and I grin at each other.

As I listen, I learn that Missouri lost her husband and her oldest son in World War II. She worked for the Red Cross. She led a full life, right up to her last day.

When it's over, I can't stop crying. I'm embarrassed. Everyone else is smiling, even Jack. She and Karissa come over and stand with Drew and me.

"You okay, Sis?" Jack asks.

Nurse Miller, in her gold choir robe, joins us. She wraps her arms around me.

"I should have kept my word," I sob. "I promised Missouri I'd go to her church. I didn't even do that."

She hugs me harder. "Oh, sugar. Look around. You *are* here!" She makes me look at her. "You know what Missouri told me, not 10 minutes before she passed? She said she knew you'd be here at the church. And I was to give you this." She takes the big Bible from her husband, who's joined us, and she hands it to me. "Missouri wanted you to have this."

I hug the familiar black Bible to my chest, as if it's Missouri herself. And I don't let go, not until Drew and I are in the car. A hospital napkin is stuck between pages. I open the Bible carefully and see that she's printed my name on the napkin: *Sierra.* And next to that, she's printed: *Forgive and forget.*

"We better get going," Drew says, starting the engine. "You've got an assembly to put on."

When we get back to school, middle-school kids are already filing into the high school for the assembly. Ms. Wilcox, the art teacher, meets me in the hall and says the principal is looking for me.

I am pulled along by forces already set in motion. I flow with the crowd to the gym. I'm motioned onto the stage. Ryun and Kenzie are already there. Sitting together, side by side. Ryun is smiling and chatting with the mayor. He's so happy, so full of himself that I know Moser hasn't called him. Not yet.

"Great! You're here!" Principal Waters rushes up to me and gives me last-minute instructions.

I nod and sit where I'm told. Without thinking, I scan the crowd. They blur together in a noisy throng.

Then I see Jack. She's sitting next to Karissa. She shakes her head when we see each other. *Don't do it.* That's what she's saying.

The program starts. Principal Waters welcomes everyone and says how proud he is to have the mayor here. He introduces Officers McCarthy and Williams. Williams gives a brief report of how Ryun and Kenzie risked their lives to pull me out of the car.

Then Mayor Cellars says a few words about heroes and asks Kenzie and Ryun to stand. He hands them each a plaque and shakes their hands. Ryun smiles, as cameras flash near the stage. Kenzie's hard to read. I think she keeps sneaking glances at me, frowning. Even when the mayor's speaking to her, she looks like she doesn't want to be here.

I don't want to be here. But I'm here. This is where I've brought myself. I've made this happen. This is the day I've waited for since I got my memory back. This is my moment to get even. To get my revenge.

Forgive and forget. It's like I can still see Missouri's scrawl on the napkin. But I don't know how to do either one. I don't think I can.

"Sierra wants to say a few words and give her own thanks to our two heroes," Principal Waters says. "Come on up, Sierra."

I stand up. My legs carry me to the podium. Kenzie and Ryun are standing next to me. I try to think of what I've planned to say.

The microphone hums.

Hums.

I see Jack in the audience and Drew. I wonder if they can hear it. The humming.

"Sierra?" Principal Waters whispers.

I look at Kenzie and Ryun. Kenzie looks worried now, almost scared. Ryun is as carefree as ever.

I could do it now. Expose them in front of the whole school. Get it over with. My revenge. With the police here and everyone.

I want this to be over. I want peace. Peace like a river.

But I don't think this is the way to get it.

"Now!" the principal whispers. Only he's in front of the mike, and his voice amplifies.

The audience breaks into soft laughter.

"A lot's happened since that accident, to all of us—Kenzie, Ryun, and me," I begin. I'm just talking, not thinking first. "Not everything has been easy. Or good." I'm picturing Missouri, the way she looked when I first opened my eyes, her white hair wild around that wrinkled face.

The crowd is quiet now, waiting.

"Memory's a funny thing." In my head, the memories are swirling—Missouri, the accident, Kenzie, Ryun—but they're starting to settle too, dropping into corners of my mind. "There's a lot I want to forget about that accident. And a lot I want to remember." I look for Drew in the audience, find him. "Someone really wise once told me that life is about remembering the right things and forgetting the wrong."

I turn to Kenzie and Ryun. Ryun's not looking at me, but Kenzie's staring, her eyes narrowed to slits.

"There are a lot of things I'm going to try to forget," I continue. "But I want to remember that you pulled me out of the car. Thank you."

When everyone realizes that I'm done, that I'm not going to say anything else, they applaud.

Principal Waters thanks everyone and dismisses school a few minutes early. He shakes Ryun's and

Kenzie's hands. Then he escorts the mayor off the stage.

As soon as Principal Waters leaves, Kenzie corners me, blocking the stairs so I can't leave the stage. "You know." She spits out the words.

I look at her, and at first I really don't know what she's talking about.

"You haven't lost your memory. You've known all along about the accident! I don't know what kind of game you're playing, Sierra. But I'm tired of playing it with you."

"I'm tired too, Kenzie. And I'm done. I don't want to play anymore." I look at her, and I don't see the person I've hated all these weeks. I just see somebody like me.

"You did it, didn't you!" she demands. "You got me fired from the Center. I knew it. I knew it was you!"

"It was. I'm sorry, Kenzie." And I mean this. "I was just so mad at you for letting me take the blame and–"

"What was I supposed to do?" she shouts. "I didn't lie. The police just assumed you were driving. And Ryun let them. He was driving without a license–"

"Why?"

"His license was suspended. I should have known you didn't know that."

She's right. I didn't know. How long had he been driving without a license? And I had no idea. It almost makes sense now. More pieces are falling into place.

"What are you going to do now?" Kenzie demands.

"I don't know," I answer truthfully, for once. "But I think you should talk to Sergeant McCarthy."

"Is that a threat?" she asks, ready to do battle.

I shake my head. "No. But I think everything will come out eventually."

Ryun comes over and taps Kenzie on the shoulder. "Everything all right?"

I haven't spoken to Ryun in weeks. When he looks at me, I don't turn away this time. He is so totally confident, fearless.

"Everything is *not* okay," Kenzie informs him. "Sierra hasn't lost her memory. She's been faking it the whole time."

"No way." Ryun laughs, like it's a joke. "She couldn't have faked that."

"I did lose my memory, at least at first. But I got it back in the hospital," I admit.

I watch this sink in. Ryun's smile fades. "Then why—?" But he doesn't finish. He's getting it. "What are you going to do now? Have you told the police?"

It's amazing. This is all he cares about—he doesn't want to get caught. No remorse. No explanations. No apologies. Just, *Have you told the police?*

"I could have told the whole town today, Ryun—police, students, parents, newspaper, everybody. And I didn't. I'm not even sure why I didn't. But, no, I'm not going to the police."

Ryun's shoulders relax. The tension drains from his face.

"But you need to know that all I've thought about since I got my memory back has been revenge. I wanted to get even." Something inside me makes me keep going. "I've done some things, Ryun, some things I can't undo. I wanted to hurt you." I look him straight in the eyes. "I've talked to Duke. I told them about your leg."

He laughs. "You did not. I don't believe you. *They* wouldn't believe you, even if you *did* tell them." He puts his arm around Kenzie. "You know what? I'm not buying into any of this."

"Ryun," I begin. But I don't know what else to say. "I'm sorry. Be careful."

And I walk off the stage.

Jack and Karissa are waiting for me.

"Bet you're ready to go, huh?" Jack asks.

I will never be able to hear the word *bet* without thinking of Missouri. "You bet."

It's not until I get home and ready for bed that I pull out Missouri's Bible. I've been saving it. It feels as if I have an appointment. With Missouri. With God?

I open it to the page Missouri has marked with the napkin. Again, I read: *Sierra. Forgive and forget.*

I try to remember everything she told me about forgiving. About forgetting. About remembering. *"Remember the right things. Forget the rest."* I think I'm beginning to see what she means. I *want* to forgive–Ryun, Kenzie. I want to try to make things better, maybe even to help them somehow, to help all of us. Maybe Dad too.

But it feels even more important that *I'm* forgiven. By Ryun and Kenzie. I have a lot to apologize to them about. We have a lot of things to try to work out.

But mainly, I want to be forgiven by God.

In the past few months, I've done so many things, things that hurt so many people. The hurting isn't over. And I'm responsible for more than my share in that. But it's not just A.A. Sierra. I've always *sinned,* Missouri would say. I thought I cared about my friends, but how much could I have cared for them if I wasn't even willing to know the tough things going on in their lives? I just wanted everything to be smooth, easy.

I don't know if God can forgive all that.

There's a knock on my door, and Jack comes in. "Are you reading it?" she asks, nodding to the old Bible, open on my lap.

I motion her to sit next to me. "Just about to. She marked the page for me. She underlined verses, Jack."

Jack sits cross-legged next to me. "Read them out loud?"

I run my finger down the page until I come to the verses. Wavy brown lines underscore Jeremiah 31:34: "'And they shall teach no more every man his neighbour, and every man his brother, saying, Know the Lord: for they shall all know me, from the least of them unto the greatest of them, saith the Lord: for I will forgive their iniquity, and I will remember their sin no more.'"

I look up at Jack. Her eyes are watery. "Jack, did you hear that? God says he'll forgive and forget. How *can* he forget? How's that possible?"

"He *chooses* to forget—to not hold things against us, Sierra. Because of Jesus." She laughs. "Sugar, that's his style."

And then I laugh. It's what Missouri used to say.

I'm not sure I understand it. Not yet. Maybe I'll go back to Missouri's church again.

I sit there with Jack and feel almost like I did when I was coming awake but still inside the cave, with voices swirling around me and ideas just out of reach. Only this time, Someone is there with me, pulling me out of the cave. Forgiving me. And I'm holding on, swimming to the surface, with a peace worthy of Missouri. I can almost hear her humming.

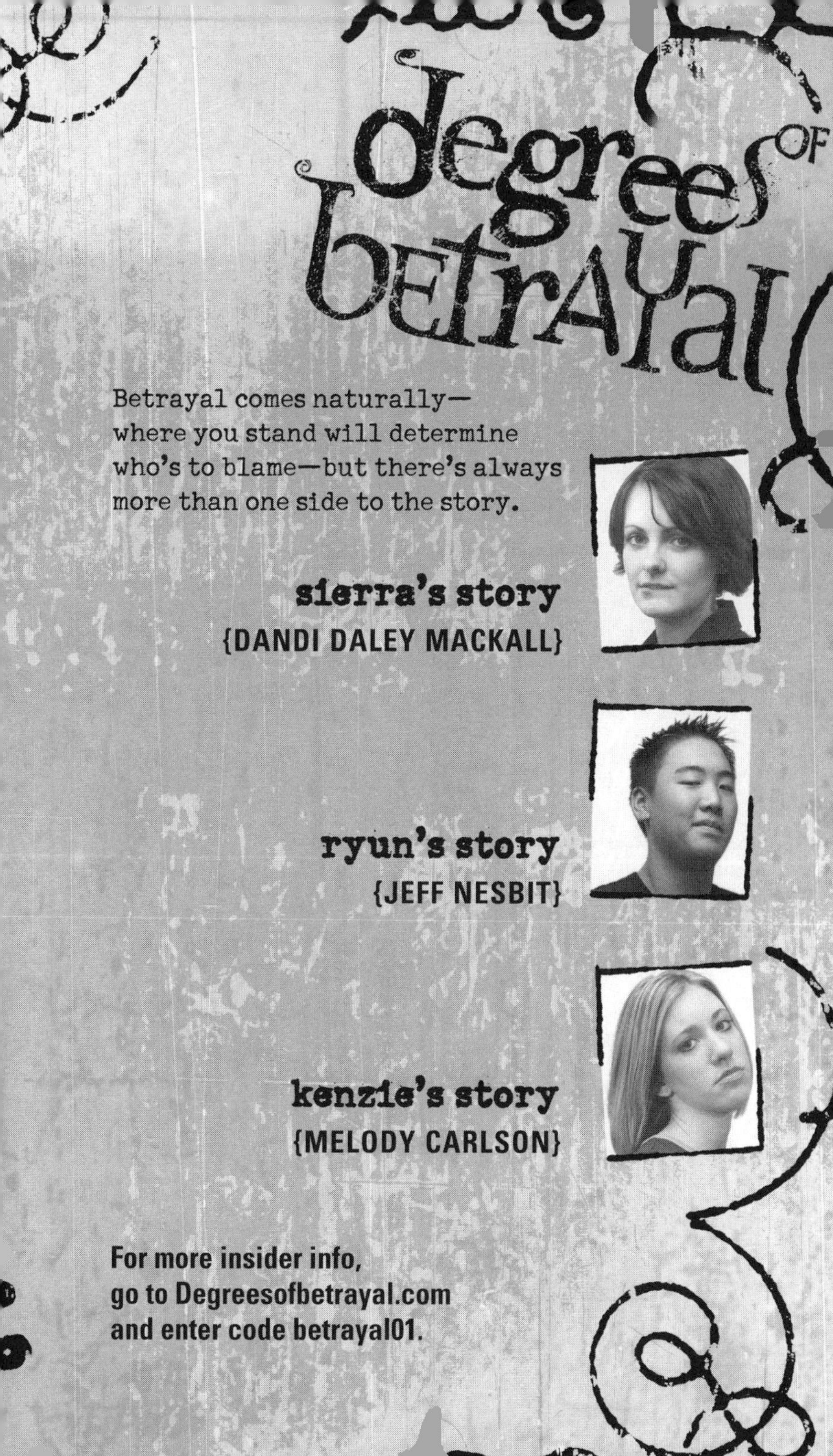
degrees of betrayal
Betrayal comes naturally—
where you stand will determine
who's to blame—but there's always
more than one side to the story.
sierra's story
{DANDI DALEY MACKALL}
ryun's story
{JEFF NESBIT}
kenzie's story
{MELODY CARLSON}
For more insider info,
go to Degreesofbetrayal.com
and enter code betrayal01.

A Sneak Peek at *Ryun's Story* . . .

I am invincible.

You don't believe me? Really? Well, watch this.

There used to be a straight road, about a quarter of a mile long, out near the airport. It was behind a couple of big warehouses. If the word got around, and you heard about it, you could watch two kids racing their cars just as it was getting dark.

They'd hit 120 mph or so, hope they didn't slide or fishtail at the end, and then get out of there before the cops could catch them. Every so often, a kid would roll, get mangled, and die or something.

Then the cops started hanging around, waiting. The city put up speed bumps. Finally they cut the road in half.

But beneath that road is a huge empty water pipe. I don't know what it was used for. Maybe carrying sludge from one of the factories to a stagnant pond at the other end.

But now the factory's gone, and the pond is only dirt and trash. There's nothing at either end of this long straight pipe. It simply sits there. Waiting quietly, never complaining.

The pipe is just big enough for someone tall, like me, to walk through. I'm 6′2″, taller than almost every other kid at Highview. I can walk through that pipe and my straight black hair doesn't even come close to touching the top. When I spread my arms wide, they barely touch either side. If you shout at one end, your voice disappears at the other.

I don't ever walk through that pipe, though. No, I leave an old Yamaha motorcycle out there, and I ride whenever I feel like it. I don't wear a helmet. I don't need to. I never wear a seat belt in a car either . . . I told you–nothing touches me. I always come out on top.

Anyway, the old Yamaha is one of those sport bikes where you have to ride low, your head down. I got it from one of my friends I play soccer with–a lawyer–who was bored with it. I picked up a little extra cash from my folks to pay for it.

They don't know I own it. My folks, I mean. There's a lot they don't know, actually. There's a lot *everyone* doesn't know . . . well, maybe except for my little sister, Joon, but she'd never give me up.

Here's how it works. You start at one end of the tunnel on the bike, get going, no lights. Then you kick into another gear. The bike jolts forward a little.

You put your head down lower. The light starts to dim. It gets darker.

Then you hit a time—maybe just a few seconds, maybe forever—when it's pitch dark. There's only the sound of the bike coming off the walls of the tunnel to guide you. You hope the bike is going straight, but you don't really know. You aim at the tiny dot of light at the other end of the tunnel and hope you have it right. Maybe you do—maybe you don't.

But I always have it right. I always hit that spot of light at the other end of the tunnel. The bike doesn't wobble or pitch. I don't ever have to adjust. I just aim and ride through the darkness. And I hit it perfectly every time.

It's such a rush. Light to dark to light. Fast to faster. And then—you *rip* out the other end into the brilliant light, going at least 80 or 90 mph across the dirt toward a line of trees. Plenty of time to stop the bike.

I can do it 100 times, a million times. I never get tired of the feeling. There's a point where you can't be afraid, because you know that if you are, you'll lose it. The bike will roll or tilt, and it will all end. Your life, I mean. But when you know you're invincible, you're not afraid. You just go, as fast as you can, until you blast out the other end.

It's funny what happens when you live your life this way, as if you're untouchable. When I'm on a soccer field, there are times when I *know* I cannot be stopped. There may be one or two—or even three—defenders in my way. But I simply go around them, through them. I carry the ball with me as I go, and then I put the ball near post, upper 90, wherever it needs to be.

I've never told this to anyone. I'm not sure anyone would understand it or even believe it. I'm not sure anyone would even care. It isn't an easy thing to explain.

We all die some day. I know that. But not me right now, not this way. I am invincible. I can do what I want, when I want. It's just the way it is.

A Sneak Peek at *Kenzie's Story* . . .

I tried to act natural, but I was in total shock. I'd come down to the University of Virginia thinking this college visit would be pretty boring, but then someone (my guardian angel maybe) went and paired me off with none other than the guy of my dreams—Highview High's soccer king *Ryun Lee!*

Talk about unreal! Who would've thought something like this could happen to me? But there I was, staring into the face of the coolest guy on the planet—the guy I'd had a secret crush on for, well, like forever. I casually said, "Hey," as I joined him in the backseat of our escort's car, but I couldn't help thinking, *What is up with this? Have I died and gone to heaven?*

Just the same, I couldn't figure out why Ryun Lee would be wasting his time visiting a college like the

University of Virginia when everyone knew he was getting some incredible scholarship offers from the really big schools—like Duke.

I had to remind myself to play it cool. No way was I going to blow the new image I'd worked so hard to create over the last couple of months. You are a new woman, McKenzie Parker, I told myself. And your time has finally come!

"How's your game going this summer?" I asked as our escort, a Billy something or other, put the car into gear.

Ryun gave me a confused look. "It's going fine."

I nodded and leaned back, thankful that I'd decided to wear the sundress Sierra talked me into buying on our most recent shopping spree. It was a two-piece number with a halter top that fit like skin and an adorable little skirt that swirled nicely and showed off my tanned legs. Sierra assured me it was perfect for me and even said the color brought out the gold flecks in my brown eyes. She also insisted on picking out the coolest shoes I'd ever owned in my life—Nine Wests with high heels and skinny straps. Of course, because Sierra helped, they went perfectly with the sundress.

As I sat in the car, I felt like laughing. Ryun looked so dazed and confused, like he couldn't place who I was or how I knew him. It was obvious he had no idea who the strange chick sitting beside him really was. I felt sorry for him, so I finally gave him a break. "You don't remember me, do you?"

He made a funny face. "Well, I'm not sure. You seem familiar."

I stretched out my hand. "McKenzie Parker."

He nodded and shook my hand, holding on a second or two longer than you'd normally do. And the feeling of him holding my hand like that and looking into my eyes made me feel warm and tingly all over. Almost dizzy.

"McKenzie Parker," he repeated, but it was obvious he was still clueless.

"Remember we worked on the yearbook together?"

His raised eyebrow showed he was even more surprised. *THAT McKenzie?* I could tell he was thinking. But since he's a gentleman, he didn't even mention my prior life as the invisible girl.

Still, it was fun watching him study me, as if seeing me for the first time. And I got this feeling that he liked what he saw too. Just the same, I was careful to keep my distance. I mean, as much as I liked Ryun and have always liked Ryun, I didn't want to move in on Sierra's turf. Everyone knew that she and Ryun had been a "thing" since the spring of junior year. And I knew enough about Sierra and her friends to know that it wouldn't be good for me if I did something sleazy like that. But it sure wasn't *my* fault we'd been stuck together for the evening. Besides, we were only doing a little tour of the campus and then heading over to a party at a frat house. Totally innocent.

After a few minutes, I couldn't help but bring up Sierra's name. For one thing, I was curious. If they were still dating, and I assumed they were since she hadn't told me otherwise, then why didn't he invite her to come along with him? Besides that, I wanted to see how he reacted. Because, although I certainly wasn't an expert on these matters, I thought Ryun Lee was actually *flirting* with me. He'd already complimented me on my new look several times. There was just something about those smoldering dark eyes that told me he liked the new me.

■ ■ ■

Before the night was over, I could feel myself falling—make that plummeting—in love with the guy I'd had a crush on for ages. The guy I talked to in my dreams and in my head every time he walked by.

We talked for several hours, but it seemed like minutes. I felt like Cinderella, knowing our time would end and we'd both turn back into ourselves and go back home to Highview. Then Sierra, the incredibly cool and popular Sierra, would have her guy back by her side again and I'd just be on the fringes, where I usually was. Still, Why not make the best of tonight? I asked myself. Really make it a night to remember?

About the Author

Dandi Daley Mackall has published 330 books for children, teens, and adults, with sales of three and a half million in 22 countries. In addition to *Sierra's Story,* she's also written *Kyra's Story* in the Degrees of Guilt series for young adults (Tyndale). Her fiction best-sellers include eight titles in the Winnie the Horse Gentler series (Tyndale), including *Wild Thing, Eager Star, Bold Beauty, Midnight Mystery, Unhappy Appy, Gift Horse, Friendly Foal,* and *Buck-skin*

Bandit. She was creative director of the teen fiction series *TodaysGirls.com* (Tommy Nelson) and author of *Portrait of Lies* and *Please Reply!* She's also written three nonfiction books for high school students on having success in the workplace: *Problem*

Solving, Teamwork, and *Self-Development* (Ferguson).

Currently Dandi conducts writing assemblies and workshops across the U.S. She writes from rural Ohio, where she lives with her husband, Joe, and three children—Jen, Katy, and Dan—as well as two horses, a dog, a cat, and two newts. You can visit Dandi at **dandibooks.com.**

thirsty
™

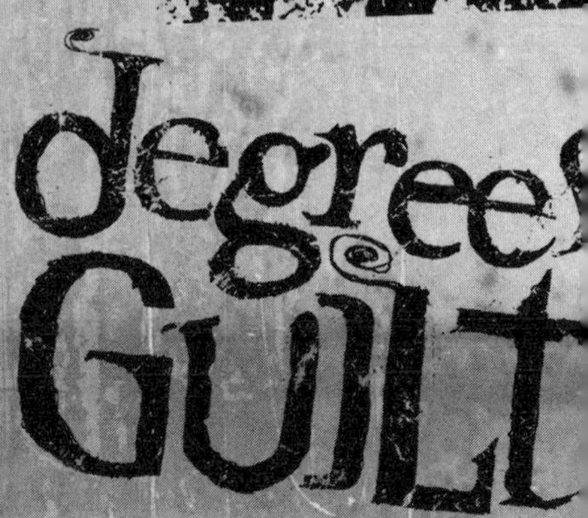

Sammy's dead. . .they each played a par
Kyra, his twin sister. Miranda, the girl h
loved. And Tyrone, a friend from schoo

WHAT'S THE REAL STORY

There's always more than one point of view—read all three.

kyra's story

{DANDI DALEY MACKALL}

ISBN 0-8423-8284-4

miranda's story

{MELODY CARLSON}

ISBN 0-8423-8283-6

tyrone's story

{SIGMUND BROUWER}

ISBN 0-8423-8285-2

degreesofguilt.com

ANOTHER NEW TITLE FROM 

Jennifer Knapp
ZOEgirl
Ginny Owens
Stacie Orrico
Superchic[k]
Jaci Velasquez
Rebecca St. James

Ever worry about where your life is going?

Some of the most popular singers in Christian music face the same types of struggles you face—loneliness, materialism, feeling ugly, difficult friendships, body image, popularity, and more. Here some of your favorite musicians share their stories and what they've learned from God in the process.

Open the book and step out with friends for a deeper, more intimate relationship with God.

You can't begin a journey without taking a step . . .

are**U**thirsty.com

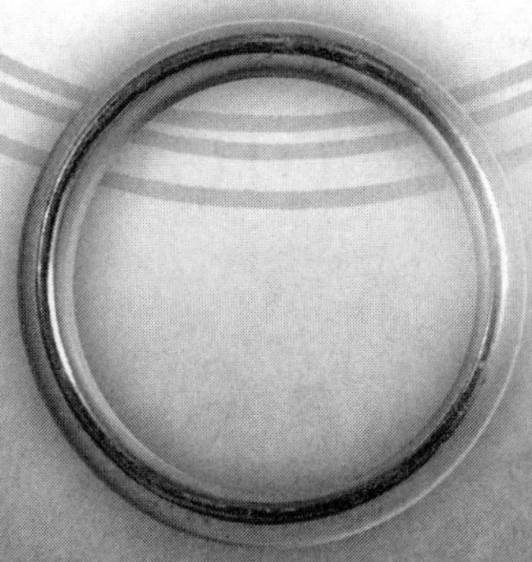